I Don't Want to Talk About It

I Don't Want to Talk About It

Jane Lovering

Book 5 in the Yorkshire Romances

Where heroes are like chocolate – irresistible!

Published 2016 by Choc Lit Limited
Penrose House, Crawley Drive, Camberley, Surrey GU15 2AB, UK
www.choc-lit.com

A CIP catalogue record for this book is available
from the British Library

ISBN 978-1-78189-279-4

Printed and bound by CPI Group (UK) Ltd, Croydon, CR0 4YY

To Prince, Saddie, Perry and other sock-headed, broomhandle-bodied, woolly-maned facilitators of imaginary gymkhanas – and the grown up little girls who loved them.

Acknowledgements

With my special hugest thanks to Sharon White, Senior Speech Therapist, for the help with Alex's stammer, and cups of tea, and Tom Quinn, for the books on engraving styles and pictures of the old mill. Without you both, this book would have been a lot shorter and had lots of gaps, where I probably would have written '*fill in information here. If necessary, torture someone until they tell you things*'.

Thanks also to the Tasting Panel members who passed *I Don't Want To Talk About It*: Megan, Betty, Heidi J, Janice B, Lucy M, Sarah N, Linda.Sp, Jennifer S, Saada and Janyce.

f

Facebook

Alex Hill

My mother's let her holiday cottage to someone writing a book about graves! I bet she's all black lipstick and dodgy footwear. Who writes books about graves, anyway?

Matt Simons likes this

Comment: Matt Simons Your mother is all black lipstick? Introduce me …

Comment: Alex Hill This woman writing about graves, dickbrain.

Comment: Matt Simons Aye aye, you could be in there, man! She'll be someone who doesn't get out much …

Chapter One

*'Northern stone, being harder – like the locals, some
would say – lends itself less readily to the flourishes
and overblown decorations found further south.
Nevertheless, the Churchill family somehow managed
to find a stonemason capable of producing something
more appropriate to the pages of an illustrated
manuscript for their daughter Beatrice. Deceased at the
age of 29, there is a local rumour that she died giving
birth to an illegitimate child, and that the somewhat
over-decorative nature of her stone was her father's
attempt to distract attention from this unpalatable
fact. Whatever the circumstances of her death,
familial affection is obvious in every deep-cut line.'*
—BOOK OF THE DEAD 2

It's not every epitaph that can carry off the 'explosion in
an eyebrow factory' look, but, as I moved the ivy which
made the age-angled gravestone look like a drunk in a bad
toupee, a host of earwigs scuttled across the surface and,
when I looked through the camera viewfinder, Beatrice
Churchill (1747–1776) was giving infestation her best
shot.

'What are you doing?'

I jumped and turned around. There's not usually much
of an audience in a graveyard, or, if there is, I don't want
to think about it, but, standing behind me and half-hidden
by more ivy, was a little girl.

'I'm taking photographs of this grave,' I said, slightly

unnecessarily I felt, given that I'd been crouched in front of the stone with a camera and there were a limited number of other things I could have been up to in the circumstances and in broad daylight.

The girl came a little further into the sun. She looked, to my inexperienced eye, to be about eight, blonde messy hair with a cycle helmet crushed down onto it, the splash of freckles that said she probably spent a lot of time out of doors, and one hand holding a hobby horse with a red corduroy head and an expression of good-natured stupidity stitched onto his face. 'Why?'

I turned away and took another shot, now that the earwigs had reconvened somewhere other than all across the sandstone. 'I'm writing a book. I write books about graves. Haven't you been told not to talk to strange people?'

The little girl came further out from under the ivy. I could see now that, along with the cycle helmet, she was wearing a striped jumper, leggings and a pair of wellington boots. The hobby horse continued to wear his inane grin.

'You aren't strange. You're called Miss Winter Gregory and you're renting Grandma's little cottage in the High Street.' She dramatically threw one knee in the air as though she was having some kind of fit, dragged the stick horse to a bush and pushed his plastic reins over it, and I realised that she'd been dismounting from an imaginary, and quite large, pony. 'I'm Scarlet, and this is Light Bulb. He's part thoroughbred.'

I stared at the broom handle, fabric and vacant embroidered smile. 'Light Bulb is an unusual name,' was all I could think of to say, doing that peculiar half-crouch that people who aren't used to children do when trying to make up their minds whether to bend down to talk to them or not. Children had never really featured much in my life and, at thirty, I hadn't quite made up my mind how I felt about them.

'So is Winter,' Scarlet replied, sensibly enough, I suppose.

I went back to trying to get an un-entomological shot of Beatrice's stone and hoped that Scarlet would take the hint and go away. Like I said, I didn't know much about children, otherwise I would have realised that, in the land of the village-bound child, a newcomer is conversational gold.

'I like your scrunchie. And …' a pause, as though she was giving my usual outfit of jeans and T-shirt a once over, in search of something at least vaguely complimentary to say, 'your boots.'

I glanced down at my strictly practical Converse trainers. 'Are you supposed to be here on your own? Isn't someone …' I glanced around, and saw a resounding lack of responsible adults, 'looking after you?'

'Only Alex,' the little girl said, with an insouciance that seemed to say that 'Alex' was so regularly neglectful of her that she'd already learned to cook, pay the bills and do basic DIY. 'It's all right. He's working on the Old Mill across the road over there,' a toss of blonde fringe towards the building site beside the river. 'And he knows that Light Bulb sometimes runs away with me.' This time the head-toss went in the direction of the hobby horse, propped blamelessly against the overgrown yew. 'Alex is my uncle and he helps look after Light Bulb and I live with him. Alex, I mean, but I live with Light Bulb too, but I'm not allowed to sleep in his stable because Alex says it's unhygenous.'

Oh boy. It's like Sesame Street *meets* This Is Your Life.

4

'Uh-huh,' I tried to grunt in a conversation-stopping way, swivelling around to get Beatrice Churchill and her interesting engraving in a shot to show this corner of the churchyard, triangulated by a wall slumped around it like bored shoulders and overgrown with feathers of grass and cow parsley. Some unkempt trees shaded it and hung their lowest branches over the grave markers.

'You've got wiggly hair,' observed the child, and I finally laid down the camera.

'Look, Scarlet. I'm trying to get this picture done so that I can go back and struggle with the next bit of my book. Please, can you just let me get on?' I hadn't meant to sound so abrupt; the words came out cropped by annoyance and snipped into sharp edges by my desire for solitude. There was silence from behind me, and when I turned around to check that she'd got the message, she was standing very still with one thumb in her mouth and the other hand twisting a piece of hair that stuck out from under the bike helmet. She looked small and hurt and I felt like the biggest pile of pooh on the planet. 'Sorry, sorry, I'm just … Look, why don't you come and hold this ivy back for me so I can take a proper picture?'

The thumb came out with an audible 'pop', and her mouth stretched into a grin as she ran over and dragged the leaves away from the stone with an enthusiasm that would have any botanist gritting his teeth. 'Like this?'

'Fabulous.' For the look of the thing I took some more pictures. I'd already really got more than enough of Beatrice, whose lettering wasn't *that* interesting, but I wanted to give Scarlet something to take that 'lost' look from her eyes.

After that, she ran from stone to stone, yanking at undergrowth and overhanging branches with shouts of 'do this one now!', leaping the snaggled upthrusts of broken grave-kerbs with an almost elemental enthusiasm. She hugged marble angels and whirled around a granite obelisk as though engaged in some kind of morbid country dance, finally flinging herself down alongside a new-looking pale stone which hadn't had the chance to grow more than a border of ivy and a slight lichen-tan. 'You have to do this one too!'

I looked sideways at the marker, its clean white lines sharp against the green backdrop, like a lost tooth embedded in an apple. 'No. I'm writing about pre-nineteenth century headstones, this one is far too recent.' My glance slid away from where she sprawled and found the comforting endurance of Beatrice again. 'It's not interesting enough.'

The silence came over the little girl again but this time the thumb stayed away from her mouth; instead her fingers bunched and grasped at the fabric of her leggings. Her easy slouch pulled tight into a curved defence. 'This is Mummy,' she said, 'and she's very, *very* interesting and you are horrible.'

Ah. The bitter smell of torn ivy was suddenly very pungent in the still air.

Nothing in my previous experience had given me any hints as to how to manage this situation, so I was more delighted than I should have been when a large man came crashing out of the yew-and-conifer undergrowth. The fact he had no shirt on, a light shading of brick dust being all that covered his well-muscled upper torso, didn't hurt either. He had dark hair lightened by powdered stone, and an expression of dusty annoyance. On seeing me he froze into immobility, as though being seen by a human turned him to stone, like a troll.

'Alex!' Scarlet scrambled to her feet. 'This is Winter who's in Grandma's cottage, but she won't take a picture of Mummy!'

Welcome to Precis-land. 'Scarlet was just helping me,' I began, although why I felt I needed to justify anything to a man who'd left a child in his care to roam willy-nilly across a main road, I wasn't sure. The man opened his mouth but didn't say anything, closed it again, and held out a hand to the little girl, who gave him a weary look and fetched the hobby horse from his tethering post on the bush.

'All right.' She mounted, with the same exaggerated gesture as she'd got off. 'We're coming.' Then, adopting a high-kneed trot, she hurtled off, followed by her silent guardian, and I heard her shout out to me as she disappeared through the overgrown graveyard. 'He's not weird, you know!'

Well, you could have fooled me. But then, I was taking pictures of graves, so, you know, maybe it takes one to know one.

Daniel Bekener @EditorDanB
RT @TheBookseller: Next yrs list from publishers of 2014's surprise hit Book of the Dead @ShyOwlPublishing. Can they do it again?

Chapter Two

'*These remote churchyards are less subject to vandalism than those in conurbations, but their isolated locations can mean less in the way of conservation and protection of the stones. One very interesting example of Primitive carving with triangular terminations has become so overgrown that it took some effort to determine that it had been erected to the memories of children in one farming family, who had all died before their third birthdays. There were seventeen of them. One can only imagine ...*'
—BOOK OF THE DEAD 2

f

Facebook

Winter Gregory Author Page

Does anyone know whether J.R.R. Tolkien ever visited a North Yorkshire churchyard? Because some of the spiders I'm seeing look like Shelob's descendants. Honestly, this research should come with an award for 'Bravery in the face of Numerous Legs'.

I flipped the computer shut and sat down on one of the very 'holiday cottage' chairs in the tiny living room; old-fashioned wooden backs and seats padded with home-made cushions in 1940's tea dress fabric. The room was so small that there was no space for anything more upholstered and the rest of the furnishings looked like dolls house seconds.

I'd got the fidgets. The ideas were there but somehow

the writing-down of them had got clogged, and the build up of words was making me restless. This little market town, with its cobbled streets, jagged roofline and notable lack of tourist attractions, was providing me with lots of lovely material for the book, but not a lot of recreational activities, unless I wanted to join the Bowls Club (I didn't). Pacing around the room wasn't much help either, not enough floor space and too much furniture, and the bookshelves were filled with local guidebooks, maps and the odd Jeffrey Archer, Scrabble and puzzles. Nothing that would occupy my mind. Nothing that would provide focus for thoughts which, left to themselves, would circle and snap at me from the shadows like hungry wolves.

I'll talk to Daisy. I felt a bit guilty at having the idea now. As though speaking to my twin was only something I did when there was nothing else, when I'd run out of books and there was nothing on TV, rather than it being something that was second nature.

'Hi, Daze!'

A small pause before she answered. 'Hey, Winnie.' Sounded normal, sounded as she always did, apart from maybe that little gap before her reply being longer than usual. 'Are you bored again? You only want to talk to me when you're bored these days.'

'That's rubbish.' My eyes wandered over to the picture on the mantelpiece, me and Daisy aged about five. My favourite picture of us, wearing identical pink dresses and identical ice cream-smeared grins. I'd rebelled shortly afterwards at our mother's liking for dressing us the same and had immediately gravitated towards jeans and T-shirts, while Daisy had continued with the pretty florals and floaty fabrics. She said I looked like a boy, and I countered with the fact that she looked like curtains. 'It's

9

just, you know, after what happened with Dan ... I never wanted us to fall out about it. It was nothing to do with you.'

She laughed now, and her laugh was unhesitating and unconsidered, unlike her speech. 'How could I fall out with you, Winnie? You're so totes adorbs in every way.'

I snorted. 'Don't overdo it. How's things for you, anyway? Are you okay?'

'Busy, busy, busy, you know how things go. How's the book coming along?'

Daisy, predictably enough, had gone into fashion design. Having spent our teenage years wearing stuff she created herself and embarrassing me half to death by draping herself in rugs, our dad's cast-off shirts and random bits of knitting, she'd found herself a dream job working for an up-and-coming 'name' in designer fashion. It was dramatic, creative and wildly exciting but also had moments of sheer drudgery, all of which my sister accepted calmly and worked through methodically. The only real drawback was that it was in Melbourne, Australia, but it was so 'Daisy' that it had been an unmissable opportunity, with the chance to create her own clothing lines and work with so many talented people. It was my idea of hell, but then I worked on my own and, apart from the obligatory book tours and radio and TV slots, rarely spoke to people who weren't dead, buried and immortalised by an interesting gravestone.

'The book's going okay. I travelled around a bit looking for the perfect place to write and now I'm in a village called Great Leys. It's not that great, and I don't know what leys are, but the material is good.' There was a knock at the front door, which opened directly into the living room, and behind the glass lights I could see a female head. 'Got to go, Daze. I think my landlady is paying a visit.'

'Laters, Win,' and, uncomplaining as ever, Daisy went back to doing whatever it was she did. It was one of the few advantages I'd ever come across with being a twin, we could talk or not talk, agree or not, and yet when we did communicate, everything felt as though it was part of an ongoing conversation, something we could dip in and out of and always have that feeling of connection.

I opened the door to see Mrs 'Call me Margaret' Hill and, much lower down, Scarlet. She was being held by the hand very firmly and there was no sign of Light Bulb, so I assumed that the news of her earlier adventure had travelled.

'Hello. I was just taking Scarlet home and I thought I'd pop by and make sure everything was all right for you in here. Have you found the bin liners? Only the bins have to go out every Monday, like it says on the notice, and it's Sunday today and so I wanted to remind you, and I wondered ...'

Margaret had the tightly managed hairstyle and slightly random clothes of a woman whose life consisted of more wayward arms than a spiral galaxy and the little worry-crease between the eyes of someone who isn't sure they're doing a very good job of holding it all together.

Scarlet made a face at me. I returned it. Margaret was still talking.

'... and if the bin lid isn't down they won't take it away. We've complained to the council but there's not much they can do now it's all contracted out. Oh, bother, and I forgot, I've got to call in at the library while they're still open and take those books back and put up that notice about craft shops for Alex, only they close at twelve on a Sunday.'

'I'll stay here then, Granny, with Winter. I can help her find the bin liners while you go to the library.' The little girl slipped out of her grandmother's grasp and into the living room, where she plonked herself down on a chair and looked around with evident curiosity. 'I know where everything is,' she said, despite the wide-eyed taking in of the scene that gave the lie to her words.

'Oh, no, I can't leave you with Miss Gregory, that wouldn't be ...' Margaret trailed off, the worry-crease deepening into a veritable gulley.

'I helped you in the graveyard, didn't I?' Scarlet appealed to me, turning surprisingly adult-looking grey eyes to mine. 'I'm useful, Granny. And I really *hate* the library. Mrs Cookson said I drew in the pony books.'

'She can stay with me,' I said, hoping that my expression implied that I had things to be doing and it had better not be an extended stay. 'It's fine.'

'But your work ...' Of which, I knew, there was no conspicuous sign. My laptop was closed, the pictures were still in the camera and there wasn't so much as a notebook to hint that I was actually doing any. In fact, apart from a couple of photographs and my pyjamas neatly folded on the end of the Spartan bed upstairs, I might not even be here. I gave an inward wince and made a mental note to tell Daisy that I was travelling so light these days that I seemed to have more mental baggage than physical.

'Hurry *up*, Granny. I need to turn Light Bulb out soon!' Scarlet had got up again and was looking at the framed pictures I'd propped up on the shelf above the gas fire. She stopped short of picking them up and squinting at them but I knew she wanted to. People always did, as though identical twins were an optical illusion.

'Are you sure? She can be a bit of a handful.' Margaret

was backing out of the door, but slowly and dubiously. 'I'll only be a few minutes, the library is just over there, next to the little bistro, and I really ought to put these posters up for Alex, he's hoping that the Old Mill can be turned into craft shops when he's finished.'

'We'll be fine. Scarlet's right, she's been very useful.' And I felt a bit sorry for her being described as 'a handful' in front of me. Surely parents, grandparents, should keep their opinions of their children to themselves? I knew mine always thought of me as the strong, capable, practical one while Daisy was the artistic one, but they never said as much to either of us, although my mother had said that we'd fallen into our chosen professions because of the sort of people we were, and that was the nearest she ever came to acknowledging our differences. But then, she'd been the one who'd tried to dress us alike until the incredible temper tantrum I'd thrown, now notorious in our family as 'Frockgate'.

The door closed and Scarlet grinned at me. 'Granny fusses,' she said. 'Why are there two of you?'

I jumped. The skin around my shoulders prickled as though I was being hugged by a frost. 'What?'

She pointed at the picture. 'Here. It's you when you were little.'

Relief. Stupid relief, from a feeling that was just as stupid. I'd thought she'd meant that there was someone standing behind me. 'It's me and my sister Daisy. We're twins.'

Scarlet picked up the other picture. 'And this is you when you're grown up.'

I took it from her. 'No, that's Daisy.' Long wildly curly hair tied back, boyishly slender figure lightly tanned in a bikini. Blue-green eyes and wide mouth laughing at the camera.

'Are you sure?' Scarlet narrowed her eyes at me and I laughed.

'Yes, I'm sure. It's Daisy. She lives in Australia and she emailed me that picture last Christmas, to make me jealous. It was freezing here and she was having Christmas dinner on the beach.'

'Looks exactly like you though.' She lost interest and wandered into the tiny kitchen. 'The bin liners must be in here. Granny keeps hers in the cupboard under the sink.'

'That's how identical twins work,' I couldn't let it go. 'We are the same. Everything. Well, Daisy's hair is a bit longer than mine, and she's thinner than me, prettier ...' I tailed off. Cleared my throat. 'But we're very alike.'

'Is she coming to see you?' She had her head in the cupboard now, her voice muffled and the room full of the smell of drain-cleaner – my knowledge of childcare was limited, but just about everything I bought said 'keep out of the reach of children'.

'I'll find them, don't worry,' I said, hastily. 'Would you like a drink of ...?' What did I have that I could offer to a child? Did I have *anything* that could be drunk by anyone under voting age? 'Milk?'

'Yes, please.' Scarlet hitched herself up onto the square foot of work surface. This cottage was *tiny*, no wonder it was advertised as only suitable for one person. If that person had had a dog, even a small one, someone would have had to eat outside. 'And a biscuit. Do you like horses, Winter?'

Her small, booted feet swung against the lower cupboards and I suddenly realised her rather eccentric clothing choices weren't indiscriminate: her leggings, wellingtons and bike helmet were all approximations of riding clothes.

'I used to ride, when I was younger. Daisy and I had a pony called Jack when we were growing up. We had to share but she was a lot keener than I was, so she rode him more than me.'

Scarlet's face turned to me as I poured her a mug of milk. She had a rapt expression, as though her eyes had found me magical all of a sudden. '*Really?* What was he like? Have you got any pictures? Did you do gymkhanas?'

'Er, no, but I did do a lot of falling off.' I dredged through my memories of growing up. We'd lived in the countryside just outside London, small house but near enough to fields to make childhood a stretch of free running and kite flying, dam building and paddling. Never short of a playmate because Daisy and I did everything together, except riding Jack, when some of our most fierce arguments took place, one of us having to cycle alongside or sit on the fence and watch while the other got all the fun. I started telling Scarlet about it – about the time Daisy fell off and cried, about jumping bareback, about leaning against the barn eating an apple while my sister tried to make our small, fat pony do dressage in the lumpy grass of the orchard.

Her eyes grew rounder, as though I was letting her into the secrets of the universe, as she sipped at her milk and ate her biscuit, her rubber-heeled feet clonking against the cheap vinyl-covered cupboard door. 'Alex and Granny won't let me have riding lessons,' she said, eventually, turning her gaze to her toes. 'Mummy would have let me.'

I wanted to know. I wanted to know about Alex, all god-like shape and stone dust like a Michelangelo statue in a slut's household, about her mother, now under that bland grave, about Light Bulb and his fabric face but I didn't know how to go about asking, and before I got the chance to worm my way around the subject, there was another knock at the door and Scarlet slithered off the side, her upper lip masked with milk. 'Granny's back.' She made her way through the maze of furniture. 'Thankyouverymuchforhavingme.'

But it wasn't Margaret out there in the bustling street. It was Alex. He'd got a shirt on now, a red T-shirt with a misshapen neck and splashes of something across the front, but his hair was still pomaded with fine sand. I smiled. 'Hello.'

His mouth opened, then he saw Scarlet over my shoulder and shut it again.

'Alex stammers,' she said, squeezing past me in the doorway. It was very matter-of-fact, not defensive or ashamed. 'So he doesn't say much.'

Alex rolled his eyes. 'I c- ...' and the pause was longer than I'd expected. We'd had a boy at primary school who stammered and our teacher had told us not to interrupt him but give him time to speak, although, in the careless way of the young, we'd usually ended up talking over him, or not listening at all. But that had been then, and I hoped that the ways of the world had softened me a bit over the years, although Alex being six feet of gorgeous didn't hurt either. 'Came to fetch Sc- ...' He didn't seem frustrated by the stoppage of the words. More as though he was using their staccato delivery as time to formulate the rest of his sentence. 'Scarlet.'

'Did Granny tell you I was here?'

There were similarities, I thought, watching him as he looked down at his niece. He had the same grey, serious eyes and the same generous mouth. His slightly crooked front teeth spoke of a similar thumb-sucking habit, although hopefully his was long gone.

'Look, it's fine if you want to leave her with me.' Then, remembering the pictures I had to download and the text I had to write, added, 'Sometimes. I mean, not right now but if she ever wants to pop in.'

He smiled. He had a similar expression to Scarlet's as well, I realised now as he lost it in favour of a grin that showed dimples and made his eyes gleam, a slightly wary look as though he suspected that someone was creeping up on him, just out of sight. 'That w-would be great. C-can I email? Or f- ...'

I really hope he's going to say Facebook. It's way too soon for anything else.

I found one of my business cards lurking in the back pocket of my jeans and held it out, figuring it was better to pre-empt the ending of that sentence thinking the best of him. 'It's got my email and my mobile and my Facebook author page and everything.'

He took it. His fingers were coarse with engrained rock dust and his nails were ragged and I had a sudden, awful flashback to long, careful fingers and the way they'd curved around the coffee cup, stirred a single sugar lump.

'Won't you?' Scarlet was hopping from foot to foot. 'Winter?'

I breathed deeply. My heart was settling now, its slurring pulse no longer deafening me. 'Sorry? Let you come again? Yes,' I said without thinking, without having heard anything but my rising blood.

'Yay!' I was the sudden object of a rushed hug. 'Thank you! Come on, Alex, Light Bulb needs a haynet and Granny won't let me use her plant holder so we need to buy some oranges or something. And some hay.'

Alex smiled at me again over the top of the child's

over-excited head and raised his eyebrows. 'You're a s-star,' he said. 'I'll …' and he flipped at my card.

As he led the bouncing Scarlet off down the road towards the main run of shops, I wondered what I'd agreed to do. I closed the door on the street and felt the quiet settle back around me. Time to turn on the computer, check my emails. Tweet my new project to keep the interest of those who'd, inexplicably in some opinions, made my last book a huge hit. Make sure my editor, make sure *Dan* knew I was working.

But instead I turned on the small radio. Listened to some indie music and let the noise fill that empty hole that surrounded any thoughts of Dan.

Chapter Three

Daniel Bekener @EditorDanB
@WinterGAuthor
How's the book going?

Facebook
Dan Bekener – Winter Gregory Author Page
Hey, how are things? You've not been in touch lately. I know I'm not your favourite person right now, but it would be great to hear from you.

From: DanBekener@ShyOwlPublishing.co.uk
To: BethanyAnnBekener@wolmail.com
Subject: How are you doing?
Hey, Bethie

Glad to see that voice recognition kit is working out for you. Let me know if you need a more up-to-date package and I'll grab one, Greg won't mind. He sends his love, by the way, everyone at Shy Owl says 'hi' and me …

No, I'm doing okay. And, before you start nagging, yeah, I've tried to get in touch with Winter. She's back in the country, so I guess she's working but I'm not getting involved any more than I have to, hey, only so much punishment a guy can take, right? Right. But you know something? Yeah, course you do, you're the only one who really 'got' what I had with Win, so I don't need to put it here, do I? Jeez, I miss her, Bethie. I miss her like someone put a twelve inch spike through my gut … but I couldn't do it. In the end, it wasn't me she wanted, I wasn't enough for her, I guess.

Anyhow. Mum says the meds are working for you and you've got a new chair. Hope next time I come round you're gonna race me round the yard like when we were kids … and, for the record, I *know* you used to let me win.

Love 'n stuff

Danny Boy

'Daze?'

'You should be asleep. What time is it over there? Three? Four?'

'Half three. I can't sleep.'

'What's up? I told you, you shouldn't read those books before you go to bed, all those ghoulish goings-on in graveyards … wow, that is a really good sentence, you can have that one.'

I rolled over in the bed. In keeping with all the other furnishings in the cottage, it was about three-quarter size. I was beginning to feel like Alice blundering about among all these tiny things. 'I was talking to a little girl today about when we had Jack, the pony? Just remembering what fun it all was; how long the summers seemed to go on for. Oh, and you falling off that time you tried jumping without stirrups and crying all the rest of the day.'

'Winnie, I'd broken my wrist. It's no wonder I cried all day.' Daisy sighed. 'And, yes, looking back is all very well but you mustn't dwell.'

'Am I dwelling? I don't think I am.' I drew the covers up around my shoulders. September was getting well dug-in and this far north the frosts came early.

Another sigh. 'You are, of course you are.' My sister's voice became faint for a moment, then strengthened. 'And it's only because the writing isn't going well, and you know what you need to do about that. You need to talk to Dan.'

'I can't *not* talk to him, he's my editor.' But my hands were sweaty at the thought, and the hair at the base of my neck prickled. 'But I don't have to see him again. Do I, Daze?'

She 'humphed'. I could picture her right now, sitting in her second-floor apartment which was strewn with fabric swatches, the Australian spring sun putting her in a warm spotlight of colour and texture. Her long legs, with those bony knees that caused both of us many hours of anguish as we tried to find tights that wouldn't make us look as though we were built of hinges, would be drawn up and she'd be fiddling with her toes. 'Don't expect me to tell you what you should do, Win, you already know. Now, I have to work and you need to sleep, go away.'

Now it was my turn to 'humph'. 'Charming.'

But she'd already gone, and she was right. The pressure was on to come up with another winner, the follow-up to last year's *Book of the Dead*, a book I'd come up with on the spur of the moment, pitched and been commissioned to write all within a matter of weeks, because Dan … I tossed my head on the pillow but the image remained … because Dan had had faith.

Dan. In his perpetual long black coat and motorcycle boots, hair that stuck up from his head like a dark aura. The hands of an artist, the soul of a poet and the business sense of a well-tuned laser; lover of indie rock music, snowstorms and sunset colours. The man who had taken my hand and told me I could be something.

The man who had made me choose ...

Chapter Four

✉

From: AlexHillStone@wolmail.com
To: WinterGregoryAuthor@teddymail.com
Subject: Just to say thanks
Hello

Thanks so much for looking after Scarlet yesterday, and it was very kind of you to let her help you do your photos. You mustn't let her be a nuisance – although, having written that, I'm damned if I know how you prevent an eight-year-old from being a nuisance sometimes, it's kind of inbuilt, isn't it, like the whole 'pink' thing and a love of One Direction? She's adorable in a kind of 'force of nature' way, not loving Scarl would be like not acknowledging gravity, but then, I'm her uncle so I would say that! Anyway. Upshot and point of this whole mail was just to say 'thank you' for keeping her company – she'd hate me for saying this but she can be a bit lonely sometimes. Life in a small town like Great Leys can be hard enough, when everybody remembers your family back three generations and every single transgression any one of them ever made, it's even worse when there's some kind of tragedy in the background for them to carefully 'not mention' in every conversation! So, any time you feel like dropping by the Old Mill for a slow chat please do.
Thanks again
Alex

I reread the email. Was it just me reading between carefully typed lines, or was Alex hinting that it wasn't only Scarlet who was lonely in the small town? Or was he nicely shacked-up with the local beauty, bringing up

23

his niece as his own amid a brood of Greek godlings and mini goddesses? He didn't seem like the kind of guy who'd trawl through incomers for a potential hit-and-run affair though, he'd seemed *normal*. Right up at the good-looking end of the spectrum, obviously, but still, normal.

Which was a nice change, really.

And, as though the word 'normal' had ricocheted through the aether and set off some kind of chain reaction, my in-box pinged again.

✉

From: DanBekener@ShyOwlPublishing.co.uk
To: WinterGregoryAuthor@teddymail.com
Subject: Hey …
Seriously though. I mean, seriously. Progress check would be nice, you're on a deadline, y'know.
D

Very carefully, and with great deliberation, I deleted the email from Dan. Even so, my hand shook slightly, as though even an electronic message could carry some element of him through to Great Leys. *It's no business of yours where I am, Daniel. I'll write the book because I have to, because I said I would, and whatever else you may say about me, whatever nasty little lies you may tell to anyone who will listen, I keep my promises. Yeah, great, you think you were right, 'course you do. You ALWAYS think you're right, Dan. I tried to tell you, tried to explain about the whole 'twin' thing but you just couldn't get it, couldn't understand that what Daisy and I have between us is … I can be certain of her. Whatever I do, whatever I am, she will be there for me. You may try, Dan, you may have given me promises, assurances, but they would never be the absolutes that I have with my sister. You could leave, after all, isn't that what you did? Didn't you just prove my case?*

Go to hell.

I wished I could have written all that. Put it in an email and sent it back, imagined the look on his face when he opened it, his dark eyes widening, maybe a hand rumpling distractedly through hair already frantic in its own right. But I couldn't. To communicate with Dan would be like forgiving him, and that was never going to happen.

I uploaded the pictures I'd taken for safekeeping. I'd once had a camera die on me and eat the memory card as a last meal, so now I was rigid about backing everything up, keeping a copy, not letting things vanish. Then I sat back, the hard wood of the chair digging into my spine. *I know the room's a bit small but an armchair would fit in. If you cut the arms off. And probably the back. So, a stool, a comfy stool, is that too much to ask for?*

But the cottage was cheap. At this back end of the year, in this tiny town with its lack of attractions and so small that it couldn't even be called a romantic hideaway, unless you were actually hiding from the object of the romance, and even *then* there wasn't a lot of room for concealment unless you got under the bed. And *even then* you'd need to be under five feet tall and really skinny.

Outside the window the bustle of the High Street was dulled a little by a thick mist which had come down from the moors. They overhung the town and loomed like a visit from an opinionated relative to the south, while the north was a river plain which stretched to Newcastle. Great Leys was the last picturesque place before the countryside degenerated into factories and refineries and was therefore a really great location to be studying grave fashions, as the eighteenth century's version of the nouveau riche had moved out of the unhealthy cities and into the countryside, bringing their modern fashions with their dead bodies. It also made a great centre for travelling to the counterpoint graveyards up on those moors, where farming families had lived for generations and engraved their headstones in the same traditional ways as they always had. Fashion didn't apply when you were trying to scratch a living from a six-week summer and sheep and believed caps to be essential wear.

I went back to the churchyard, walking through the mist which decorated my sleeves and my hair like a hit-and-run beading fanatic. The shops were opening for Monday business and a knot of children in brand-new uniforms waiting for the school bus turned to watch me, but then it can't be every day that you see someone go into a churchyard with a laptop. Maybe they thought I was going to conduct a very high-tech seance.

In fact, I was going to write. The text to go with the photographs would hopefully come a lot more easily when written in situ, when I could see the decorative calligraphy in daylight. Beatrice Churchill had clearly had a loving family who had seen fit to not only carve her name and dates in a gothic style which took over most of the stone, but also a nice little homily in English style text, and then to beswag any available clear surfaces with the kind of decorative edging more usually seen as piping around cushions. It was a bit of a dog's dinner as far as tombstone lettering went, but it gave me a lot to say.

I sat cross-legged on the damp grass, closed my eyes, and tried to feel my way around the emotions of those who'd had the stone erected – it was this 'speculative' angle that had given my previous book the edge that had made it the best-seller it had been, rather than the dry, scholarly tone of many books on such subjects. I'd tried to put myself in the mindset of these long-gone people, tried to put their voices across, collated from such disparate sources as the position in the graveyard, the condition of the graves, lettering style and any general family research that I could dig up. And, with the current fashion for genealogy, readers lapped it up.

Beatrice Churchill had had a notable father. One with no taste whatsoever, apparently, but someone about whom I could write. I opened my notes as a separate document and began to type, slowly, slowly putting myself back into the head of the man who'd lost his only daughter at the age of twenty-nine.

Ping.

I had an email. How could I have an email? Who turns a churchyard into a wireless hotspot? And, more to the point, *why*? I wriggled my shoulders to loosen them and only now felt the damp that had seeped through my jeans while I'd been working. Two hours? How had that happened? And not many words to show for it, either.

Ping.

✉

From: DanBekener@ShyOwlPublishing.co.uk
To: WinterGregoryAuthor@teddymail.com
Subject: You probably won't even read this but ...
Okay. Okay. I get it. You don't want anything to do with me and I guess it's pointless for me to plead my case. But, Winter, you must have seen how it was for me, how I couldn't think straight after ... shit. I just said it was pointless and yet, here I am, trying to make you see my side of the story. And that's all I want, y'know? To tell you how it looks from my perspective. I mean, I

know what I did was wrong. I know I hurt you. The whole Daisy thing, I shouldn't have got involved … yeah, doing it again, guess that's my mindset for you, pleading that whole pointless case. But you and me, we were *good*, Win, we were strong, we were that thing that everyone wants, a unit. We were tight. Remember that day in Rouen? With the drunk guy coming on to you, and I offered to punch him out for you and then he floored me and you had to call the police? Guess this email is my equivalent of that, my attempt to punch out the drunk.

Please don't call the police.

Dan

I had to put the laptop down on the grass because my hands were shaking so hard I was worried I'd drop it. *Dan.* For a moment I thought that the mist was back, blurring the lines of the stones in front of me, but then I felt the damp touch of tears against my cheek and realised I was crying. *Crying? Over Dan? No. No more tears shed over him, he doesn't deserve them. He shouldn't be able to affect me like this, not now. Six months is too long to keep that ragged cutting edge of sorrow sharp enough to slice through memories. Enough.*

Enough.

I sniffed, wiped my eyes on the back of my hand and bent to pick up the laptop.

'Winter? Oh, I'm sorry, are you working? I was just, well, it's a shortcut through here and I was going to pop in and see Alex, such a shame he can't use a mobile but well, he's a little impaired with the spoken word so it's difficult. Did you find the bin liners? If you miss the bin men they only do domestic every other week and it builds up, you know.'

Margaret Hill, wearing something startlingly pink,

approached me down the churchyard path. She stopped short of stepping on the still-damp grass and sort of hovered around the edge of the path, almost vibrating with something. Curiosity, possibly, given my damp crotch and sniffing, although it was possible that she'd reached such a stage of fuchsia that the earth was rejecting her physical presence.

I was so shaken by the email from Dan that I seized upon her as though she was my long-lost best friend. 'Oh, hello. Yes, I was working, but my battery is pretty nearly flat now so I was just going to go.' As I spoke I walked to the path, uncomfortably aware of my moistness. 'Where can I get a really good cup of coffee in Great Leys?'

'Well, there's the Costa, but they're a bit corporate for my liking. There's a little independent coffee shop down near the river but they don't open on Mondays. Are you writing a book about inscriptions then? Because, if you're interested, you could talk to Alex, he does some stone carving, he's done the entranceway to the Old Mill with the poem on it. He's been working on that place for years now, Do you know he used to be a stonemason? Did very well but now he just does the odd commission.'

Wow, a conversation with Margaret was like playing Twister with a pipe cleaner. 'Maybe,' I began, cautiously, in case she was about to launch into rhyming couplets on the subject of Spam or something, 'I could come and talk to Alex? I could have a coffee at the same time.'

She was suddenly still. Her grey eyes, so like her son and her granddaughter, were shrewd. 'Alex has a stammer,' she said. 'Ever since Ellen,' and her voice tripped over the name, 'since his sister died, he's had problems communicating. It's called psychogenic stammering, they think it might have been brought on by the trauma.' Now her speech had lost the twists and turns, it was straightforward and her voice was sad. I wondered if the butterfly attention span she'd so far displayed was a protective thing, to keep her from thinking too deeply.

'Yes. We've met and chatted.'

She smiled a tight smile. 'He feels guilty, that's what it is, I'm afraid. Ellen died when a delivery of stone fell, and Alex blames himself for not warning her, for not making her stay away; she was only popping by to drop in some milk; she was bringing Scarlet over to me after school one day and she got out of the car and …' a flick of fingers. 'I'm sorry. I have no idea why I'm telling you this.' And now her words were slow, anchored by tears.

I know why you're telling me. You're warning me not to mess with your son. You might not even realise it, but that's what you're doing. I'm not sure whether you're telling me to stay right away or to be careful and not hurt him, but you are being a concerned mother of a damaged son, and I suddenly like you a lot more than I did before.

'It's fine. It's nice to meet a man who thinks before he speaks,' I said, and she let out a sudden giggle.

'You're right! Let's go and see him and he can make you a cup of coffee, and then you can have a chat about stony things.'

I averted my eyes from her pink outfit, which was beginning to make my vision strobe at the edges, and we walked out through the churchyard and across the main road. I'd passed the Old Mill site several times but, apart from a stone archway with the words *'The stones move like hearts beat, And love is ground'* carved into them, there wasn't much to see from the road. Once we walked under the arch though, I could see the old flour mill, its wheel still dredging into the stream. From the newness of much of the stone it had been almost completely rebuilt, and now looked like a posh barn conversion, with huge doors of glass opening onto a paved yard. Pulley arms jutted high on the walls and an old door at second storey level looked like the place where grain sacks had once been hauled, to be poured down into the mill mechanism.

'Alex is going to let the units out as craft workshops,' Margaret said. 'The bank manager said he should make his money back in ten years.'

Yes, all right, you're trying to persuade me that your son is a dateable guy, not sell me a second-hand car. But I smiled and noted the eco-friendly solar panels on the roof, the sweeping wooden arch of the timbers that curved from the ridge to provide a sheltered seating area outside the doors and the two huge millstones in the centre of the yard. 'It's beautiful.'

'Th-th—' Obviously a difficult one because Alex stopped there, walking towards us from the half-built wall towards the back of the mill. He smelled of hard work, of dust and an earlier shower that had left his hair damp; his shirt was checked and the sleeves were rolled to reveal dusty forearms. His knuckles were red and slightly cracked and his jeans were tight over the muscles that a physical job gives you. He looked like a man who's spent his whole life in the gym and has then fallen into a sandpit. I'd never been much of a one for muscular men before, my type had always been more cerebral. Tall, verging on the lanky, but with a mind that could win a Scrabble game with a 'Q' and no 'U's, speak four languages – all of them with a Lincolnshire accent – and a charisma that would charm everyone from old ladies to small dogs. I shook my head. Muscles were where it was at, now. Yes. No more of the dark, no more of the chaos. No more of the *Dan*.

'Hello, dear.' Margaret kissed the stubbled cheek in an offhand way. 'Winter would like a coffee, if you're not busy, and I think she wants to talk about stonemasonry, but I'm not very sure. Can you pick Scarlet up from school this afternoon? I have to take Mr Park to the hospital for his prostate again, they're really going to have to do something about it, he's just wee wee wee all day, maybe they can put a tube in it.'

'I've got a d-delivery c-coming.' Alex led us in through the double doors into the building which smelled of new wood, a clean, citrusy scent. 'Can't Mr P-Park's p-prostate wait?'

'You wouldn't say that if you had to sit next to him in meetings. Quite frankly, he's starting to smell, besides he's got an appointment and it took me weeks to get him to make one this time and I don't want him having an excuse not to go, even though all he seems to do is go, if you see what I mean. Can't the delivery wait?'

'I'll fetch her,' I found myself saying. 'If that's all right,' I added as both pairs of eyes turned to me, and I wasn't sure if they were looking at me as a lifesaver or a potential child-abductor. 'And if someone tells me where the school is.'

'Well, that's—' Margaret began, but Alex cut her off.

'If y-you wouldn't m-mind, Winter. It w-would be such a help.' He laid a hand on my sleeve and smiled, his face moving up an attractiveness-category as he did so, a half fan of sun-puckered lines spreading from each eye and his dimples deepening as that wide mouth curved into a proper grin. 'Y-you'll have to p-put up with Light B-bulb though, and he's often a b-bit fr-fractious after a d-day at school. He k-kicks, you know.'

Margaret sighed. 'You shouldn't encourage her to keep playing with that thing,' she said. 'It's silly.'

'It's all she's g-got, Mum,' he said, quietly. 'I'm g-going to p-put the k-kettle on n-now.'

'Right, well, I'd better get back to town, I've got a library committee meeting this lunchtime before the hospital run and I must remember while I'm there that I wanted to borrow that book. You know, the one with that purple cover that Sally recommended when I was in the fruit shop, something to do with wine tasting or something and then there'll be Mr Park and his wee to contend with so I'll see you tomorrow, probably, Alex, and I do hope they've taken your bins, Winter. It's such a worry, what with rats and things.'

She moved off back out of the building, pausing to stroke a hand over some timber supports as though checking for dust. The outfit became more bearable and less pink the further away she went, like an illustration of redshift. 'She's b-b—' began Alex.

Broke? Bradford? Buggering the librarian? I cursed my brain for its impatient tendency to fill in the worst possible permutations of words.

'—bonkers,' he finally managed, 'but she's been th-through a lot, what with El-Ellen, and th-the stammer, and h-having to look after S-Scarlet. She w-wanted to t-t-take her but ...' A shrug. 'My d-dad had n-not long d-died. She d-didn't c-cope w-well.'

I thought about the woman as she'd been in the churchyard. Quietly sad. 'It must be hard for her. It must be hard for all of you, especially Scarlet.'

A shrug. 'W-we do our b-best.' Then a headshake which sent drying hair flicking flakes of stone outwards. 'Now. C-coffee.'

He led me through the building, which was in various stages of completion with electricians working in one section while another had no roof and only three walls, to an office space in what had obviously been the mill itself. Old beams creaked overhead as someone walked on an upper floor, and there was still a smell of flour, wet sacks and, faintly, mice. There was also a cutting-edge computer system, photocopier and printer and, where I had expected a kettle and a couple of chipped mugs, a vast coffee machine. It grumbled and burbled and shot occasional jets of steam from a chrome nozzle, but the smell made my mouth water.

'That's a bit heavy duty, isn't it? For a building site?'

Alex hesitated, then grinned. 'I have a h-heavy duty habit to s-sustain,' he said. 'It's temperamental b-but makes b-bloody good c-coffee.' At that moment the machine let out a noise like Everest achieving orgasm and Alex was just in time, shoving a pot underneath the nozzle to catch a stream of coffee which frothed out. 'As I s-said. Temperamental.'

'Dangerous, I'd have called it.'

With one leg he hitched a chair over from beside the desk on which all the equipment rested and poked it my way, then swung himself up to sit on the desk itself. 'M-milk? Sugar? I've got a huge d-d—'

For God's sake, Winter, stop it …

'—delivery coming in a bit, so I c-can't chat for l-long but …' He poured two mugs of the fragrant coffee, raised an eyebrow at the milk bottle and, when I nodded, added a slurp. '… if you've got any q-questions, I'm always h-here.' Then he gave a peculiar half-laugh. 'Yeah. Al-always here,' he repeated, and now those grey eyes weren't looking at anything in the real world, they were seeing something old, something that seemed to be ghosting through his brain.

'Thanks for the email.' I wanted him to stop thinking

whatever thoughts were making his cheeks pull in like that, stop his eyelids drooping down as though to cut the world out. 'Like I said, I really don't mind having Scarlet, if it helps you out. Not when I'm working or anything, obviously, but you know, if you find yourself stuck. Ever. Or your mother has to go to the wee clinic.'

Now the grin was back again. It was obviously a more normal expression for him, judging by the way his face had tanned around the laughter lines, and when he stopped they showed up as pale indents along his cheekbones. 'You might n-not be so k-keen when sh-she's going on about h-horses,' he said. 'She c-can be a b-bit s-single-minded, Scarlet.' And the grin died again, it was like watching the sun rise and set, days passing across his face. 'Ellen used to l-love horses.'

'When did she die?' I sipped. The bitter, burned taste of fresh coffee swung me back to meetings at Shy Owl, me pitching ideas, Dan picking them up and running with them; laughing and jotting notes, throwing speculative titles at one another, *coffee falling into drinks, a meal, a kiss in a parked car and then—*

'Are y-you all right?' Alex was frowning at me. 'Y-you went all b-blurry.'

'Sorry. Flashbacks.' I swallowed. The coffee seemed to have solidified in my mouth. His expression was now a mixture of carefully reined in curiosity tinged with a sadness that made me say more than I should have done. 'Ex-boyfriend. My editor. Oh, that makes it sound as though they are two separate people in a fist fight, but they're not. Daniel, he … there was …' *Careful, Winter.* 'He never understood. I have a twin, you see, Daisy. Dan … he thought I relied on her too much. She moved to Australia, so I spend a lot of time talking to her, to make up for not being able to ...' That was as far as I could go. As much as I could vocalise about what had happened. 'I've never really told her what happened, she just knows we split up, I mean, none of it was her fault but I can never forgive him. *Never*,' and I surprised myself with how vicious I sounded. If I'd been Alex I'd have been hiding all the sharp objects, or at least covering the steam spout from the coffee maker.

'Y-yes, I kn-know the feeling. I was d-dating s-someone when El- ... when it all h-happened. We b-broke up b-because I c-couldn't h-handle ...' He stopped speaking and wrinkled his nose into his mug. 'Only d-difference is th-that I c-can't forgive *m-m-myself*. Well, th-this is turning into a b-bit of a th-therapy session for b-both of us, isn't it?' He leaned forwards and gave my knee a quick rub.

I felt the weight of his hand, the heat of it and, although I knew the intent had been an expression of sympathy I couldn't stop the blush from rising to my face and dropped my mouth back into the mug to try to conceal it.

'And El-Ellen died three years ago. S-Scarlet was five. Long enough, you'd th-think. A l-lifetime for a l-little girl.' And then a direct, cool stare. 'I do my b-best.'

And you're worried it isn't enough. You're trying to do all this, renovate the mill and get a business up and running and still give enough time to that child, and it isn't really working, hence today when the childcare arrangements fell apart and you'd have had to what? Find someone at short notice, or rearrange the delivery? You've had guilt fitted as standard.

'I actually do want to talk about stone carving though.' I finally remembered, dazed as I was by all the turmoil and the dimples and everything, why I'd come in the first place.

'You m-mean it w-wasn't a p-ploy? Now I'm d-disappointed.'

'Don't flatter yourself, sunshine.'

I hardly know this man. Okay, he's cute, has the requisite amount of deep feelings and an incredibly nice chest, but that means nothing. Even Dan had deep feelings and a good body. Didn't make him a nice guy though, did it? And yet, I've told Alex more about what happened with Dan and Daisy than I've said to almost anyone else, except my mother. All anyone else knows is that we're no longer a couple. He's still my editor, for now, but that's only a matter of time.

'Like I s-said, I have this d-delivery d-due, that's g-going to hold me up for th-the rest of the d-day so I c-can't really chat much n-now. I've g-got some b-books though. I'll sh-show you when you b-bring Scarlet b-back.'

'And Light Bulb.'

'Ob-viously.'

I drank the rest of the coffee slowly. Alex got called to some on-site problem and left me with a grin and a flipped hand in the company of the evil coffee dispenser, which growled threateningly at me and refused me a refill. Between that and the hobby horse, I was beginning to think that Great Leys was run entirely by inanimate objects.

Chapter Five

*'The Wilkinson family seem to have had a particularly
eventful life. Miles Wilkinson (1738–1800, when he
probably died just for a rest) married no less than five
times, with each marriage producing seven children.
The eldest offspring from each of the various marriages
was named after Miles, so for anyone tracing their
family tree and finding a Miles Wilkinson on one
of the branches – the very best of luck to you.'*
—BOOK OF THE DEAD 2

Both Alex and his mother had forgotten to give me
directions to the primary school, but it wasn't too hard to
find; I just waited until half past three and then followed
the screaming. Scarlet was waiting inside the gate, holding
the hand of a woman wearing what Daisy would no doubt
have had trendy words for, but I could only call a smock.
In the other hand she held Light Bulb.

Scarlet's face lit up when she saw me, and the thumb
she'd been sucking slid out of her mouth. 'Winter!'

'I've come to get you, your uncle has a delivery and
your grandma, well, I'm not quite sure what's going on
there but it seems to involve quite a lot of widdle.'

The woman holding Scarlet frowned at me. 'I'm afraid
I can't let this young lady go anywhere with you without
parental permission.' She couldn't have been much older
than me, or possibly younger but with the slightly tense
look that some primary teachers tend towards giving her
a prematurely crinkled forehead. 'Which we don't have.'

'But it's Winter,' Scarlet said, baffled. 'And Alex must have told her to come and get me, otherwise how would she know where to come?'

The woman crouched down. 'Sweetie, you know we can't just let you go with anyone, can we? Remember the talk we had last term? About keeping safe?'

Scarlet looked as nonplussed as was possible for an eight-year-old. 'I've got Light Bulb. No one can hurt me while I've got him,' and she patted the stick in much the same way as I imagine a ninja would stroke his nunchuk.

'But what if someone wanted to take Light Bulb away and hurt him?' There was a patience in this young woman that impressed me. She genuinely seemed fond of Scarlet, and anybody who could treat that cloth and broom handle as a sentient being was either eight, insane or born to childcare.

Scarlet made an illustrative face, ninety per cent teeth, and with fingers held up like claws. I didn't know about anyone wanting to hurt Light Bulb, but I wouldn't have tackled her.

'Could you not go and telephone Alex, perhaps?' I suggested.

When I used Alex's name the woman straightened and looked me up and down in a kind of half-assessing, half-cautious way. *Oh. I see. That's how the land lies, is it? But then, I shouldn't think eligible single men come on the market all that often in a place this size – Alex must be the local equivalent of El Dorado. The proper one, obviously, not the rubbish TV programme.*

'Alex doesn't do phones. 'Cos of his stammer,' Scarlet supplied. 'You can phone Granny, I s'pose, on her mobile.'

'She was going to the hospital though, she won't have her phone on in there, will she?' I sighed. 'Look, Miss …'

'It's Ms. Ms Charlton,' and then, softening when I didn't raise my eyebrows at the Ms bit, 'Lucy. Look, school policy is not to let children go with anyone other than a named adult.'

'Can't I go by myself?' Scarlet was stroking Light Bulb's unresisting ears. 'The big ones do, they walk home by themselves. I could walk home by myself with Winter.'

We adults looked at one another. I could see Lucy trying not to grin and I was fighting my own inclination to snort. 'If you're sure,' Lucy said. 'And if you make sure that Light Bulb is careful near the road, you wouldn't want him to get loose in traffic, would you?'

She went up in my estimation again right there, although I still wasn't sure about the smock. Never mind what Daisy might say about fashion, it made her look pregnant. Unless she was, of course, but even so it was a crime against *Vogue*. 'I promise I'll keep an eye on her. I'm taking her to the Old Mill anyway, so you could always come past on your way home and check she's safely there.'

'That's a good idea,' and the speed with which she took my suggestion told me I'd been right to suspect that Lucy Charlton had a bit of a 'thing' for Alex. But then, who wouldn't? I mean, I found myself smiling at the thought of his rock-dusted hair, and doing something a bit more basic at the memory of his bare chest, and he wasn't even my type. 'I haven't seen Al … I mean, Mr Hill, for a while, I'll do that. Be careful, Scarlet.'

Scarlet mounted Light Bulb in her usual exaggerated fashion, and we literally trotted off down the road. 'He's a bit fresh. He has to spend the day in Mr Moore's office, but it's all right because he has a haynet.'

Light Bulb shied dramatically at a rubbish bin as he and

Scarlet dashed along the pavement. The mist had cleared with the afternoon and the sun was warm, which was just as well because Scarlet was only wearing a summer dress. Her bare legs were scraped and scrubbed with rashes and the grazes of childhood and were very vulnerable-looking under the pink checked cotton and above the ankle socks that I bet had started the day as white.

'Shall we get an ice cream?' I found myself asking, unexpectedly.

'Ooh, yes!' Light Bulb performed a dressage manoeuvre and circled back along the pavement towards me. 'Can we eat them in the park?'

Great Leys has a park? Why? Ninety per cent of it is countryside anyway, what have they done, bunged a set of swings up in a field?

It turned out that that was pretty much exactly what they had done. We sat on a bench and ate Cornettos, while Light Bulb grazed, or at least lay face down on the grass in front of us. Without the bike helmet Scarlet's hair was curly and had obviously been cut by someone with more enthusiasm than talent – it was slightly lopsided at the back and her fringe looked more like an amateur comb-over – but she seemed entirely unselfconscious as she sat next to me, digging one sandalled toe into the peaty earth.

'Where do your mummy and daddy live?' she asked me unexpectedly, staring at two big lads shouting at one another from the swings.

'My parents split up five years ago. My mother lives in France and my dad went back to America, where he's from.' *And I still feel the pain of their divorce, although they've tried not to bother me with it.*

'So you must get really nice holidays then.'

'Well, I've just spent six months in Paris with my mum,

but it didn't really qualify as a holiday. I was plotting out the new book.'

'Has your dad taken you to Disney World yet?' She was licking her ice cream with determination and regarding me from those curiously adult eyes, but without the adult level of prurience that I was used to from personal questioning. She simply wanted the facts, ma'am.

'I'm a bit old for Disney World, I think, besides he lives in Maine and that's quite a long way away. I think,' I added, hastily, since my knowledge of the geography of the United States was a bit shaky, even given my parentage.

'My mummy and dad split up before I was born. He was called Jamie.' It was hard to know how Scarlet felt about anything, I realised. Those eyes, unlike her uncle's, gave nothing away, and besides, I was far more used to reading men than eight-year-old girls. She could have been trying to make me understand how it was to grow up with no parents or she could simply be giving me information. 'So now Alex and Granny look after me.'

'So where do you live?'

A frown, as though she had never really thought about it. 'Where Mummy and I lived before. With Alex.'

'And where does Alex live?' This being the information I really wanted. Did he live at home, with his mother, in his old childhood room with an entire adolescence-worth of … let me think, he didn't look the type for girlie-mags … *Doctor Who* merchandise all over the surfaces and a *Star Wars* duvet cover?

'At the Old Mill. Up at the top. I'll show you my bedroom if you like, and Light Bulb's stable.' A last chew saw the ice cream gone and she was up and on her feet again.

The park was swarming with children now, all in various

stages of disrobing from school uniform, climbing on the wooden frame, draping themselves over the tyre swings, while adults chatted and watched with half an eye. No one approached us, I noticed. None of the children came to talk to Scarlet, not even some of the pinker little girls, with their hair in complicated plaits, who looked around the same age. They were sitting together making daisy chains, while Scarlet had collected Light Bulb from his prone position and was trotting him round and round in a circle. His benevolent expression was already beginning to get on my nerves.

'We'd better go. I don't want Ms Charlton to find you're not at the Old Mill when she gets there, she looks the type to call out the police first and set homework later.'

Scarlet obediently followed me out of the park and along the tree-lined lane that led to the main road and the Old Mill. Great Leys was only about half a mile from end to end, residential streets orbiting the High Street, through which the river ran like a self-conscious tourist attraction, green banked and beducked as it was. The main road which passed through on its way to the industrial north wasn't even that main, a B road which clipped the eastern end of the town, over the old iron bridge and then away. Even the traffic didn't want to hang around Great Leys.

Different. Not like London. This would all be cars and buses and yelling; dropped litter and the taste of diesel in the air, grass contained in parks not containing sheep. And shops. And museums and art galleries and railway stations.

I realised I hadn't driven my car for three days. Hadn't even checked it was still where I'd left it – parked up near Margaret's Victorian villa just off the High Street. I shrugged to myself. If anything had happened to it, I'd bet Margaret knew the names of the offenders, their addresses and, probably, their library card numbers.

Scarlet swung in through the archway to the Old Mill, Light Bulb's wooden stick bobbing about as she cantered up the yard. Off to one side I could see a big lorry disgorging a load of timber and, as we went inside the building, I saw Alex supervising the unloading. The lorry's engine was running and a hydraulic crane ground its gears as it lifted the wooden beams, so everything was being done with hand signals. He'd taken his shirt off again and was wearing a safety helmet and gloves, which made him look like Mr September in a construction-man pin-up calendar. He'd obviously worked most of the summer with the shirt off, his torso was tanned evenly under the customary cosmetic dusting of stone.

I wondered how old he was. He had the laughter lines and worn hands of someone in their late thirties, but the body of someone much younger; the way his jeans hugged his thighs and the nicely-rounded contours of his buttocks said late twenties. No grey tones in his hair. I supposed I could just ask Scarlet, she'd probably tell me his shoe size and taste in music too without much prompting.

I was slightly embarrassed when he looked up, across the lorry, and caught me staring at him. I tried to do an expression of surprise, as though my eyes had been wandering around and had only recently settled on him, rather than having been running over his bare midriff for what felt like hours. He grinned and gave me a double thumbs-up, then one of the other men helping unload tapped him on the shoulder and he bent low to hear what they were saying, so I figured this was a good time to stop staring and find out where Scarlet was. Possibly rescue her from that coffee machine, which looked more than capable of holding a child to ransom.

She was waiting for me in the big atrium. 'Up here.'

'I'm not sure.' My brief had been to bring her home, not go through his CD collection. *But I can't just leave her, can I? Alex is busy, what if she falls down or the coffee machine gets her?* 'Okay. But I can't stay long, just until Alex finishes.'

'I want to show you my bedroom.'

It was a flat on the top floor of the mill. One wall still had the door I'd noticed from the outside, for hauling grain in, and the roof was all beams and hooks, high above our heads. Open plan, one end was a swish kitchen, the rest filled with sofas, a TV, and more shelves of pony books than anyone outside The British Horse Society could live with. Scarlet opened a door and ran through into a corridor, charging on down to the end and giving me not much choice but to follow her, staring around me all the time at the Farrow & Ball paint choices and the framed pencil sketches on the walls. It was all so nicely done that I wondered if Alex was secretly an interior designer.

Such a contrast to Dan's flat which was all windows. Where we stood and looked at the view over the park as the sun flowed across us like a river of light. One huge couch and a rug, all scattered with papers, the smell of age-old dog fur and cigarette smoke from previous inhabitants layered through the rooms. Casual, unstudied, like Dan himself. And on one wall, the hand-drawn sketches for the tattoo he bore on his wrist, a design he'd created and immortalised on his own body. 'Chaos,' he'd said when I looked. 'The secret of the universe.'

'Here!' Triumphantly Scarlet threw open the door at the end of the passage to reveal ... well. To say she had an obsession with ponies would be to underplay the decor to quite an extreme level. There were posters of ponies. Pony wallpaper. Model ponies. Pony duvet set, pony curtains and a pony rug beside the pony slippers. Too long in that room and you'd slip species. 'And this is Light Bulb's stable.' A walk-in wardrobe, possibly, on the architect's plans, its polished wooden floor strewn with straw, an old orange-net filled with hay tied to a beam, a plastic tub of water in the corner. On a shelf stood an old hairbrush and plastic dog comb.

My heart ached.

Scarlet propped Light Bulb against the wall, removed his plastic bridle and began brushing his wooden stick body with the hairbrush. 'He gets a bit sweaty when he's excited,' she explained. 'I should have made him walk home, but he loves to canter.' *Oh, Winter, you should have stuck to the dead people. You know where you are with them.*

'Did,' I began, carefully, watching her start to brush out the string tail, 'did your mummy give you Light Bulb?'

She didn't even hesitate in the brushing. 'It was my birthday two days before she died. I was five and Light Bulb was my present.' Now she'd got a swathe of fabric, something like a piece of old fleece. 'You'll have to wear your rug until you stop being sweaty, or you might catch a cold,' she advised the horse-designate.

'Don't leave his rug on,' I found myself saying.

'What?'

'When you're hot you don't put something on, do you? Let him cool down first, then rug him up.' *What am I doing? He's a broomhandle with a stupid face!*

Slowly Scarlet peeled the fleece off. 'It says in my horse book that they have to cool down slowly,' she said, somewhat sulkily.

'But I bet your horse books are aimed at … ummm … little children? Not the sort of grown-up books that you need now.' An idea. Sudden, not all that welcome, and not sure where it came from, unless it was kicked into being by those eyes, so much like her uncle's. 'Look. Next weekend, if Alex says it's okay, why don't we go into' – I mentally blundered through the local map in my head – 'York, and look for some new books on horse care?' *Winter, Winter, you don't even like children! You've never even thought about children! Actually, that's not quite true, is it? With Dan, just that once, when you lay looking at him sleeping and you imagined that jawline, that curve of nose, those beautiful eyes transposed onto a child, your child. Yours and his. That one moment, before you thought about sleepless nights, where you'd live, how you'd be able to write and research with a baby, but in that one, breathless moment you thought about having Dan's baby.*

Scarlet was rotating with delight. 'Alex will let me! Can we go to McDonald's too?'

Oh, the privations of a small town life, which make McDonald's look like a treat. I was floundering my way around a reply when Alex came into the room, still shirtless but now minus the safety helmet. From the way Scarlet launched herself at him, armed with a stream of words about how much she wanted me to take her to York and how Light Bulb had behaved that day and how she'd got a list of spellings to learn, I think he wished he'd left the helmet on.

'I'd better go. Got some stuff to get on with.' I didn't really, such work as I'd done was backed up for the day and all that remained to do was to eat something, watch the tiny television and go to bed, but I needed some space.

Eight-year-old enthusiasm and energy made me want to lie very still for a while.

'I …' Alex waved a hand to indicate the still-talking Scarlet, 'I'll m-message you. Th-thank you, Winter, you've been g-great.'

As I walked out of the room I had to move past him, still standing in the doorway with Scarlet doing her impression of a small moon orbiting a gas giant. He flashed me that smile, and I could feel the heat from his body, smell the dust and timber on his skin giving my libido a good kicking. Even the sight of a Fiat 500 driving into the yard with Lucy Charlton at the wheel and skidding to a halt that Schumacher would have regarded as a bit reckless didn't kill it. In fact, the feeling stayed with me all the way back to the cottage, a feeling that had been in abeyance since Dan and I split up.

I needed to talk to Daisy.

Chapter Six

'There's this bloke,' I started carefully. 'He seems sweet, he's nice and cute and available, but I have absolutely no idea if I fancy him or not. Or if he fancies me. Or if it's even a good idea.'

Daisy sounded slightly distracted. 'I don't think you should. You've still got issues, haven't you? With Dan?'

I flinched. 'No. Have I? Maybe. But can't I just ignore those and go straight for the kill with Alex? Honestly, it's a waste of a terrific body, having it hanging round on a building site like that when it could be ...' My imagination supplied a couple of the things it could have been doing and I felt my cheeks fire up.

'But it's not just him though, is it? He's got a little girl to think of too.'

'I hate your advice. You should be telling me to go and rip this man's clothes off with my teeth. Honestly. He's got the full set, you know, gorgeous eyes, a fantastic torso and thighs like ...' I tailed off again. 'He's pretty ripped, Daze. Even the stammer is cute.'

'So it's purely a physical thing then. You've never been one for the muscles and the action before, Win. What's made you suddenly come over all Thor fangirl?'

'Look, he might have biceps like a bouncy castle, but he's bringing up his niece. She's got a bedroom that looks like a show room in World of Pony, he doesn't say a word about her going round on a hobby horse that has its *own stable in the house*, it would be hard for him to be any sweeter without producing a diabetic coma in susceptible onlookers!'

Daisy was quiet for a moment. 'But your judgement might be a bit skewed, don't you think, Winnie? You thought Daniel was totes gorge too.'

'Yes. I remember.' *And now you can't even hear his name without the spectre of a sour taste on your tongue, without your mouth drying in remembered horror.* 'But, honestly, he's just so good with her.'

'Well, she is his niece. He would be good with her, he's presumably known her all her life. Doesn't mean he'll be boyfriend of the century, and there's still the fact that he's going to care for Scarlet forever, which leaves far less room for a girlfriend. And he really doesn't sound like your type of guy, Win, unless he's hiding his MENSA certificate under those pecs.'

'Shut up. You're too logical. I hate it when you're logical.'

'It's why you love me.' It sounded as though she was grinning the Daisy-grin, which should have been identical to mine but, through some fluke of muscular genetics, was wider and friendlier. 'And you know you really can't move on until you've got closure with Dan.'

'I'm not listening to you ever again.'

She was right. I knew she was right. I sat with my laptop open, Dan's last email on the screen, and tried to think of a reply. Composed lots of pithy one-liners in my head but, when it came down to it, I just couldn't bring myself to write them. The sight of his name there next to the little blue icon made me feel sick, paralysed me, and anything I tried to type looked stupid. *You used to be able to talk to him. Stuff you didn't want to talk over with Daisy, stuff about the book, your parents' divorcing, the everyday things. You used to send joke mails to one another, even when you were sitting together, daft things you picked up on the net, and all those pictures of kittens doing cute things that he endlessly forwarded to you. And now you can't even bring yourself to type his name.*

Sometimes I had to hold on hard to the memory of that last day. To the expression on Dan's face, that tough, self-justifying look in his eyes, the shouted accusations, the fact that I hadn't been able to talk to Daisy for weeks afterwards. Because if I let myself forget, all I could think of was Dan, leather coat flapping, boots all jingling buckles, long-fingered hand with the small tattoo on his wrist, shouting into the air that I was going to be 'GREAT!'

And now, here I was. I'd been great, he'd been right. But he'd wanted something else.

Facebook
Alex Hill – Winter Gregory Author Page
Thanks for everything today. I'll email you properly later.

Emily James @CatGirlEmily
@ShyOwlPublishing @WinterGAuthor Just read *Book of the Dead*. Great book.

Retweeted by @EditorDanB
I snarled at the screen, snapped it shut, and went to bed.

From: AlexHillStone@wolmail.com
To: WinterGregoryAuthor@teddymail.com
Subject: Thank you. And general chat.
Scarlet was so over-excited that I didn't get her to bed until just now, and even then I had to let her watch some DVD about

horses until she fell asleep. Not your fault, of course, obviously, she's just looking forward to the weekend so much. All I can say is thank you. Thank you for taking the time and interest in a little girl who doesn't really have a lot. Oh, she's got me, all this (I'm pointing at the Old Mill here), a grandmother who loves her to distraction, which, let's face it, for my mother isn't a long trip. But sometimes she seems so sad. I'll watch her (she doesn't know, and don't tell her) outside, galloping round the yard, she makes this kind of jumping course out of flowerpots and sticks and she'll be hurtling around and then next minute she's cuddling Light Bulb, just holding his head and whispering, or maybe crying.

It hit us all badly, Ellen dying. She was my little sister (she was seven years younger than me, think Mum and Dad had given me up as an only child and then, there she was), so pretty, all curls and smiles. Ridiculous, isn't it? I still get choked up thinking about her, even now. Don't even know why I think it's ridiculous, being a bloke, I suppose. We ought to shrug, brush it off, get on with life. Tough it out. And I can, mostly I can, just sometimes, when Scarl says or does something that's so like her mum, I just, well … I try to be everything she needs but everyone thinks I'm a bit weird too. I never used to stammer, you see, and of course everyone in Great Leys has known me since Mum moved into maternity wear, so they can't get used to it. It all started when Ellen died, when the accident happened.

It was my fault.

I had to go away after I wrote that, I've had twenty minutes on the Glenmorangie to give me the courage to write this, thank God Scarl is at Mum's, and please forgive any subsequent spelling mistakes. Yep, it was down to me that Ellen died, I was always screpulus (sod spellchecker) about unloading at the far side of the yard, where we unloaded today, but that morning … God, I was saving time, cutting corners. We had the stone lorry pull up at the entrance so they could just swing the stone off and go. Ellen got out of the car and she didn't know the lorry was unloading and she walked underneath and the cradle slipped and I tried to resssussitate her but she had a head injury. Oh God, Winter, it was horrible. Then I started stammering and they thought I must have a brain tumour or something. I had scans and tests and then they dicided it was caused by the accident. It would go in time. But I couldn't take time, Scarl needed somebody, she was there, in the car and she saw her mother die … And I lost my relationship too, someting that was importnt to me, becaus I had Scarl to take on.

My fault. Corse it was. I kind of threw myself into being Scarl's carer. She and Ell lived hre from when she was bron, y'see, an I got custody cos of Mum being a bit … she just coulndt cope. And they'll only let me adopt Scarl if I dont put a foot wrong. And I got so woried that they woud take Scarl away if I didint put all my atention into her that I broke off my relationshp, so as not to look like I wasnt taking it serously. Hurt her. Hurt me. Was stupid, but now I cant go back …

Wish I new why I have this urge to spil everything out to you. Lonliness, maybe, it gets so quiet here at night when I'm on my own with nobdy to talk to, and you seem so sweet and so understanding, its like my fingers get a life of their own wen I start writing these emails.

Sorry. Ampissed now. Better go to bede.

Al x

Chapter Seven

Daniel Bekener @EditorDanB
Going Out of Office for a few days. Stuff to sort out, guys, bear with me.

ElliottTravels @Tripsky02
@EditorDanB How're you doing? Thought you were coming over all white picket fence on us?

Daniel Bekener @EditorDanB
@Tripsky02 Things went bizarre, mate.

Sam Turner @ComfortZone6
@EditorDanB @Tripsky02 Off anywhere nice?

Daniel Bekener @EditorDanB
@ComfortZone6 Just getting things sorted in my head. Finding things out, you know?

✉

From: DanBekener@ShyOwlPublishing.co.uk
To: BethanyAnnBekener@wolmail.com
Subject: Heading out for a bit

Sorry, Bethie, but I've got to take off for a while. I'll be down to see you in a few weeks, so keep up the exercises like they told you, but I have to go north. Winter is … she's on a deadline and she's gone quiet on us.

I don't like it. So I'm going to check it out, make sure she's coming in on time with this book. Yeah, I want this one out, on the shelves but … I need to see her. Think you're the only one who gets it, Bethie. Sounds stupid when I run it through my head, she hates me, wants me nowhere near her, so why the hell do I feel like this?

I do know. Course I do. You nailed it in your last email (although there were some cracking good voice-recog cock-ups, 'that time wee ran around the garden?' Cried laughing at that one). Last time I saw Winter, I walked away.

It hurt. Hurt so much. It was her choice to make, but maybe I could have handled it another way, been more understanding. Helped her see that what she has with Daisy is unhealthy, keeping people at arm's length while she tells all her secrets to her sister when she could have … *should have* been telling them to me. But making her choose – yeah. Not my finest moment, but I couldn't take being second best, not after the way we'd been together. Winter made me feel something, made me feel like I fitted in somewhere. You know our family, everyone all niched up, the accountant, the paramedic, the scientist – only you and me breaking the mould, and now—

So, what could I do? She wouldn't let me save her, so I had to save myself. But I don't feel saved, Bethie. If I were safe, it wouldn't hurt like this.

Take care of yourself, kiddo. Promise I'll come and see you soon.

Danny Boy

f

Facebook

Winter Gregory Author Page

This is a picture of the little church I was in yesterday. Stones carved in Primitive and some *very* interesting stories to go with them!

I spent the rest of the week driving around on the moors. Mists would come down overnight and then burn away by lunchtime, so I managed to get some atmospheric pictures of headstones rearing their way up through the fog and then sit in warm sunshine to type and do the background research. Some of the little churches had records going back to the mid-1500s when parish registers first had to be kept, and I found one particularly isolated chapel which had had a vociferously anti-everything vicar in 1623, who had written snarky little notes all over his registers, which kept me happily busy for ages. I didn't see Alex, Scarlet or Margaret at all that week. I wondered if Alex was regretting his drunken heart-opening email and staying away from embarrassment, or whether, and more likely, he was just busy.

A little of the pain had slipped away now. Dan had gone dark on Twitter and it was easier to pretend he didn't exist when his name didn't pop up in my feed every time I checked. Alex tweeted every now and then, but mostly about craft supplies or building work and he clearly checked my Facebook page because he religiously 'liked' every update I put. The distance was giving me perspective, and I was realising how right Daisy had been about Alex. He may be gorgeous and kind, he might have the disposition of a saint, but his first responsibility would always be to Scarlet. Did I want that? She was lovely and everything, but she was eight, and lonely, and if she attached herself to me then how would it work if Alex and I broke up?

So I threw myself into work partly, I had to admit, to keep myself out of the town and away from Scarlet or Alex.

✉

From: AlexHillStone@wolmail.com
To: WinterGregoryAuthor@teddymail.com
Subject: Headache, guilt and York check

Hello, Winter. Wow, that sounds a bit like the beginning of a really terrible poem, doesn't it? Anyway. I really hope I didn't say anything to upset you in that last, drunken (oh my God, how drunken, I had a headache for two days!) email. I know you're busy and you came here to write and everything, so it's perfectly normal that you'd be out every time I came by. Oh, don't worry, I'm not stalking you or anything – just realised how weird it sounded, as if I was walking past the cottage every five minutes. Really just checking up for Mum, she wanted to make sure you knew that next week was recycling bins (yes, even though there are notices all over the cottage about refuse collection timetables). And, well, maybe just a little bit of wanting to see you, make sure you were all right, eating properly that kind of thing. Maybe not the eating, I put that in so that I didn't sound stalky again, sorry.

Now I'm worrying that you don't want to talk to me, that's really what it is. After I told you about Ellen. I didn't kill her, if that's what you're thinking, in case you're reading all deep stuff into that email. I mean, I know it was an accident, I *know* it was. But there's all these 'what ifs', if you know what I mean, what if I'd had the delivery where I always do, what if I'd warned her to keep clear, what if? Stupid, yes, I know. Anyway. Look. I completely understand if you're not on for Saturday any more, I can talk to Scarl and she'll be fine, she knows you're busy and she really wants me to buy a copy of your book so that she can get you to sign it for her! I've told her it's more like a history book than one of hers but she's still insisting. She can, I'm sure you've noticed, be very persistent.

Let me know though. Please. I don't want any last-minute disappointments for her.

Thanks

Alex

✉

From: WinterGregoryAuthor@teddymail.com
To: AlexHillStone@wolmail.com
Subject: Saturday

Of course Saturday is still on! You must think I'm really evil if you think I'd cancel! Oh, and is Light Bulb coming too, only my car won't take a horse trailer.

Winter

✉

From: AlexHillStone@wolmail.com
To: WinterGregoryAuthor@teddymail.com
Subject: Relief and thank you

Thank you. Thank you, you don't know how relieved I am. The thought of explaining to Scarl … urgh. No, sorry, never meant to doubt you! But I know how it can be when work gets busy, sometimes it's like having to balance things in your head, isn't it? With me it's Scarl, getting her up and to school and making sure there's something to eat and that she gets picked up and there's my life and friendships and then the workmen and getting the buildings together – we need the roof on before winter sets in – and sometimes I feel as though I'm sitting in the middle of this huge war, just keeping the peace. Her on one side and my whole life on the other. God, that sounds like she isn't my whole life, which she is, but not … I'll shut up now. We'll come to the cottage at, what, ten on Saturday? And, I'm sure you're glad to hear, Light Bulb is being turned out for the day, in Mum's garden.

Alex

✉️

From: LucyLoo@wolmail.com
To: AlexHillStone@wolmail.com
Subject: Scarlet

Hi Alex

Any chance I could pop over sometime? There's a couple of tiny issues with Scarlet, it would be nice if we could chat over a coffee or something rather than in school. Oh, and Scarlet told me that her friend the writer – is that Winter? – was taking her shopping in York? That is really sweet of her, and she does seem like such a nice lady. I'm really glad you've met someone like her, Al. It's what you both need.

Lu x

The nights were dark here. Of course, nights are sort of dark by definition, but the nights here were *really* dark. I walked along the paved way by the river, where the odd street light threw angular shadows. Dark. Less artificial light, and more stars. More stars than I could ever remember seeing in one place, bright and cold and clear, it was like the sky used mouthwash. The air smelled of a primitive kind of cold, snow and peat and stone ringing with frost, as though those high hills that rose above the little town were funnelling a new Ice Age towards us.

'Hello, Winter.' It was Margaret.

'Blimey. Why do I always meet the same people whenever I'm out?' I muttered, but she heard.

'It's a small town. Three thousand residents, over half of which are elderly, a quarter are small children and most of the rest are in the pub right now.' She gave me a smile. 'That really only leaves me, you and Alex, so it's no wonder. How is the writing going?'

Hmmm. Here we are, walking slowly along by the river at ten o clock at night. That should give you a hint that it's probably not going quite as smoothly as it should be.

'I'm having a break.'

'And you're taking Scarlet to York tomorrow? Shopping ...' She tailed off as though she knew the word but couldn't place its meaning. 'I know Alex appreciates the time you spend with her. We love her dearly but she's very much a handful. I'm sixty-three and my husband passed over a while ago, just before Ellen ... well, and Scarlet doesn't really have much of a feminine influence in her life.' Margaret gave my jeans-and-anorak get up the once-over, and seemed to be stopping herself from continuing 'not that you're very feminine'. 'There's really only Lucy.' Another tailing-off pause, as though a lot of possible futures collided in her head, but then she refocused. 'I'm just on my way to the Women's Group meeting, we're having Ewan McGregor tonight and I'm looking forward to it. Of course, he isn't everyone's cup of tea, a little bit too keen to get his willy out, but it's a treat for the older ladies, isn't it? I mean, not that he'll be there in person, of course, but it's something.'

A duck broke cover and slid, quacking, into the busily-running stream.

'Well, I'm sure Scarlet and I will have a lovely day tomorrow.' I tried to ease my way further along the path. 'I won't bring her back too late.' *Because I'll probably be deaf by lunchtime.*

'I'm sure you understand ...' – Margaret closed the gap between us again. '... how much Alex trusts you with her.

He's very … he's quite an unhappy young man. He was so different before Ellen died, so carefree and, well, although I shouldn't say it, he was a bit of a hit with the ladies, oh, they were practically queueing up for him in those days! But since then he's been so serious. Has trouble meeting *people*, if you see what I mean, of course everyone around here knows everyone else and is related to everyone else, so much so that every time we have a wedding we all have to check it's not incest, but not people from outside.'

I wanted to say that all the women must be blind if they were letting something like his stammer get in the way of getting their hands on that spectacular body, but it wasn't really something you said to the mother of the object in question, so I just nodded. 'You'd better get on. Ewan McGregor's willy will be getting cold.'

She bobbed her head a couple of times. 'Nights are the worst, you know,' she said, quietly. 'Everyone remembers more at night.' And then she was gone, neat heels, which looked grey in this half-illuminated darkness but were almost certainly pink, clicking along the stone path like a dog's claws on lino.

'Of course they do.' I shrugged myself deeper into the anorak. I'd bought it at the Agricultural Merchants earlier in the day, having nothing in my London suitcase that even halfway suited the way the temperature oscillated up and down the scale this far north. Down south we'd still be sitting out in our gardens or on balconies at this time of night, drinking wine and chatting. Here the theme from *Coronation Street* sounded like a klaxon warning everyone to don their duvet.

The dark brings out memories in the same way as it brings out the rats.

* * *

'You could read a book.' Daisy's advice wasn't up to much tonight.

'I've told you, the only things in here with me are spies, and whatever Jeffrey Archer writes about. I didn't bring my Kindle with me.' I stared at my laptop. 'And I'm too twitchy to read.'

A sigh. 'Winnie, you can't use me as a substitute for entertainment, you know.'

'I'm bored.'

'You're lonely.'

I thought about it. Was she right? I was used to spending a lot of time alone, writing books about dead people didn't involve a lot of circulating with crowds, but then I'd always had company to fall back on. People I could phone to go out for a drink, Daisy to chat to. 'Maybe. It is rather just me and the doll's house TV here. Honestly, Daze, it's like something that should be on display somewhere rather than a house, everything is three-quarter size! I feel bloody enormous.'

'Look. If you're really serious about having a bit of a "thing" for Alex—'

'I couldn't be more serious if I made a documentary about it.'

'All right. But you don't have to be *serious* serious, do you? Why not just be a bit light-hearted about it? Have fun. Just because you've met a guy who's luscious and everything—'

'With an arse to die for,' I couldn't help putting in, because she did seem to be underplaying the godlike nature of Alex.

'Still not convincing me, Winnie, it doesn't mean you have to launch yourself at him.'

'I don't "launch myself" at men!' I bridled.

'You did a bit at Dan, Win. Remember? As soon as you met him, when you went for drinks to go over the notes for the book edits, Dan was all you could talk about. And you carried on about him pretty much like you're doing over Alex.'

That first meeting. We'd talked on the phone, emailed, then decided that, since the offices were shut for the Bank Holiday, and he wasn't far away, we'd meet up in the pub and talk over a tricky issue I had. I'd seen him sitting there as soon as I walked in, almost as though my eyes had been looking for him without realising. Slim and dark, hunched over a pint, legs up on the seat opposite. Black jeans, big boots and a T-shirt with a picture of the galaxy on. Hair that spiked and fell around his ears as though he'd just got up and a face like an angel that's lost a bet with Hell. And Daisy was wrong, I hadn't launched myself, I'd fallen.

Chapter Eight

'Outside a little chapel in the north of the moors is a fabulous example of sarcasm – I can only imagine what this lady must have done to the man who carved her stone. Whatever it was, he bore that grudge until she died. The lady in question, one Jennet Hartley, seems to have been one for lying about her age, because her stone, carved in beautiful, easy-to-read classical style, reads: "Here lies Jennet Hartley Born 1819 Died 1876 Aged Forty-Three Years". I had the feeling that someone must have pried the chisel from the carver's hand, otherwise it would have been followed by the Victorian equivalent of the smiley-face.'

—BOOK OF THE DEAD 2

York with an eight-year-old came outside any reasonable experience I could have been expected to have had. Scarlet behaved like a child who's spent the last eight years tied to a table leg and wanted to go in every clothes shop, every Claire's Accessories and every bookshop we came across, and, while she was perfectly polite and reasonable in her requests, she had more energy and enthusiasm than anyone I'd ever met who wasn't on hardcore drugs.

In fact, as we went into the fourth 'cheap earrings and lip gloss' establishment that morning, hardcore drugs were beginning to look like a viable option to get through the rest of the day. I could only muster so much interest in make-up designed for tweenagers and stick on tattoos, so when Scarlet showed signs of flagging and gave in to my request to go for coffee and a bun, my relief made me cheerful.

'There can't be many books on pony care left in the shops, we seem to have done a good job of making it look like we're a pair of clueless horse owners.'

Scarlet wriggled up onto the stool and hauled her plastic carrier up alongside her. It thumped onto the tabletop, weighted down with the aforementioned pony books, but then, as I'd told Scarlet, money spent on books is never wasted. 'Can I have a milkshake, please?'

'Okay. You sit there and I'll go and order our drinks.' I left her slumping forward, resting her head on the bag. She was tired now, and I gazed along the counter where the cakes sat, thinking that a sugar boost would be what we both needed, running my eye along the polished glass, looking for something suitably sticky and gooey.

A reflection. Just a brief glimpse of someone walking past the shop, but even that glimpse made my head spin and my hands contract into fists. *Dan?*

To the consternation of other patrons, except Scarlet, who I think had fallen asleep, I abandoned my position in the queue and dashed to the door. The crowds were thickening now as people came into town for lunch, and all I could see was a dark shape, hands in pockets, moving away towards the Minster.

Run after him? Shout, call out his name? It may not be Dan, it could be some other slightly-built bloke in black and just the fact that he's on my mind so much is making me see what isn't there.

I hovered in the doorway. I wanted, so badly, to know if it was him. To face him, look him in the eye and ask him how he dared be here, in Yorkshire, even how he dared be on the same *planet* as me, after the way he'd behaved. *Just to ask him ... why? Why had he felt the need to do it? Wasn't I good enough? How had I failed so badly to be*

65

what he wanted me to be that he needed to drive a wedge between me and my sister?

'Winter?' Scarlet's voice, sleepily raised over the general chat. 'Where are you going?' And the note of panic in her voice told me that I wasn't going anywhere. I couldn't leave her, whoever the dark man might have been.

'It's fine,' I replied, but I felt too sick to want cake now. I was shaky and shocked, as though I'd been in an accident, as though the blood was being diverted from my brain to my heart. 'I'll get your milkshake.'

Scarlet sat and sucked pink milk through a straw and flipped through one of the new books we'd bought, blissfully unaware that next to her I was trying to stop my hands from trembling. The skin on my face felt tight and clammy, bile kept rising up as far as the base of my throat, and the throat-swelling of tears didn't seem too far away. *Why would he even be here? He'll be in London, working; he certainly won't be bothered wondering where you are and what you're doing. And he most especially won't be working himself into a state of hysteria because he thought he saw someone who looks a bit like you somewhere. Come on, Winter. You're in charge of the child, you can't go into meltdown because the ex who tried to get between you and Daisy might have walked down a street in York.*

'We'd better go back to the car.'

'Oh, can't we go into—'

'No!' I felt guilt as soon as I'd snapped out the word, seeing the thumb go into the mouth and her eyes become cautious and guarded. *She's eight. Don't make her suffer because you got shat on.* 'Sorry. I just think we ought to get home before Alex starts to worry.'

Slowly the thumb came out, hovering at chin level in case I was going to be cross again. She'd got pink milk all over her upper lip where she'd drunk the froth from the cup and now it was all over her fingers too, mushing down into a tight pink line like candy floss that's got wet. 'Please may I have a biscuit to eat in the car?'

She'd almost whispered the words and, once again, I felt the jab to the gut of shame. 'Of course you can.' Cautiously I thought my way through meeting Dan on the street, walking into him in the car park, yep, good, I no longer wanted to scream all the swear words I could think of and stab him with my car keys, so we were probably good to go. 'Sorry, Scarlet, I just thought I saw someone I don't like very much.'

Her eyes brightened. 'I do that all the time! Most of the girls at school, really.'

We queued up to buy biscuits. 'Yes, I saw them ignoring you in the park. Don't you get on with them?'

The thumb hovered as though it was thinking about going back in the mouth, but eventually got shoved into a pocket instead. 'They call Alex "weirdo".'

I looked down at the sticky pink face, her blonde hair pulled into two rather inexpert bunches and her ever-so-slightly too small jeans. *They tease you too, I should think. A child with a dead mother and no father, brought up by a man who must sound scary when he speaks, if you're eight and don't understand stammering. I don't really think your grandmother helps much either.* 'What do you do? When they call him names?'

Scarlet swung away, seizing the cellophane bag that the girl behind the counter held out to her. 'I hit them with Light Bulb.'

Ah.

We sat in the car, waiting to pull out of the car park into the traffic. My brain was humming, my eyes straining this way and that, trying to catch a glimpse of a flick of coat, the hint of a studded boot.

'Why are you called Winter?' She'd bitten her way into the first biscuit. A cloud of sugar puffed across the dashboard and settled like dust in the nooks and crannies of the air blower.

'When I was born it was snowing. My mum looked out of the window and knew she was going to call me Winter.'

'Oh.' Crunch crunch. A shower of crumbs fell under her booster seat and made me narrow my eyes. 'So why is your sister called Daisy? If you're twins aren't you born at the same time?'

Oh boy. How much do eight-year-old girls know about babies being born? I could traumatise her for life here. 'Twins don't … ummm … they don't come out at the same time,' I said, carefully trying to be euphemistic and yet factually correct, and, for all I knew, she still thought babies were found under gooseberry bushes. 'I was born first and Daisy took a while to come out. By the time she was born, the sun was shining and the snow had melted.'

Well done, Winter. You managed to skirt right around the whole 'childbirth' thing, she's probably going to grow up now thinking babies appear like pop-up book illustrations.

'When Granny's cat had kittens there was blood *everywhere*,' Scarlet said, with a disgusting amount of relish. 'They came out one after the other, like squeezing cheese out of a tube.'

I'd forgotten to take into account that children living in the countryside were brought up with a more robust approach to new life than we townies, clearly. I'd thought babies came through belly buttons until I was eleven. 'Riiight.'

'Do you miss your sister?' The question came around another biscuit. The car was knee deep in half-eaten raisins and bits.

'What do you mean?' My elbows trembled with the strain of keeping my hands steady on the wheel.

'I wish I had a sister.' Scarlet turned and looked out of the window, almost dreamily. 'I could go and visit her and we'd make cakes and draw pictures. Do you visit your sister and make cakes?'

I took a deep breath. 'It's different when you grow up. Daisy lives a long, long way away in Australia and she's got a fabulous life over there that she can't just drop to come here. We talk a lot though, practically all the time, but no cakes.' *And besides, Dan hovers over us like a huge storm cloud. We might ignore his presence, but it's always there, big and black and waiting to burst if we acknowledge him.*

We drove over the moors. Scarlet had put her thumb back in her mouth and was making small sucky sounds around it, her head leaning against the glass and bumping. I tried to drive as smoothly as I could, I didn't want her waking up and finding another load of questions to ask, but either she wasn't asleep or she had a kind of sixth sense, because as soon as we drove through the archway to the Old Mill she sat upright and took her thumb out. When the car stopped she undid her seat belt, turned to me with a 'thankyoufortakingmeshoppingWinter, bye!' and hurtled off through the glass doors with bags dangling from her hands, bumping and bobbing in accompaniment, leaving a child-shaped clear space on the passenger seat, outlined in bits of biscuit and icing sugar like a confectionary-based murder scene.

Alex came out to meet me. Today he was wearing a

white shirt and dark trousers that were made of a soft fabric like brushed skin. The shirt was open at the collar and his tanned skin contrasted with its whiteness like a black and white photo. 'W-would you like to c-come in for a c-coffee?'

I hesitated. Part of me wanted to slide back into the cottage, so small and snug that it was less like going home and more like getting dressed. I wanted to lie in a bath for half an hour and wash away all thoughts of Dan, the potential of his dark shape flickering through the streets of York; to breathe in the scent of bath foam and fresh air and feel the quiet. But, on the other hand, Alex looked sensational today, and I'd dipped out on the coffee earlier.

'Yes, please. If you promise to keep that coffee machine under control.'

He laughed and opened the car door for me. 'Ah,' he said, looking in. 'S-Scarlet-shaped chaos. I'll c-clean that up for you.'

I laughed. 'Don't worry about it. My boyfriend used to sit and sharpen pencils in there so ...' I tailed off, the words sinking under the rising image of Dan calmly carving off slices of wood, scattering them around him like broken wishes. 'Just the coffee will do.'

The office space was bright and humming with electrical activity. Even though it was a Saturday Alex had clearly been working. Pages were scattered around the printer and there was the smell of over-heated machinery in the air. The coffee machine sat amongst all this like a gargoyle in an operating theatre, and spat occasional gouts of ill-tempered steam at us. There were two empty cups on the side, with tidemarks of old conversations halfway up the sides. 'You've been busy,' I said, taking a fragrant mug.

'Making the m-most of Scarl b-being away.' Alex gave

me a grin over his mug. 'We usually s-spend the weekends b-baking. Or exercising L-Light Bulb. Lucy c-came over to t-talk about Scarlet's p-progress at school.' From above we could hear the sounds of Scarlet racketing up and down the floorboards. 'I f-fetched him back f-from Mum's. She'll t-take him out in a b-bit.'

I sipped. Despite the purring of equipment and the overhead thundering, it was relaxingly quiet in here. Alex was perched on the edge of the desk with his legs bracing him, which drew extra attention, if extra were needed, to his long, strong thighs. I wondered if he was doing it deliberately, advertising his attractiveness to an available potential mate, and then I cursed myself for my cynicism.

'Why not get her a pet?' I cast my eyes upwards, in case he might think I was talking about his mother, whose only need for a pet would be to have something else to fret about. 'Something real to lavish all that attention on.'

His mouth twitched, it didn't look like a smile. The mug went down onto the desk and his hands spread in a gesture of hopelessness. 'It w-would be nice, yes. B-but ...' And now his hands went up, cupped his face briefly, then he sighed and stood up. 'It's h-hard to explain.' The coffee machine burped twice, and he suddenly seemed to find it fascinating, lifting its lid to check water levels and pulling a few levers, which appeared to do absolutely nothing apart from jet steam in random directions. 'Scarl would love a p-pet but I can't c-cope with anything else. I mean we m-manage, it's fine, everything is under c-control but if things g-go wrong' – he peered into the depths of the machine's workings – 'with th-this place and Scarl. It's a b-balance, d'you see? Anything else w-would be too m-much.' The lid clattered back and he turned round to face me now. 'I s-seem to do nothing b-but talk about

71

myself with y-you. All I know ab-about you is what Scarl tells me, which is q-quite a lot admittedly, sh-she can be a bit nosey, I'm afraid.'

The more he talks, the less he stammers. As if he's gradually relaxing with you, getting less fazed by speaking; it's quite attractive. Even the way he blinks when the words jam, it's a nice little touch, stops him from being so utterly out-of-your-league gorgeous; that little hint of vulnerability.

'Oh, before I forget, I gave Scarlet a copy of *Book of the Dead*. I had a couple of author copies with me, which saved us having to comb some of the more dubious bookshops in York looking for one. You might want to check through before she starts reading it, there's a couple of stories of death that might not be all that suitable, although I don't know what level she's reading at, so she might just slide right past them, but you ought to be aware, just in case.'

He was staring at me now. Or, rather, not staring, but his eyes were particularly intent on me. 'Th-that happens a lot, p-people changing the subject. Like, b-because I stammer I c-can't keep track of what's g-going on in a conversation. B-but I can, Winter. I c-can see you change the subject b-because you feel uncomfortable w-with it, but why? I'm only a-asking for what you've told Sc-Scarlet, in your own words. Not a d-deep psychological insight.'

I sighed. 'I'm sorry. Yes, you're right, of course. I mean, Scarlet asks these questions, right out of nowhere and sometimes she sort of gets me by surprise, but, yes, you trust her with me so you ought to know that there's nothing horrendous there in the background. I'm just a writer who had one huge success that she's now trying to replicate by writing about little-known country churchyards and staying in a house that looks like the doorbell should chime "hi ho, hi ho".'

'And you're a t-twin?' He resumed his coffee drinking, after staring briefly into the cup, checking that the machine wasn't trying to poison him, presumably. 'That must be …?'

What does he want you to say here? That it must be nice, or terrible or confusing or painful?

'I don't know. I've never been anything but a twin. I mean, I know enough people who aren't to say that it's a relationship that's so strong that what Daisy and I have is …' I felt the tears come to my eyes, flattening my throat so that words wouldn't come and flaming in the back of my brain. 'Sorry, sorry.' I started sniffing, but that wasn't enough, and the tears began to fall. I hunched myself forward and groped for a tissue, encountering nothing in my pocket but a sheaf of receipts, wondered about using my sleeve but, even in extremis, realising that blowing my nose on my own clothes in front of a desirable man was not the way to go.

'Here.'

To my surprise Alex passed me a box of tissues from the desk. He didn't look as appalled as I would have expected of a man who's asked a simple question only to be met with a breakdown. I blew my nose resoundingly and rubbed at my eyes.

'Winter?' Scarlet was standing in the doorway. 'What did you do, Alex?' A very grown-up question.

'It wasn't Alex,' I snuffled. 'I just got a bit sad for a moment. I'm all right now though.'

'Oh.' She hovered for a moment, with Light Bulb swinging his head from side to side as she made a decision. 'Well. You have to say sorry, Alex, if you upset Winter.'

'I'm v-very sorry if I upset y-you,' Alex said, solemnly, and I nearly laughed around my tissue.

'Good.' And now the drama was over, life was back to normal for the little girl. 'I'm taking Light Bulb out for a canter. I put the books in my bedroom, we bought *loads*, and Winter got me some lipstick and a milkshake! Come on, Light Bulb, trot on, you've got so *lazy* today!'

'J-just in the yard, Scarl,' Alex called after her. She gave no sign of having heard but, when we peered through the doors, she was loping round and round the paved yard outside. 'I really am s-sorry,' he repeated, more quietly now. 'What h-happened?'

I heaved another great sigh, as though the incoming air could rinse out some of the poison. *No point in being coy about it. And if you ever do end up dating Alex, then he ought to know.* 'Dan. My editor. He and I were … well, a couple, of sorts. Not for very long, but …' *Long walks by the Thames, mooching through the chilly spring sunshine eating ice creams not much colder than the breeze. Laughing, always laughing, meals and wine.* 'And then the book came out and it was a success.' *Drinking champagne, the constant phone calls updating me on the sales figures, Dan chasing the publicity department to get me on TV, radio, interviews with the press. Still, the laughing.* 'And then something changed. Dan never really liked the fact that I spent so much time talking to Daisy. He was jealous, basically, of the time I gave her. I mean, I *said*, I explained, she was such a long way away, and I missed her, and I needed to talk to her to make up for her not being around. But he wanted … he said I shouldn't rely on her so much. That I had him …' I swiped the tissue over my face again. 'And he made me choose.' *Dan, never more beautiful than he was that night, standing on the bridge, his hands against the rail, head bent so far forward that I thought he might jump into the river. 'You need to make a decision, Win. If you stick with Daisy, then I have to go.'*

And I chose.

'She's my *twin*. If I separate myself from Daisy I'd feel as though I was losing something … oh, I can't describe it … something treasured. Something that has been a part of me for so long that it's not even a part any more, it just *is*. Like my nose or something. So Dan went.'

Alex's eyes were soft. 'That's r-rough.'

'So. We still sort of work together, he okayed the new book so it's his responsibility to get it out there, but after that …' I shook my head, 'I never have to have anything to do with him again.'

'I shouldn't h-have asked.'

'No! No, I'm glad you did.' *Because now I don't have to worry about slipping up and saying something, dropping his name.* 'It was all six months ago now, so, you know, old memories.'

'Winter.' Alex closed the gap between us and put his arms around me. He was tall, taller than Dan had been, broader and harder, the difference took my breath for a second. 'I'm s-sorry.' The words ruffled my hair, one hand rubbed up and down my back as though he was calming a child. The tears thought about making a resurgence but fell back as I took in the sheer glory of being held against Alex; those trousers were every bit as snuggly soft as they looked, his shirt was crisp, his skin, where it showed at the neck of the shirt, smelled of a sharp masculine fragrance and I could hear his heart beating underneath it all. A steady thump, which sped up whenever I moved, however slightly. Above everything, though, was the rising smell of coffee. 'Oh, b-bugger.'

I laughed and took a step back. 'Not recommended when you're holding a mug, Alex.' My cup had become part of the general hug and had tipped my drink down the front of his shirt.

'I w-wondered what that was. I just th-thought you came armed.' He held his arms out to the sides to free me to move back completely. 'Th-that's a sod.' Then, before I could say anything, he pulled at the back of the collar and took the shirt off over his head, slithering out of it like a snake shedding its skin.

Well.

My eyes became paralysed by the sight of the red blotch on his torso where the hot coffee had gone through the shirt, but he seemed more concerned with the fabric itself. 'I'd b-better put this in to s-soak.'

Oh, don't hurry on my account.

It was clearly the chest of a man who works hard rather than a man who gyms hard. Rather than pecs that made his nipples look like a couple of dartboard bullseyes, he had a nicely normal shaped torso, just a little perter and less ribby than some, and without the attempt to escape sideways of others. A highlight of hair dusted broadly across the top, then got its act together into a narrow line which disappeared down into his waistband. I'd forgotten the tears. Hell, I'd practically forgotten my own name.

Dan, the first time I saw his body. Taking off his T-shirt almost apologetically. 'I'm not exactly Chris Hemsworth, but I make up for it in …' a wry comedy glance downwards. 'No, actually I don't make up for it at all.' But so at ease with his athletic muscularity, so at home in his own skin that I never thought about a lack of biceps, only that it was Dan. That he was strong enough.

I shook my head free of the memory.

'I n-need to get this in w-water.' He held the shirt up to the light, causing some interesting muscles to come into play in his upper arms. 'And I'd b-better check on Scarl.'

'And I ought to get home.' *Am I really thinking of the cottage as home? I'm either going native or shrinking.* I drained my mostly-depleted mug down to the sludge in the bottom. 'I'll catch you later, maybe?'

Alex nodded. 'Th-thanks again. I'll email you. It's easier.' And then he gave me a beaming smile that turned those serious grey eyes into hazard lights.

Outside Scarlet had disappeared, but had clearly not gone far because Light Bulb was tied to a drainpipe. I looked at his befuddled expression. 'You and me both, mate, you and me both,' I whispered, and headed back to the car.

Chapter Nine

From: AlexHillStone@wolmail.com
To: WinterGregoryAuthor@teddymail.com
<u>Subject: Sorry. Again.</u>

God, you wouldn't believe how fed up I get with saying sorry
– when the stammer cuts in, and there's a whole row of faces
waiting for me to say something, and then I try to apologise but
I can't even get the 'sorry' out without stammering. But, fed up
as I may be, I still have to say it to you here. Winter, I am so
sorry I made you cry. I've come to think of you as this rather
tough girl, always alone, always so capable and just … *there*
in every situation. I've got this little mental fantasy (nothing
like *that*, obviously) of you being all sort of Catwoman. Only
probably without the stunts, now I come to think of it. But seeing
you cry … well, I'm really rather glad that the coffee got spilled
because I had no idea what the next step was going to be.
Crying made you softer, somehow, someone I wanted to hold
(hope I didn't freak you out when I hugged you!). I don't deal so
much with adults, you can probably tell. When Scarl falls over
or something, one quick hug and she's back up and running. I
forget that sometimes adults have hurts that can't be got over
with a hug. I'm guessing yours comes into that category.

You should never have been made to choose. That's all I'm
going to say on the subject. I don't know the circumstances
after all. I'd have thought that your Dan would just have to find
a way to work around things, to make sure you had time with
your sister and with him – it shouldn't be so hard really, should
it? Unless there was other stuff in his head, maybe he's just
messed up.

Okay. Now that's out of the way. A couple of things. Firstly, because I know you should always ask for favours upfront – is there *any chance at all* that you could pick Scarlet up from school on Monday? I've just had someone reschedule something and Mum, who usually picks up the slack, has got to go to Middlesbrough for an appointment. No pressure, absolutely, if you can't then that's fine and I can slip away for twenty minutes, or ask Lucy to bring her back after she's finished, only it's the bank, and I really don't want to give them any chance at all to find me unfit to run a business. It's tough enough convincing them that Scarlet doesn't interfere with my ability to earn them pots of money anyway.

Oh. And do you fancy coming over for a meal on Monday night? I know popular convention says that I should take you out for dinner but babysitting being what it is, and Mum not being able to have Scarl overnight because she's got to leave early in the afternoon for her appointment … I can cook, honestly.
Alex

✉

From: WinterGregoryAuthor@teddymail.com
To: AlexHillStone@wolmail.com
Subject: It's okay

You didn't upset me. Really. I know I cried, but it's mostly because I feel stupid. Stupid that I ever let Dan get close enough to even question my relationship with Daisy. There's something about being a twin that's impossible to describe. She's my other half. She's nicer than me, really, she's kinder and softer and she cries *all the time*. I've even known Daisy to cry at football results. When we were little my parents had to tape shut the story of the *Ugly Duckling* because Daisy used to cry at the pictures every time. She's more compassionate than me, more imaginative, more … everything. It's as though when we were in the womb and all the attributes were being doled out, she got all the nice ones, all the artistic and sensitive ones, and I got the practical ones. It does mean that I can hold my own in a swearing contest, and drink seven pints of beer before I fall over, but that's not always a good thing. She's just better than me is what it comes down to. And I know I should feel jealous, I should be all narrow-eyes and hissy whenever her name is mentioned, but I love her. Not loving Daisy just isn't an option, and *that's* where Dan went wrong. You're right, he should have just let things go on, let me have Daisy and fitted himself in around us both, but he couldn't. Maybe he was messed up, or maybe *he* thinks Daisy is better than me, I don't know.

Of course I'll fetch Scarlet on Monday, don't worry. Please send her in with a letter though, saying I'm coming, that Ms Charlton is a bit scary! And I would love to come to dinner. I trust Light Bulb won't be eating with us?
Winter

✉

From: AlexHillStone@wolmail.com
To: LucyLoo@wolmail.com
Subject: Monday
Hey, Lu
Thought I'd better let you know, Winter is coming to pick Scarl up on Monday. Mum's busy and I've got the bloke from the bank coming in. Oh, and before I forget, thanks for the chat. Glad to know she's getting on better with those spellings! You can hang on to the books you borrowed, btw, no rush to get them back.
Al x

▮

Alex Hill @AlexHillStone
Lovely woman coming to dinner, things are looking up!

Matt Simons @MattyS
Is this black-lipstick-woman?

Alex Hill @AlexHillStone
Ah, yes, turns out I was wrong about that. No black lippy, just
v cute.

Matt Simons @MattyS
Aw, my boy's all grown up now.
RETWEETED by @AlexHillStone

f

Facebook
Alex Hill
I've rather rashly invited someone for dinner on Monday. I have
no idea what to cook, any suggestions? Nothing with fish though
– hate fish.
Matt Simons LIKES this.
Comment: Matt Simons Man, I am still laughing. Your heating-up
skills are legendary, but your cooking? Not since we were at school.
Alex Hill LIKES this
Comment: Alex Hill It's never too late to learn though, is it?
Comment: Matt Simons Think the Saturday night before the date
might be a bit too late.
Comment: Alex Hill Wish there was a bloody 'dislike' button.
Comment: Lucy Charlton What about risotto? Here's an easy
one www.desperatecook/risotto
Alex Hill and 4 people Like this.

B

A.N. Editor Blog
Profile: Anonymous editor, blogging to keep sane in the crazy
book world. Lives in London, male, thirty-two, not looking for pick

ups or any more slush pile reading material, thanks, guys. Trying to believe that life is for living, YOLO, *carpe diem*, and all that crap.

BLOG POST

I've been on the move a lot lately. Getting some fresh ideas, fresh perspectives. After The Book was such an unexpected hit (none of us saw that coming; it was destined to be niche at best …) there's been an influx of manuscripts on similar subjects, a lot of people trying to cash in. Some good, some bad. But I needed to get away for a while, from the office, from London. From the questions, everyone chasing the follow-up, chasing me, chasing *her*.

My personal life took a fall. Amazing woman, terrific writer, it's like she sees the gaps in a story, she's fascinated not just with people but with what makes them who they are and I reckon that's why the book was such a success. She gets into those nooks and crannies of personality and jemmies them open so that anyone could see what makes people tick. Now she's on with another and I should be involved. But I ruined it.

Should have handled it differently. Should have been … what, more sensitive? If I were any *more* sensitive I'd be talking to the other bloody side, and sometimes, you know, sensitivity isn't enough. Sometimes there has to come a bottom line. I gave her mine. And she stood there on that bridge that night, all brown eyes burning through me and hair in the wind like Medusa and her crazy snakes and she blew me out. Just ended everything I thought we were working towards.

I offered to help her, offered everything I had to make it better but, in the end, she chose the life she'd already made. A narrow, broken path that's never going to get anywhere, just going to pull her deeper and deeper into something dark.

I wish it hadn't gone that way.

'Win?'

'Hey, Daze. You just read Dan's blog?'

'You were right.' Daisy sounded upset. 'He's completely rewritten his version of history, hasn't he? Bastard.'

My sister rarely got upset, at least, not like this. She was, for all her artistic temperament and flair and really weird clothes, much more equable than me. If anything was going to get thrown during an argument, it was always me doing the hurling and her ducking.

'He's putting it all down to me. I notice there's no mention made of the ultimatum. He's making it sound as though I'm something to be *pitied*, and for what? Not ending up with him?' I was finding the anger useful, it pushed all the other feelings away.

'We've got each other though, Win. He tried, but he couldn't do it, he couldn't keep us apart, so we won in the end.' Daisy was calmer now. 'We just have to remember that.'

'And forget about him? You agree with me now, that I keep as far away from Dan Bekener as I can? I'm relieved about that, I thought you were going to nag me to ring him or something.' The unknotting of my muscles told me how relieved I really was. There had been that tiny hint of dissention between my sister and I lately, whenever we'd spoken there'd been that little breath of blame in everything she'd said. As if my talking to Dan would have resolved something. 'Daze, he wanted you out of my life! No amount of talking was going to change that, you know what he's like.'

'Single-minded. Determined.'

'Yes.'

'Sexy as all get out?' She sounded as though she was smiling now.

'There was that too, of course.' I smiled back. 'But being more attractive than a softly-melting bar of Galaxy on a no-carbs day doesn't mean he's not as mad as a badger, does it?'

Now she laughed. 'Why are you always so totes logical?'

'Because I'm the oldest, and don't you forget it.'

That's better. When Daisy had gone, I could properly appreciate the lifting of my spirits, the extra bit of brightness in the day. *You can't fall out with Daisy, not over this. We need each other, that's what Dan doesn't get. He thought it would be a simple thing – you never speak to your sister again and that would be it. Boom. Plain sailing. But he never got the 'twin' thing, the fact that we spent nine months together, jostling for space in the womb, two people who came from one conception, one act, how could we ever be separate? Even when she's far away and you're here, we're still feeling one another in some stupid, semi-mystical way, and that, Mr Bekener, is forever. When you and your fancy drainpipe jeans and your hard-man boots and your chaos-symbol tattoo have vanished into nothingness, we will still be together, Daisy and me.*

So shove that up your red-pen comments and your track changes.

On Monday I found myself struggling to write, with one eye on the clock. I could feel the ideas, almost taste them; they were there, hanging in the air in front of me. But whenever I tried to pull them into existence with my keyboard they seemed to vanish, puffing into the air as though they'd always been ghosts. As though I was trying to make the unreal real and just couldn't do it, just couldn't do justice to the beauty and the shape of them, like trying to nail clouds onto paper using only the power of the apostrophe.

Eventually, at three, I packed up. I could no longer ignore the itchy feeling telling me that I'd only got another thirty minutes, even though the distance between the churchyard, where I was working, and the school could have been covered in infinitely less time, by someone with only half the number of limbs I possessed. *Is this how Alex feels all the time? Is this what it's like to be a parent, this constant rule of the clock?*

I wandered up to the school alongside a drift of mothers, some pushing buggies, some walking in little knots and clusters. Almost every single one looked me over and dismissed me, which gave me a momentary desire to snarl, until I realised that I was wearing jogging bottoms with my recently-purchased anorak over the top, and looked less like a massively successful author than the kind of unfortunate who shouts at cars. *Maybe you should have got dressed properly? These other women all have full make-up on, fading summer tans and designer flip-flops, you look as though you just got off* The Jeremy Kyle Show.

I hung back to let the School Gate Massive have the space they clearly wanted. Lurked around in the newsagents for a while, bought a packet of little toffee chews for Scarlet and read *Your Dog* magazine until I heard the raised voices from the direction of the school, and then wandered down.

This time Scarlet was standing inside the building with a man. He had 'Head Teacher' written all over him, from the thinning hair to the ever-so-slightly askew tie. They were waiting for the playground to clear, and as soon as the final drifts of children had been swept up by parents, or run off together towards the park, he approached the doors. But before he had a chance to usher Scarlet out, Lucy Charlton appeared in her floppy smock and I could see their lips moving behind the glass as they launched into a conversation. They had the unnaturally cheery expressions that told me they were talking about Scarlet without wanting her to know. She was gripping Light Bulb by his stick so hard that his floppy corduroy ears were almost rigid, whilst in her other hand a vivid green nylon book-bag trailed to the floor, and she was scuffing her toes along the corridor lino in a 'bored and wanting to go home' way.

The Head eventually made the sort of face that goes along with the words 'if you must' and surrendered Scarlet, shuffling off into some inner reach of offices, and Lucy opened the door to launch Scarlet out into the world, floppy-headed hobby horse first.

'Winter!' Scarlet was clearly relieved to see me. There was a red streak across her face, cheekbone to cheekbone and one grubby sock was flapping as though the elastic had given up the ghost. 'Can we get an ice cream again?' She seemed cheerful enough, if a little less keen to gallop off down the road than usual.

'Miss Gregory?' Lucy hooked a couple of strands of her blondish hair behind an ear. 'Could I have a quick word, please?'

I looked from her to Scarlet. 'But I'm not ... I mean, I'm only picking her up as a favour.'

Scarlet cantered a small circle around a painted shape on the playground, concentrating furiously. I knew this meant she was probably listening as hard as she could to our conversation, although her expressionless face, between the bobbing, oddly lumpy plaits, gave nothing away. Lucy clearly thought the same. 'Just ... in here.' She indicated the lobby inside the doors. 'Scarlet, stay this side of the gates, please.'

The little girl threw us a look, and pirouetted in her own length. 'Okay.' She had affected disinterest, but I foresaw some probing questioning in my immediate future and was glad I'd bought the toffees.

'I just wanted to ask you something.' Lucy tucked more hair behind her ears. It was wispy and too fine to stay tucked anywhere, I noted. Along with the pointed little chin and big blue eyes it made her look a bit like a slightly simple Siamese cat.

'You need to talk to Alex,' I said, hastily.

She blinked, and both hands dived into the muff-like front pocket of the smock. 'I'm sorry? Has he …?'

'I mean, I can't really tell you anything about Scarlet. I'm only picking her up from school as a favour.'

Blink blink. 'Oh, I see.' More hair tucking. I wondered what was making her so nervous. 'No, it's more that I just wondered … Alex has invited you to dinner?'

Oh. *Oh*.

I looked out of the window so as not to read her expression. I really didn't want to see anything combative in her eyes, not when I didn't have the faintest idea how I even thought about Alex yet. 'Just to say thanks for looking after Scarlet.' I tried to make myself sound neutral, uninvolved. 'We're just friends.'

A moment, then an embarrassed throat-clearing made me look at her again. 'So are we.' She was holding out a piece of paper. 'It's a recipe. He was on Facebook, not knowing what to cook, I thought he might like to try this.' And now her gaze was steady, still big, blue eyes but now holding something else. 'I'm very fond of Alex.' Not a challenge, not yet, but a warning. 'And Scarlet.'

And I like the way he looks. I like the fact that he's approachable and pleasant and, let's face it, I haven't spoken to many men in the last six months, let alone good-looking ones, so I can't make you any promises, Lucy.

I took the folded paper from her hand. 'He's a nice bloke.' I let my voice hold no more expression than hers, but an equal lack of challenge. I wondered whether Alex knew that Lucy wanted him; I knew she spent time around at the Old Mill, surely even Alex must have picked up on the fact that women don't just 'drop in' on men unless they fancy them? Or maybe Great Leys was the world centre for platonic relationships and it was me getting the wrong end of the stick. 'I'll give him the recipe when I drop Scarlet off.'

Lucy smiled and there was a touch more warmth about her face now. 'Thank you.' She turned to open the door to the outside. 'Is Alex coming to pick her up tomorrow?'

I shrugged, but the anorak absorbed the movement, so I said, 'I would think so.'

'That's good.' She turned to walk back inside, speaking to me over her shoulder as she went. 'Perhaps you'd tell him that Dad … that Mr Moore would like to have a word with him? About Scarlet?'

Well, I didn't think you were going to be correcting his spellings and giving him a maths test. 'Is she all right?'

We watched her bouncing along, performing some complicated dressage move on the playground, staring solemnly between Light Bulb's ears as her legs danced along another painted line. 'She … there are some issues. I've already mentioned it to Alex, but Mr Moore wants a proper meeting up here at school.'

I walked on to catch up with Scarlet, and held out the bag of toffees. 'Here. I thought it might be a bit chilly for ice cream. Sorry about having to chat to Lucy.'

''S okay.' Bounce, bounce. 'She wants to snog Alex.'

'Does she?'

'Mmm. She and Alex used to go out together. Lucy was Mummy's friend.'

I had a moment of creeping prurient interest that told me I was likely going native and was only a London childhood away from taking up sheep-dip as a hobby. So, Lucy and Alex had a past, did they? But then again, they were similar ages, neither was a gargoyle, why was I surprised? I felt the edges of crumpled paper in my pocket, the recipe Lucy had given me, to ensure Alex's dinner with me went off well; she was either a very generous lady or, despite Scarlet's beliefs, had no interest in Alex any more.

I changed the subject. 'What happened to your face?'

'Nothing. Let's go home.'

'Scarlet, I ...'

But she seized the toffees and wheeled suddenly away. 'Light Bulb! Oh, he's taken a hold I can't stop him, Winter, he's too strong,' and she hurtled off along the pavement, leaving me to shuffle in pursuit all the way back to the Old Mill. When I arrived, Light Bulb was face down on the small patch of grass along one side. Through the glass doors I could see Alex inside, talking to a man in a much better suit than the head teacher's, earnestly indicating a piece of paper and making marks on it with a biro. The door was ajar, as though Scarlet had hurled through and gone upstairs. Alex was clearly in full spate with the man from the bank, so, pushing Lucy's recipe down into the depths of my anorak pocket, I turned back through the archway and headed back to the cottage.

'She's being bullied, Daze, I'm positive. Remember when you used to get picked on at school?'

Daisy giggled. 'Only until we swapped places that first time. They didn't know what hit them.'

'I told you you should have fought back. They never gave you any trouble after that, did they?' I sipped at my tea and leaned back into the chair. They'd never be comfortable, it was like sitting on a skeleton's lap.

'No, but I had detention every playtime for half a term. There's nothing you can do, Win. I know you like her and you're drooling after him, but—'

'Hey, who's drooling? No drooling. Absolutely none. He's a bit tasty, that's all. And he's invited me to dinner tonight.'

A pause. 'Are you taking your toothbrush?'

I stopped to consider. Did I want to sleep with Alex? That well-muscled body promised a good time but ... *but what? He's sexy, he's tactile, more importantly he's available, and we all know how rare nice, straight, good-looking men are once you're over the age of twenty-five, so why is there any hint of a but?* 'It's a bit soon. We've not known each other that long yet.'

Daisy snorted. 'Remember, when you were nineteen, that bloke on the train? And Johan, on the Uni exchange programme, didn't you sleep with him within about ten minutes of meeting him?'

'Well, yes, but ...'

'You're still comparing every man to Dan, aren't you?'

'Daisy, you need to stop bringing Dan into every conversation that we have. I am so over him, if I was any more over him I'd be in orbit, all right? Please, can we stop mentioning him, or even *thinking* about him, yes?'

Daisy made a rude noise, and was gone. I went back to trying to put into words the sudden, and rather ignominious, end of a chap buried in one of the churchyards up on the moors who'd been killed by a herd of sheep. Despite his family's clearly not having much money, he had a dramatic stone, so italicised and decorated that the details were hard to read, and topped, rather thoughtlessly I thought, by a ram's head.

Daniel Bekener @EditorDanB
@WinterGAuthor Please just let me know that you're okay.

WinterGregory @WinterGAuthor
@EditorDanB I'm working.

Daniel Bekener @EditorDanB
@WinterGAuthor That's fine. It's good, I'm glad.

I waited, but nothing else was forthcoming. All right, so maybe he was just checking on his investment, I'd had quite an advance for this book and a deadline of Christmas, any failure to hit it was going to make Dan look daft in front of the entire publishing community. Particularly when he'd taken such a huge gamble on me when I'd submitted *Book of the Dead*, which I *knew* was fun and different and everything but I'd never foreseen it being a huge hit. I'd written it when I'd come into some money, Mum and Dad's split and divorce and subsequent relocation to different continents having released some family cash and I'd got sick of my research job. The idea for *Book of the Dead* had come to me when I'd been standing in a graveyard, wondering about some of the people buried there and ... well, that was pretty much it.

And Dan had seen it too. Cajoled and persuaded the publishing company he worked for to make an offer and the rest was publishing history. And now we both had the pressure on us, follow that up with something equally spectacular or go down as the one hit wonder a lot of the critics supposed me to be, and the unpredictable, unconventional risk taker everyone said Dan was. But it hadn't mattered when we were together. We'd just giggled at the thought of being a flash in the pan. *Book of the Dead* had made money for me, for the company, and I wasn't sure I really wanted to write another one. But Dan came from a family where no one ever stopped. His father had dropped dead at his printing works, his mother still worked with special needs children, all his siblings had stepped into employment straight from school or university and none of them had ever, as far as I could tell, even taken a day off hungover in their lives. The government could have used them on posters. So, he'd talked me into writing another book, then another, and we'd keep going until …

Until I couldn't do it any more. Shit.

I changed out of my writing clothes and into a respectable blue shift dress and heels. It felt strange not having trousers on. The sturdy breeze which swept down from the moors and scoured through the little town curled around my bare ankles like the ghosts of a thousand affectionate cats. I'd pinned my hair up, but London hairdos were not equal to Yorkshire wind and by the time I got to the Old Mill I had the feeling that I looked a bit pre-rumpled. Not that I was expecting Alex to rumple me, but I did look as though I might have had a tuppenny tumble in the bus shelter on my way over, which wasn't quite the sophisticated look I was going for.

'Hello, W-Winter.' Alex met me at the door. The lights inside were turned down so that the whole building seemed to glow softly, the seasoned timber almost shone. 'You l-look l-lovely.'

'Well, since all the local females seem to wear designer stuff just to get their kids from school, I thought I'd better make an effort. Besides, turning up in an anorak and jeans would have been ungrateful.' I slipped out of my London coat, beautifully shaped and fitted but with only two front buttons, which had let the wind in and flapped like a turbine all the way here.

'They're all v-very nice w-women really,' he said, turning to lead the way through to the stairs up to the flat.

Yeah, if you're a sexy single bloke with a come-to-bed physique and eyes like snowclouds. 'Was Scarlet all right when she got home?'

Alex laid a finger to his lips and inclined his head, indicating, I thought, that Scarlet was probably sitting in her bedroom listening for any mention of her name. 'I've m-made risotto,' he said. 'Or m-more precisely, the s-supermarket m-made it and I heated it u-up.'

'Ah. Thought you said you could cook?'

Another one of his blinding smiles. 'I was wr-wrong. Turns out it's h-harder than it l-looks.'

'What the hell do you and Scarlet eat, then?' I handed my coat to Alex, who draped it carefully over the back of a chair. A proper, upholstered chair; the desire to ruin the spines of the nation was clearly his mother's and didn't run in the family. 'Cereal and buns?'

'Eight-y-year-old girls l-like b-breadcrumbs, b-batter and b-brown, anything else is d-disgusting, apparently. If it isn't ed-edible as a result of twenty m-minutes at 180, then f-forget it.'

There was gentle overhead lighting in here too. The plain wooden flooring reflected the overhead bulbs but everything was dimmed and subtle – he probably wanted to disguise the dust and the sheer number of pony books. Up at the kitchen end of the room I could see a table, laid for two, thankfully no candles though. I wasn't quite sure I was ready for that yet.

Alex peered, rather unnervingly, in through the oven door. 'P-probably done, come and sit down.'

I sat, taking in my surroundings more fully as I did so. The flat was beautiful, underneath the trappings of 'small girl'; lots of bare, plain wood, lowlighters and uplighters and top of the range fitted kitchen. A good, workmanlike room softened with planks with the bark left on, the pale yellow gleam of ash contrasting with dark oak, all very easy on the eye. As, indeed, was Alex himself, wearing those brushed-cotton trousers and a pale shirt with just a trace of pattern along the weave. His eyes, when they turned my way, looked dark in this half-light.

'This place is lovely,' I said. 'Did you design it yourself?'

'Yes. W-well, Ell and I d-did it t-together. But b-before Scarlet. It's n-not the best place for a ch-child.' He turned back to dish out the food. 'If I'd known what w-was going to happen, I'd have b-built a bungalow.'

'She seems happy here.'

He made a sort of sideways shrug. 'Would you like w-wine? I'm afraid I d-don't drink when I h-have Scarl, but d-don't let that stop you.'

'I'd love a glass, thanks.'

Walking carefully, as though carrying a plate of hot food was an alien experience, Alex came over and placed the risotto in front of me, and followed it with a large glass of white wine. 'I d-daren't drink, y'see,' he said, sitting down opposite me. 'In c-case Scarl gets up in the n-night.'

I raised my eyebrows a bit. I remembered both my parents getting decidedly tipsy on several occasions – oh, nothing dramatic, no tales of drunken beatings or coming home from school to find them unconscious on the sofa, just the memory of Christmas sing-songs and anniversary parties, of Daisy and I laughing ourselves silly at Mum's off-key rendition of *Hark the Herald Angels Sing*, with alternative, rude, words provided by Dad. But then, there had been two of them.

'That's a shame.' I sipped the wine. It was pleasant, rather than delicious. The risotto sat in front of me, heaped on the plate like a pile of soggily-hatching maggots. 'And this looks nice.'

'It l-looks like it should h-have "could do b-better" on a little s-sticker. Sorry, W-Winter, I should have g-got caterers in or something.'

'Don't be daft.' I forked up a couple of mouthfuls. What it lacked in the *Masterchef* presentation stakes, it made up for in flavour. 'No, it really is nice.'

Alex smiled that thousand-watt smile again. It made the little creases in the corners of his eyes pucker and spread the grin even further, as though his whole face smiled, not just the mouth and eyes. 'G-good. I—'

'Hello, Winter.'

We both jumped. I'd been far too intent on those grey eyes to hear Scarlet appearing in the corner of the room.

'G-go back to b-bed.' Alex dropped the smile. His shoulders dipped a bit and a resigned expression crept in, forcing a careworn expression onto his face. 'P-please, Scarl.'

Scarlet stood in the doorway. She was wearing an all-in-one sleepsuit with, predictably, a pony pattern all over it, and her thumb was hovering around mouth-level, as though she wasn't sure of her reception. 'I just wanted to say hello to Winter.'

'Hello, Scarlet,' I said. Her eyes went from me to Alex and then to the risotto, then back to Alex again.

'Is that the rice stuff? Can I try it?'

Alex gave me the kind of shrug that must be performed by condemned men when the hangman asks them if they'd rather have a reef knot or a rolling hitch. The shrug of a man so reconciled to his fate that nothing really matters any more. 'J-just one m-mouthful. Then b-bed.'

Scarlet ran over, took a forkful from her uncle's plate, made a face, and then dashed back to the door. 'It's 'sgustin,' she said, assuredly. 'Goodnight.'

'Goodnight,' we chorused, and then sat in silence until we heard the very quiet sound of a bedroom door being closed.

Alex gave a deep sigh. It sounded as though he'd been holding his breath since Scarlet appeared. 'I'm sorry.'

'Why?' I went back to the risotto. Given the size and age of the oven in the Tiny House, I'd resisted cooking any real food since my arrival, and had been surviving mostly on soup and coffee, with the odd bar of chocolate thrown in for energy reasons. The risotto was making my stomach complain about this, vociferously. 'It's not as though I didn't know she was here, is it?'

He shook his head and stared down into the depths of the risotto as though he was trying to foretell the future though rice-based products. 'No. B-but … it's hard to be a g-grown up and do adult things when S-Scarl could come b-bursting in at any minute.'

I gave him a hard stare and waved my fork. 'I've only come for dinner, Alex.'

A slow smile now, not the high-voltage one but

something softer. 'True. But d-do you see what I m-mean? How hard it is to m-meet anyone and then take things any f-further?'

'I think a hundred thousand single mothers would probably agree with you there.' I drank some more wine and eventually he dropped his eyes back to his own plate.

'You're r-right. It's not just me. It's only sometimes it f-feels that way.'

I suddenly remembered Lucy's face, those blue eyes trying to weigh my intentions. 'Lucy gave me a recipe to give you, but I think it might be a bit late now.'

'Oh?' He didn't look up, just kept eating. 'Th-that was k-kind.' A grin. 'I p-probably shouldn't h-have p-posted on F-F-Facebook that I w-was having you ov-over.'

'You and Lucy?' I asked, carefully.

A sideways inclination of the head. 'On-once. But l-like I s-said, Scarl m-makes it h-hard to b-be n-normal. Ev-everything has to r-revolve around h-her.' And then, with a shrug that said more than the words, 'They c-could still t-take her away f-from me. I-if I don't c-come up to s-scratch.'

We cleared our plates, chatting quietly. I didn't know about Alex, but I was very, very conscious that at any time Scarlet could come sliding back through, and it put a bit of a crimp in my conversation. Oh, I wasn't about to ask what he thought of frottage or whether he considered handcuffs an interesting addition to a bedroom repertoire, but I did have to stop and think before I swore or mentioned anything that an eight-year-old girl shouldn't overhear, even accidentally.

Alex's attention was very flattering, I had to admit. He was very pleasant to look at, this nicely abstract lighting making the contrast between his hair and skin and eyes look multi-toned and artistic. He didn't stammer nearly as much now, and we talked softly over things like hobbies and what had been in the news recently – nothing controversial or too involved, just pleasant dinner-table chat while we ate and I drank and, at last, the plates were empty and it was approaching that time when a peck on the cheek could accelerate into a pleasant waste of time for a few hours.

'This has been lovely. Thanks for inviting me over.' I pushed my chair away from the table. 'Now I really ought to weave my way home.'

Both of us had an eye on the door through which Scarlet had come earlier. Although I was *almost* positive that she'd gone back to her room, for all I knew she made a habit of crouching down in the hallway and bursting into the room suddenly at this time every night. Alex was almost as twitchy. 'Thank you for c-coming. And for everything y-you've done for Scarl.'

You could kiss him. Just lean over across the table and give him a nice, friendly cheek kiss. He's sexy, he's cute, he's …

What is he? Why are you hesitating? A couple of years ago you would have had him over the back of that sofa pleading for mercy by now, with a chair against the door to hold back young girls and another bottle of wine in the fridge for afterwards. Okay, you don't have to do that, but you could give him some signal that you're interested, couldn't you?

I picked up my coat from the back of the chair but Alex took it from me and held it so that I could put it on. *Maybe that's why you don't want to make any sudden moves. He's a gentleman.* As I slid my arms down the sleeves, I suddenly noticed Light Bulb, tucked into a corner behind the sofa. 'Not in his stable?' I nodded towards the hobby horse.

Alex settled the coat across my shoulders. 'He was too w-warm. He's cooling down out h-here and I'll put him away l-later.'

I gave a little laugh. 'You're as bonkers as Scarlet.'

'Maybe.'

Light Bulb had a slightly lopsided look about him tonight, his head seemed to be slightly askew on his stick, and I suddenly remembered Scarlet, with a mark across her face like a smack, and Lucy's words. 'Lucy said the school wanted to talk to you tomorrow about Scarlet. I think she might be being bullied, you know.'

He froze. Moved away from me, his hands falling to his sides as though weighted. 'J-j—' he started, blinking rapidly, his face almost bending in his effort to get the words out. 'J-j ...' A sudden, vicious shake of his head and his fisted hands beat against his legs. 'J-just don't worry about it, Winter.' The words came in a rush.

'But she—'

He hustled me to the door, moving me with his body, so I either left the flat or he climbed up me. 'Goodnight, W-Winter,' he said, and closed the door, leaving me standing at the top of the coiled staircase from the big hallway like Ginger Rogers with stage fright.

'Goodnight,' I said to the door, for manners' sake, then went down and outside into the newly chilly air.

Chapter Ten

Facebook

Comment: Matt Simons Well, how did the date go? Did you poison her?

Comment: Alex Hill No, but I was a dick. Why do I always think that any time anyone says something about Scarlet, that they're calling my parenting skills into question? Why can I not just smile and nod and take it on board? I am, sorry to say it, a shit.

Comment: Matt Simons Nah, you're just oversensitive, mate. You gotta learn to shake it off. Unless they really are insulting your parenting skills, then you can smack 'em.

Comment: Alex Hill Thanks. I think.

Comment: Lucy Charlton Next time I see you I'll teach you how to make a soufflé!

✉

From: AlexHillStone@wolmail.com

To: LucyLoo@wolmail.com

Subject: Advice

It's not a soufflé I need. Winter picked up that Scarl is having problems at school and I bloody nearly bit her head off. What can I do about the whole bullying thing? Am I letting Scarl down?

Al x

✉

To: AlexHillStone@wolmail.com

From: LucyLoo@wolmail.com

Subject: Advice

You are NOT letting Scarlet down. It's not easy for you and

you are doing an amazing job – I wish all the parents were as dedicated as you are, some don't even listen to their children read because they think that's our job! Look, do you fancy having a coffee one evening? We can discuss a strategy for managing Scarlet's behaviour at school and how we can help her. I might even bring a soufflé recipe! Oh, only if you think Winter will be okay with us meeting as I don't want to upset anything between you – am presuming you've told her we're just friends these days?

Lu x

✉

From: AlexHillStone@wolmail.com
To: WinterGregoryAuthor@teddymail.com
Subject:

Hi. How are you this morning? Still upright, no signs of acute rice poisoning?

I know I hate saying it, but I'm going to have to do it again … I'm sorry. Sorry about last night, about so much of last night you cannot imagine. Sorry that I'm too chicken to admit that the last time I cooked a proper meal was in school, partnered up with that Shakespeare of Facebook, Matt-bloody-Simons, sorry that I didn't share a bottle of wine with you, sorry that Scarlet ruined the mood (although she couldn't help it, she didn't know there was a 'mood' to ruin, only that her friend Winter had come over). And, most of all, I'm sorry about the way I acted.

I've got this thing, you see. This I don't know what you'd call it. An inferiority complex? Something like that. The permanent feeling that I'm getting it all wrong. I love Scarlet. Unquestioningly, I adore her. I want you to know that, here, upfront. I would die for that little girl. But. Oh, and now I've had to have another drink (it's okay, Mum has Scarlet tonight, she does sometimes, when she's in early, when she's 'feeling strong' as she puts it, as though Scarl is some kind of Incredible Hulk who destroys furniture and knocks down walls). But. Scarlet isn't mine. She's not my daughter, you know that, she's my niece. Would it be different if she was mine? Maybe, maybe that genetic thing would cut in and make it all easier but she's Ellen's daughter. Ellen and some loser from up north somewhere, who only hung around long enough for the positive test, then buggered off again. So, when Ellen … when El died, who else was there? She couldn't live with Mum, and I wouldn't … *would not* have her taken away from the only home she's ever known and taken into care. But I didn't know, I still don't know, how to look after a little girl. I'm doing my best, I'm pretty rubbish at the clothes thing, and I have no idea how this make-up effort is supposed to work, but hell, she's only eight, I've got years to get the hang of all that before she needs it, yes?

And the guilt. The absolute knowing that I'm getting it all wrong. It's constant, Winter, the gnawing little thoughts that Scarl should have her five a day, her vitamin tablets, her proper calcium intake, the sunblock and the vitamin C and a good education and friends and pets and brothers and sisters and … you know, there's a list somewhere. Probably being kept by all those people who tut when she rides Light Bulb into the supermarket or reads nothing but those pony books – you know she can spell Lipizzaner but she can't spell competition? So every time anyone says anything about Scarl … oh, can be something like 'she should have a coat on' or 'she looks a bit pale or tired or sad' … I take it personally. Like an insult. As if they're saying 'you can't look after that child, can you?' And every time I'm called into school, every time Lucy mentions her behaviour in the classroom, it just heaps more shame onto my head. And then I think, 'what if they take her away? What if they decide that she really *would* be better off in a family? *What if I lose her?*'

It's stupid. I'm stupid. I know you didn't mean anything, I know you were just trying to show concern, but all I could hear was 'you don't even realise she's being pushed around in the playground, do you?' And then there's the guilt about that. Oh, they pick on Scarl because of me, I know that. And because she doesn't have a mummy or a daddy, and, you know what? That's my fault too. So it's all on me. I was a rude, ungrateful bastard. Sorry. Again.

Alex

I'd just finished reading the email when there was a knock at the door that made me jump. At least the glass panelling gave me a good idea of who was there, which was something to be grateful for, because flinging it open to Margaret without a moment's priming wouldn't be recommended, especially with today's outfit of something knitted which was the nearest I could come to a definition.

'I came to see if you need any tea towels washed,' she said, stepping down into the living room. 'Because you've been here nearly a fortnight and that's a long time with nothing but a J-cloth. And we don't have a laundrette for miles, I think the nearest might even be in Stockton, there used to be one on the High Street but I think it burned down. Or went bankrupt, I just remember there was smoke involved.'

'Hello,' I said, somewhat weakly. I was rather relieved that she'd come for something as, well, yes, it was completely peculiar, obviously, but at least it wasn't an attempt to talk about Alex. 'I think I'm fine on the tea towel front, actually, thanks.' I couldn't tear my eyes away from her costume, which was either a woollen dress or a very large and slightly camp fisherman was missing his jersey. 'That's a very nice … umm … you've got on.'

Years of Daisy's affliction with fashion had given me an acute eye for people who were 'trying something new' in the clothing department, which usually meant dressing ten years younger or older. In Margaret's case it seemed to be dressing pink and Icelandic. She looked like a boiled Bjork.

'Thank you, dear. A friend made it for me on her machine. I like something bright at this time of year, livens things up a bit, don't you think?'

Well, yes, but so does crystal meth and orgies.

Margaret gazed around the room. 'Oh, are you working? I shouldn't have interrupted … there was just another *tiny* thing? I wondered, well, it's rather an imposition I know, but we were supposed to be having a lady from Newcastle who writes about Victorian sad people, but she's had to cancel. We get so few creatives through Great Leys, though Mr Park likes to think of himself as a writer, but he's only ever managed a rather angry letter to the editor of the local paper, so he's not really suitable. We're having a meeting tomorrow, you see, and if I could tell them that you were in agreement then it would be a feather in my cap, so to speak.'

No. Not feathers. Not with that knitwear. It would be like the blue bird of happiness dying a terrible death. 'I'm sure I'd be happy to do whatever it is that you're asking me to do,' I said, being as tactful as I could.

'Oh. I'm sorry, yes, of course. Just to drop in at the book group on Wednesday, maybe give them a bit of a talk? You'd be very welcome to sell your books there, they always like to buy one or two from authors, although I can't say we've had very many. We nearly got John Grisham once, you know,' she said, proudly, as though they had been hunting him through the undergrowth for weeks and he'd scampered away from their spears at the last moment.

I looked over at the laptop. The December deadline was beginning to look as though it was peering in through the window at me, but publicity was publicity. 'Of course, I'd be glad to,' I said.

Glad is probably pushing it. Grateful for the opportunity to procrastinate is more like it.

'Wonderful!' Margaret turned on the heel of her comfortable shoes. 'Now I'd better go and see if Alex is in. He promised to come and help me move a table today and I haven't seen hide nor hair of him yet.'

I wanted to put a hand on her arm, ask her if Alex was really as worried about bringing up Scarlet as he'd seemed in that email, as anxious and self-doubting about her wellbeing, but I stopped myself in time. She didn't seem to be particularly well-bundled in the concern and reassurance department – which, now I came to think of it, might have something to do with the way Alex had turned out, a childhood of that kind of parenting was going to leave a bit of a mark – and I didn't want her to turn up on his doorstep full of a 'what's this I hear?'

I just smiled instead. 'Tell him thanks for dinner.'

She gave me a swift nod and went off out again, her dress bulging and rippling as she walked as though she had a couple of large boa constrictors in there with her. With Margaret, that wasn't totally improbable either.

Oh well. Could have been worse, I could have been standing in for Ewan McGregor.

I slumped for a bit longer, but the shaft of lengthening sunlight which had been growing across the floor for the last hour or so decided me. I'd go up onto the moors, pop in to a couple of small chapels that were marked on the map but I'd not yet had a chance to see, take some more pictures and generally enjoy the brightness outside. Being out of doors might just jazz me up enough to get down to some writing. Last time round Dan had been there to cajole me out of the mid-book slump, now it was down to me, and if I couldn't cajole myself then I had no business calling myself a writer.

I got into the car, which was still festooned with the remnants of Scarlet's biscuit extravaganza. *You should do something about that.* The thought was there, but I just couldn't work up sufficient disgust in the state of my passenger seat to do anything like hoovering, so I just turned a blind eye and headed out of Great Leys and up onto the road that ran over the high moors, a track so old that it was grooved into the landscape with the centuries of passing traffic. The high sun cast brittle shadows from the ancient marker stones and crosses which marked the way and the road was so empty that I could almost imagine myself riding across the moors, leading a string of pack ponies down towards the town.

I suppose I must have been daydreaming a bit, lulled by the straight road, the flicker of the passing stones, the warmth of the sun, because the next thing I knew a horn was blaring at me. On the opposite side of the road a big four-wheel drive thing had been forced to put two wheels up onto the verge to avoid my somewhat erratic approach along a part of the road not quite wide enough for two vehicles to pass easily. I should have pulled over, even slowed down, but my fugue state had meant that I hadn't even registered the road's degradation from smooth two-lane tarmac to single track. The sudden slicing of the horn into my thoughts made me jump and flick the wheel, so that we passed each other at speed, narrowly avoiding clipping wing mirrors, and adrenaline was dry and powdery in my mouth as I realised what could have happened. A quick glance in my rear mirror showed me the other car driving slowly down off the grass and heading the way I'd come, but the brief glimpse I'd had of the annoyed other driver was what was really sending those iced-acid pulses through my blood.

Dan.

I pulled into the little lay-by and put my head down on the steering wheel. *It can't have been Dan. You're just being stupid now, transposing his face onto every dark-haired man you see. You went by far too fast to get a proper look anyway, and Dan drives an Astra, not that big silver monstrosity, the kind of thing favoured by people who tow caravans or ferry umpteen children to a private school.*

I repeatedly licked my lips, trying to bring some fluid back into my mouth but my tongue was sticky with lack of moisture. *Not Dan. Just a bloke with a similar haircut. You're losing it, Winter.*

I had to speak to Daisy.

'Daze, I keep thinking I see Dan everywhere.'

'Define "everywhere". In your bathroom, hiding in the boot of your car?'

As everything settled down I began to feel ridiculous. 'I might be overreacting a bit. It might not have been him – it can't have been him now I come to think of it. Dan doesn't understand the countryside and he thinks sheep are out to get him.'

Daisy sighed. 'How long are we going to have this going on for? Win, you have to get over him, however you choose to do it, confront him, ignore him, burn down his house. He shouldn't be able to make you feel this bad just by existing. I mean, *so what* if you did see him? He can't do anything, not now, not as long as we're strong. He can only affect you as badly as you let him, can't he?'

With my sister's wise words ringing in my ears, I restarted the car and headed towards my original destination, the overgrown churchyard which lay off this hardly-used bit of roadway. The wheel was still clammy between my hands but the panic had abated. Daisy was right, of course she was. In fact, she usually was. That artistic temperament that should, by rights, have made her flighty and inconsequential had in fact given her a sensible and rational outlook on life, which was why I loved to talk things over with her. She'd see what lay behind my knee-jerk reactions and force me to see it too.

It wasn't Dan. It can't have been Dan. And even if it was, so what? He can't touch us now.

Chapter Eleven

The graveyard was wonderful. Twisted old crab apple trees hunched over stones like elderly mourners, their leaves beginning to buckle under the weight of autumn. The monuments themselves were austere, the lettering proud of its basic handcraftedness and the legends little more than curt dates and reminders that we'd all be dead, one day. Grass skirted the graves and bramble bushes coiled and buttressed around stones, trees and the chapel itself, providing a *Sleeping Beauty*-esque look to the pictures I took. I found myself relaxing more and more, talking sense into myself as I wandered around trying not to disturb anything in this almost breathless place. I was fine. Of course I was fine. It was men, they were the problem: Dan and our unpleasant break-up yet having to stay vaguely in touch until this book was done, meaning that the longed-for 'clean break' was going to be a while in coming; Alex and his guilt, his stress over doing the right thing; even bloody Light Bulb was male, although, apart from that relentless chain-stitched grin, I couldn't really accuse him of anything.

By the time I drove back to Great Leys I was positively insouciant.

✉

From: AlexHillStone@wolmail.com
To: WinterGregoryAuthor@teddymail.com
Subject: Are you free?

Hi Winter

I wondered if I could have the benefit of your experience on something? Well, not experience, exactly, not unless you've got half a dozen children you're not admitting to! It's to do with Scarl and this bullying thing going on at school, which seems to have escalated just recently. Lucy came over yesterday (she does pop over from time to time but don't get the wrong impression, we're just friends now) and she's worried about Scarl and what's going on. I really don't want to try to cover it in an email, it doesn't seem fair either to you or to Scarl, a little bit as though I'm talking about her behind her back – is that ridiculous? Anyway, if you're free tomorrow, could you come here, sometime during school hours, yes, I know I said I didn't want to talk about Scarl behind her back, but I can't really talk about this with her in the room.

I really would just like another perspective on things, and there aren't that many people who could give input. Mum can't really get her head around any of this and I really just want to offload on someone neutral. Not that you're neutral exactly, it's weird but in my head I have you as sort of orange and flame and, yes, still Catwoman. So, like Catwoman if she was on fire, which, now I think of it, is a bloody stupid analogy and I'll leave the creative writing to you. Don't worry about emailing me back, I'll be in all day tomorrow, just pop in and pour yourself a coffee and I'll be round.

I really, truly appreciate everything you've done for us, Winter.
Alex

I didn't really know how to feel. Alex seemed to like me. He kept on with this Catwoman thing until I'd had to Google her, never really having been much of a one for the comics or the films. I'd sort of imagined a woman who had loads of cats, and was ever so slightly amused, and a little bit shocked, to find pictures of a very slim woman in black lycra. I hadn't been that thin since I was about five and in something that body-hugging I'd probably look more like a shrink-wrapped egg-timer.

Which gave rise to an interesting question – well, interesting if you were me, anyway. Did Alex really like *me* or was he seeing me as something I wasn't just because I was the first woman he'd met that he hadn't grown up with? Because I liked Scarlet and was unaffected by the stammer? It was obvious that he and Lucy had had something going on, might even still have something, although two-timing anybody in a place the size – and with the gossip-quotient – of Great Leys was like walking down Oxford Street wearing a T-shirt that says 'I'm Cheating'.

He didn't really know all that much about me, other than what I'd told him the other night or he'd gleaned from Scarlet, he didn't know my favourite music or authors or colour or food. Maybe he was trying to talk himself into liking me, because I was the nearest thing he thought he was likely to get to a girlfriend, and overlaying me with cartoon characters because it was easier to relate to me that way than in real life? I snuck another look at the Catwoman graphic on the computer, and then looked down at myself. Nope. Not even if there was a sudden Manga-attack and liposuction event would I ever have eyes that huge or a body that tiny.

And then I checked all the places online that Dan usually hung out. His Twitter profile had gone quiet, there was nothing on his Facebook page or his blog, since the last post. Nothing to indicate that he'd decided to come to Yorkshire, nothing that gave any hint as to his current state. *Is he angry?* I ran over his last string of messages. *He doesn't sound angry. He sounds regretful. Sad.*

I shook my head and gritted my teeth. *So he should, so he bloody should!* But my heart wasn't in it, although the hurt ran deeper than my heart; it was coursing through my entire circulatory system, lodging in my veins and winding tight silver coils through my arteries. I'd thought I was falling in love with Dan. What had started as a fun, light-hearted friendship had started to deepen. When we'd slept together for the first time he'd taken my hand and solemnly told me that it meant we were bound together for life by a memory. And he'd been right. Only now it was a memory I didn't want any more, a memory that flashed through my head as I fell asleep or tried to concentrate on words. *Dan kissing my neck, running those slim fingers over my cheekbones, fixing my eyes with his black gaze. Grinning that manic grin, tinged with something else, something softer, as he undressed me, so gently. Lifted me and lowered me onto the bed, pinned me there with words of beauty and kindness and whispered me into making love ...*

Thank God for the knock at the door. Otherwise I might have talked myself into messaging him, although I had no idea what I could possibly say. *And besides, after all you went through, it would be disloyal to Daisy to have any contact with him again. She suffered too, the splashback of vitriol from his accusations and dislike; for all she told you to reach some closure, she wasn't intending you to have* that *kind of contact, was she?*

At the door stood Margaret, again, and Scarlet. Light Bulb was nowhere in evidence and Margaret looked a bit tense. 'I'm sorry, Winter, but Scarlet wanted to say hello.' She sighed an exaggerated sigh. 'There, Scarlet, I told you Miss Gregory would be busy, she's a writer and it's not something you can just pick up and put down like a casserole you know. Now, just say hello and we'll go back and you can have those fish fingers until Alex gets that wall up.'

Scarlet looked smaller than usual, somehow. She was

wearing her school uniform dress, red checks like a blood-drawn chessboard, with a red sweatshirt over the top, heavily embellished with the school name and a logo that looked as though a graphic designer had gone a bit trigger-happy on a tree. Her grandmother was holding her hand as if it were sticky.

'Why don't I walk Scarlet home?' I suggested, and watched her brighten. 'And then you can get back to …' I groped for inspiration, which Margaret's knitted outfit wasn't providing, unless she was off to trawl for cod.

Margaret's face relaxed. *She feels restricted by duty too,* I noted. *Trying to do the right thing, the required thing, having a life thrust upon her that she could never have imagined.* 'Well, I *was* going to drop in on Mr Park's mother, who's got a problem with legs, not her own legs, of course, these are china.' Margaret was practically smiling now. 'And I know Scarlet would love it.'

'I would, I would! Please take me home, Winter, and then you can talk to Alex some more about building and cooking and things.'

So she was listening to us talking before she burst in. Good job you hadn't got round to propositioning him then, but to hear her recap does make you sound like the world's most boring conversationalist. Building and cooking, good grief, is that who you are now?

'Come on then.' I reached behind me into the room, which practically put my hand in the oven, grabbed my anorak and pulled it on. Margaret released her granddaughter into my care by passing her hand over, as though she was marrying us. I'd been right, it was sticky. 'We'll go straight over there and I'll wait with you until Alex has finished whatever he's doing.'

'Alex made me leave Light Bulb at home today,' Scarlet

said, bobbing along beside me like an excited cork. 'It's only 'cos I hit Angel Williams, but Angel Williams hit me first, so it's not fair that I had to not have Light Bulb when she never even had to not have pudding, is it?'

'Well, it does sound a bit harsh.' I pulled the door closed behind us. 'But I suppose it rather depends on the pudding in question.'

'Alex had to go into school this morning when he took me in, to talk about it,' she said, confidentially. 'Mr Moore let him sit in his office. I bet he didn't give him a Polo, Mr Moore only gives Polos to people he likes.'

I zipped up my anorak. There were school mothers dotted randomly down the High Street, I wondered if they were a crack Fashion Squad waiting to put a hit on me. 'Why doesn't Mr Moore like Alex?' I asked, trying not to squint evilly at School Mother Number One, a tight-jeaned WAGalike gazing in the window of the jewellers as we passed.

'Mr Moore is Miss Charlton's dad, and Miss Charlton used to go out with Alex but Alex went off her, and then Miss Charlton married a man who used to hit her so she came home and Mr Moore thinks that Alex thinks he's too good for her,' she said, with a vast amount of satisfaction.

Hm, Alex, are you playing us off against each other perhaps? 'How do you know all that? Scarlet, do you listen at doors or something?'

A moment's consideration, then she cast her eyes down and her warm hand clenched in mine. 'A bit. Sometimes. But people *will* whisper and roll their eyes about and sigh and everything, as though I couldn't possibly understand. They forget, I *am* eight.'

Maybe Alex and I were better off sticking to discussing cookery and buildings. This child knew far too much to be good for her.

Walking along with Scarlet, but without Light Bulb, felt strange. She kept hold of my hand, although she'd tug and leap about at the end of my arm like a small dog scenting strangers, and she kept up a running commentary about people, things, cars, the shops we were walking past. The constant chatter reminded me of Daisy when we'd been about ten or eleven and she was nervous about our impending move to the senior school. I'd looked forward to it, she'd dreaded it.

'Is everything all right at school?' I felt compelled to ask Scarlet.

Her little hand went limp against my fingers. 'Yes, of course,' she said, but her tone was dull. 'Why wouldn't it be?' Her other hand flew up to her face and her thumb found her mouth, but she kept her eyes on the pavement in front of us.

'You just reminded me of my sister then, when she was a bit worried about school,' I said, trying to talk myself out of the hole I'd dug. 'She was small for her age and she had a bit of a hard time.' *Maybe, if she's being bullied, hearing that she's not the only one will help her to open up.*

'Oh.' She removed the thumb and looked up at me. *Are you really suitable to be the person she talks to about this? Surely it would be better to be Alex or her teacher or almost anyone else, really.* 'But if you're identical twins, why weren't you both small?' *Oh all right then. We'll drop that line of enquiry for now.*

'We were. But I was a bit more down to earth than Daisy. She used to burst into tears very easily.'

'Oh.' Another moment's thumb-based thought, then, 'Only babies cry.'

Oh, Scarlet, no. Grown women cry too. So hard that sometimes they feel as though it isn't tears, it's blood.

We got to the end of Stepford Street. I imagined the head of each School Mother turning on an immobile neck like something out of a horror film as we passed, but I refused to give them the satisfaction of taking any notice, and was very smugly glad to walk through the archway to the Old Mill as though I owned the place.

There was a whole gang of blokes taking down some scaffolding, a cement mixer rumbled in the middle of the yard and there was no sign of Alex. 'Will you make me fish fingers?' Scarlet led the way into the glass-fronted hall. 'I'm quite hungry.'

I followed her up the stairs to the flat with a sense of dislocation. I'd come here to write my book, not act as a surrogate mother, but there was a lot about Scarlet that called out to me. Her bravery, even if she didn't know that's what it was, in the face of loss. Her hanging on to the memory of her mother through the medium of a cloth-headed horse, giving him life through sheer will and imagination, as though the power of her belief could somehow keep that connection to her parent alive. *Poor little girl. Poor, lonely, emotionally-neglected little girl.*

Once inside the flat Scarlet bounced to the freezer and produced a pack of fish fingers, then placed them expectantly beside the cooker, cocking her head to look at me, as though she was an exceptionally able dog. 'I'm not allowed to turn on the oven, otherwise I'd cook them myself. I can cook already.' And then bravado waning into realism, 'Well, I can do cornflake cakes and toast. If Alex is there.'

'Good for you.' I read the instructions on the packet. Fish fingers weren't really in my repertoire. 'Okay, they're in. Twenty minutes at 180 and brown. Should suit you down to the ground.'

Scarlet gave me a grin that told me she'd heard that bit of my conversation with Alex as well. 'I have to go and change now. I'm not allowed to wear my uniform out of school, in case I tear anything.'

I nodded and she belted off down the corridor. The door to her room slammed in a much more definite way than it had the other night.

'Oh, h-hello.'

I jumped. 'What the hell *is* it with your family appearing unexpectedly? Have you got vampires in your genes or something?'

Alex smiled. 'Yes. Th-they call us the Silent H-Hills. It's a j-joke. Name of a c-computer game.'

'It's not a joke if you have to explain it, you know.' But this was banter. It felt normal. It felt good. 'I just put fish fingers in the oven and Scarlet is changing. I'll be off now.'

Alex came further into the room. The baggy-necked red T-shirt was back in evidence again, smeared with what I hoped was woodstain, which also adorned his bare arms like a tribal tattoo, if the tribe in question was massively tree-based. 'Oh, no, s-stay, please.'

Oh, no, I couldn't possibly, I have to hurry back to the House of Tiny and imagine that my ex-boyfriend is stalking me. 'Okay.'

Scarlet hurtled back into the room, carrying Light Bulb by the neck. 'Hi, Alex. Winter brought me home because Granny was being boring. I'm going to do some jumping now until my fish fingers are done,' and then she was gone, rattling down the stairs with the hobby horse hitting the wooden rails all the way down.

We waited until the echoes died away. 'Why not have that talk now?' I suggested. 'It will save me coming over tomorrow.'

Alex made a down-turned mouth. 'Th-that was going to be th-the high p-point of my day,' he said. 'I'd p-primed the coffee machine to ex-expect you.'

'I'm not ruling it out, just saying that now would be good, if you want to offload and avoid a sleepless night.' I sat down on the sofa and tucked my legs up. *Yes. Comfortable. I feel comfortable. And safe.* 'Come on, Alex.'

He looked a lot more serious, suddenly. Less of the Greek god and a bit more like the businessman he must be, under all the stone dust and the stammer, to have a place like this. His eyes lost all the smiley lines and gained a serious darkness. 'I f-feel it's unfair to you. Y-you're this lovely w-woman who's just b-blown into our lives, so kind and …' he tailed off, 'but I need h-help. I c-can't do this on my own.'

Oh God, I hope he's not going to suggest that I become his nanny. Well, not his nanny, obviously, unless he's into any of that really weird shit with nappies and breastfeeding … I found myself staring at him, wondering just what he *was* into, and then realising that he was still talking, 'and I don't know w-what to say to her. It's g-got worse because she b-brought you into it, you know.'

And then, to make me feel even worse than a fantasy of Dan, he told me that Lucy had come to tell him there had been invitations being handed out at school yesterday. One of the children in Scarlet's class was having a birthday party and every other child had been invited, except for Scarlet, and how, when Lucy had remonstrated with the invitation-giver, Scarlet had said that she didn't mind, because her friend was a famous author and was coming for tea on that day, so she couldn't go anyway.

Some children had taken exception to Scarlet claiming

a Famous Friend that nobody had ever seen – obviously I hadn't looked anything like famous when I'd collected her from school. Fame doesn't wear an oversized anorak or grotty jog bottoms, which probably comes as a shock to J. K. Rowling, and a fight had ensued. Scarlet had, apparently, given as good as she got, but obviously it was a situation that couldn't continue.

'She h-has nightmares.' Alex had flopped down on the sofa next to me. 'D-dreams that I die and she's on h-her own. And I d-dd …' A resigned look and a shrug and he didn't even bother to try to finish the sentence. The muscles around his jaw twitched with the unsaid.

I tipped my head forward and cupped my hands over my face. 'You're right,' I said. 'I came here to finish my book, not to get tied up in something that sounds like an episode of *The Archers*.' Then I let my hands fall, turned to look into those grey eyes. 'But I like you, I like Scarlet and I'm not particularly keen on any of those unnecessarily glittery mothers or their shiny nylon children, so I can at least try to fix this particular bit of your niece's life.'

Alex relaxed, just a little. I saw his shoulders drop and a little hope creep into his weary face. 'I l–like you too, if that helps.' One hand crossed the cushion which lay between us and onto my lap, loosely covering my fingers with his own. 'I r-really do.'

I turned my own hand so that it bowled upwards and curled into his rough palm. 'I just don't think I'd be any good for you. I'm not …' *Not so many things. Not ready to settle down in a small town, not keen on taking on a child, not quite ready yet to live this kind of life.*

Not over Dan.

'Not good at relationships,' I finished, chickening out of a proper explanation.

'You and D-Dan ...' Alex gently drew his fingers in, enclosing my hand completely. His skin was hard, calloused from a proper job, like the bark of a tree. 'I understand, honestly I d-do. The way he b-behaved, the way he treated you and D-Daisy.' He leaned a little further forward, so that our faces were very close. 'I would never, *never* d-do that.'

Stone dust had fallen into the little lines around his mouth, decorating his stubble with sweat-beaded balls. His lips were still moving, soundlessly now, his grasp on my hand firming with every inch he leaned in and his breath, scented with coffee, played across my mouth, promising heat and yet raising chills down the back of my neck. Closer. I closed my eyes.

A microsecond of pressure, of warmth and moisture, and then the stairs let out their fanfare of rattling as Scarlet whirled her way back up and hit the door running. Alex and I jerked apart as though someone had electrified the sofa. 'Is my tea ready yet?'

'She's got a spy camera in here. It's the only explanation,' I muttered to Alex out of the corner of my mouth, and he smiled back with his eyebrows raised in a rueful acknowledgement. The chills had migrated and joined the warmth that had spread upwards. Somewhere around my middle there was a minor hurricane taking place as I began to acknowledge this desperately sexy man as something more than just a shadow in a corner. Somebody real, not only a set of broad shoulders, an exquisitely well-formed backside and thighs like a set of architectural supports, but a breathing, feeling person with whom I may, just *may*, have some real kind of connection. If I wanted it.

'I'll see if it's r-ready.' He stood up and the space next to me felt like loneliness.

'I'd better go.'

They both swung round. 'Oh, can't Winter have her tea with us, Alex? Winter, Alex has some proper food in the freezer, he likes that kind of chicken in that yellow stuff, you could both have that.' And then, with a prescience that she'd so far failed to exhibit any signs of, 'I can go and play outside again.'

I smiled. 'Sorry, Scarlet, but your grandma has asked me to talk to her book group tomorrow, so I ought to do some preparation for that, check how many copies of *Book of the Dead* I've got hanging around, decide what to say and make sure I've got something clean to wear, that kind of thing.'

'Oh.' Scarlet jutted her lower lip at the plate of incipient brown Alex was preparing for her. 'Well, I suppose that's all right then.'

'H-here. Tea. I'll just show W-Winter out.' Alex put the plate down on the counter and came with me to the door of the flat. Outside, on the landing, he put out a hand to stop me from walking straight down the stairs. 'Hey.'

'What?'

'D-do you really think y-you can do something about the b-bullying?'

He was keeping me talking, I was fairly sure of that. Didn't want to see me leave. 'Not all of it, but maybe some. I'll talk to the school.'

He walked in closer. 'Th-thank you,' he whispered, and that hurricane gained more storm force as he put fingers to the back of my neck and drew my mouth up to his, beginning a kiss that made my clothes feel too tight and massively too hot. When we finally stepped apart I felt like a ghost.

'Wow.'

Another wide smile, a wink, and he stepped back inside the flat, closing the door gently and slowly on that gigantic grin. I stood and fanned myself for a moment before I set foot on the stairs and caused a conflagration.

'Wow,' I said again, to myself. 'This just got *complicated*.'

Chapter Twelve

*'Gravestones can be heart-rending, funny, an attempt
on behalf of the stonemason to try out every type of
lettering he's learned; they can be decorative and inspiring.
But up here, on the North Yorkshire moors, in one of
the highest, most bleak parts of the country, there isn't
much time for fancy, either during life or after death.
The Osborne family, who lived, worked and died up
on the high moors, seem to have got this down to a fine
art. Witness one William Osborne, whose stone reads
simply: 'Wm Osborne. Died Jan 1815. Killed by bull.'*
—BOOK OF THE DEAD 2

'He *kissed* you?'

'Yes, Daisy, I just said that.' I leaned my back against the wall by the bed. It was dark, it was late, but I couldn't sleep until I'd updated my sister with this latest development.

'And how did it make you feel?'

I took a deep breath. 'Oh, he got it just right. None of that awful groin-thrust that some of them do, no trying to lick the face off me. It was sweet. It was *kind*.'

'Hmm.' Daisy sounded slightly annoyed. 'That's not what I asked, Win. I asked how it made you feel, not what his technique was like.'

I shuffled my feet under the duvet, but kept my back against the plaster of the wall for the cool reassurance of its solidity. 'I feel ... Seriously, Daze, I *like* Alex. He's calm and pretty stable, if you don't count all that guilt he's got going on, which, and I hate to admit it, makes him a little bit more human. Otherwise he's just this well-built bloke with the looks of an action hero, a gorgeous home and a future of financial stability.'

'And?'

'Does there have to be an "and"?'

Daisy sighed. 'Yes, Winter, I think there does.'

'Okay, okay. I think I fancy him, but I just don't know if I trust what I feel any more. But then again, I'm old enough to know what I think, so—'

'Two buts, Win. You know you're only allowed one, with a possibility of a half a one for "but he's too rich and successful and glamorous, and or famous". Two buts mean he isn't for you, you're just trying to talk yourself into it.'

'Look, I've only just met the bloke. He might even have something going on with Scarlet's teacher, I haven't really got to the bottom of that yet. We've had one dinner and one little kiss – I think I can give things a bit longer before I have to decide, don't you?'

'Okay.' She sounded as though she was smiling now, which was a relief. I'd hesitated about talking to her until I got to bed, slightly worried that she might have given me some kind of moralistic homily about how I was rebounding and it wasn't fair on Alex, etc etc. Instead she seemed to be taking it all quite seriously. 'Just be careful, Win.'

'It's all right, he's not going to throw a Dan on us. He's more laid-back than Dan anyway, a bit more … I can't explain it. Less …' I made a sort of 'clutching into my stomach' gesture which, of course, she couldn't see.

'A bit more and also less.' She was definitely smiling now. 'Sounds more like a French perfume ad to me. ''E is a leetle more … and yet 'e is also a leetle less.'

'Shut up or I shall never speak to you again.' I was laughing at her terrible French accent.

'Yeah, right. Laters, Win.' And she was gone, like the ethereal being she was.

I picked up the photo I had beside the bed and grinned at her in it. It was us on our twenty-first birthday, nine years younger, nine years slimmer, arms around one another. We were both bending with laughter, me wearing a classical green dress that swept the floor and left my shoulders and arms bare, Daisy in her trademark mini-dress, very retro, very 60s, all geometric circles that made us both feel sick to look at by the end of the evening, but beneath it her legs had gone on forever. 'Night, Daze,' I whispered to it. Then I curled up under the duvet. Well, I had to curl up, if I'd stretched out my feet would have been on the landing.

That was the thing about being a twin. One of the things that Dan hadn't understood. I was never alone. Oh, she wasn't here in the room with me, but I always knew that, wherever she was, wherever *I* might be, my sister was there for me. We were two different people, led two very different lives, and yet the inexplicable connection played between us. It lay, like a permanently open telephone line that ran heart-to-heart, as though within us we each carried a part of the other.

Besides, she knew all the bad stuff about me, and vice versa, we had a lot invested in keeping each other close.

f

Facebook

Winter Gregory Author Page

You know that feeling when something happens and you're not sure how you feel about it, or how you *should* feel about it? That.

134 people liked this.

Wednesday morning dawned through a drizzly grey mist. I sat in front of the laptop for a few hours, mostly spent on Facebook, ran a tiny iron over the dress I'd decided to wear to talk to the book group, and turned out half a dozen copies of *Book of the Dead* that had been sitting in the boot of my car. I washed my hair and tried to make myself look presentable, and was just making myself a quick cup of coffee when Margaret's head appeared beyond the glass panel.

'Oh, good, you're ready. You are ready, aren't you? I mean, is cleavage very "novelist"?'

I narrowed my eyes and considered saying that John Grisham wore a Zara maxi-dress to do all his talks that gave him a cleavage like the Grand Canyon, but decided against it. 'I haven't got a lot of suitable clothes with me,' I said, being very tactful in the circumstances. 'Besides, it shouldn't really matter, as long as I look professional.'

I put my two-buttoned London coat on over the dress and followed Margaret as she led the way across the High Street and down a narrow lane beside the river. 'We meet in the old hall, by the bridge,' she said over her shoulder. 'We've got some new additions this week. One is a gentleman who's just visiting Great Leys and is staying with me. On a B&B basis,' she added, as though I might assume she'd acquired herself what she would doubtlessly call "a fancy man". 'The other is a couple from up on the moors. I think she wants to get out more,' she added, although whether this was an opinion of Margaret's or whether the lady herself had said as much, I couldn't tell.

The hall was up a flight of stairs, and Margaret ushered me into a small cloakroom. 'I'll go and introduce you, then you can talk for a bit, show off your books and then we'll have tea and biscuits,' she said with relish, as though the tea and biscuits were the main reason for the gathering. 'We've got chocolate digestives tonight.'

I hefted my bag of books and checked my reflection in the mirror. In the hall I could hear Margaret, surrounded by a buzz of conversation and the clank of tea cups, starting to call the meeting to order, and, having reassured myself that my hair was tidy and my dress didn't show a ridiculous amount of cleavage, I stared out of the first floor window down into the darkening street while I waited for my intro.

The dismal weather was making dusk come early. Lights shone from the shops still open across the street, the road was highlighted with the shiny black of damp tarmac, and if I looked down I could see the cars parked along the river's edge, all neatly slotted and aligned as though marking the boundary between water and land in glossy metal. I let my eyes unfocus and run dreamily along as I ran through what I wanted to say about writing *Book of the Dead*. Easy stuff, stuff I'd done a hundred times before. As long as no one asked me about the sequel, about how work was going, I reckoned I could cruise through … and then my eyes got a horrible jolt of familiarity. A big, silver SUV, very much like the one I'd nearly run into yesterday up on the moor.

Hastily raked-over memory refused to reveal any telltale details. It had been a big silver four-wheel drive, that was all I could come up with. I had no real knowledge of cars and their makes and I'd been too dreamy to really take in much yesterday, all I knew was that it looked similar, and then I had to scold myself for being so paranoid. *This is*

*the countryside. Where people tow horseboxes and sheep
trailers as part of everyday life. There must be a million of
those things round here, and even if it were the one you
saw yesterday, what are you afraid of? That the driver is
going to come looking for you to give you a good talking
to about inattentive driving? He wouldn't recognise you
any more than you'd recognise him.*

'… so it's my pleasure to introduce, Winter Gregory!'
said Margaret in the other room. I took a deep breath,
shook my head and walked through into the meeting
room.

Where the only thing, the *only* thing I could take in was
the fact that Dan was sitting at the back.

People were clapping, a bit half-heartedly, over the
buzzing in my head. I felt my stomach clench and beads of
what felt like wax settled across my cheeks as I gripped the
edge of the table in front of me.

*He looks ill. Pale, anyway, and he hasn't shaved in days.
In fact, he looks as though he's slept in his clothes.*

'Winter?' Margaret stood next to me. 'Are you all right?'

I straightened my back. Pushed my chin up and took a
sip from the thoughtfully placed glass of water on the table.
*He's not going to stop you. Whatever he's come here for,
whatever he thinks he's playing at, you can top him, Winter.
You are stronger, you are certain, you are his equal.*

'Sorry.' I swallowed the water. 'Bit of stage fright, that's
all. Big crowd.'

She looked at me dubiously. Apart from Dan, who
was sitting right at the very back of the hall, half in the
shadows, with his crazy big coat pulled tightly around him
as though he was cold, the 'crowd' consisted of an elderly
couple, two men in their mid-fifties, a small collection of
late-teens/early twenties writer wannabes, judging from

their earnest expressions and notebooks, and Margaret. I must have given the impression that I usually only spoke to one man and a dog – and that the dog wandered off halfway through. So I cleared my throat, fixed my eyes on the people sitting at the front ... *I will not look at him. I will not* ... and began the talk I'd given so many times already since the book came out.

I ran through my own writing history, how I'd left university and gone into advertising, then research, how I'd come up with the idea for *Book of the Dead* and how I'd written it. I left out Dan's part, snipping mentally around the edges of the story until the part he'd played curled in on itself like old paper. Left out any hint that anyone else had had any input, apart from the publishing company who had taken the book on, all the while adamantly refusing to even acknowledge the corner of the room in which he sat. He made no move either, as far as I could tell with my careful avoidance of any eye contact; he seemed almost to be asleep on that chair, his legs stretched out and crossed at the ankles in a way that, if he wasn't careful, would link the buckles on his boots and cause much staggering when he tried to stand. His coat was almost doubled around his body and his hair was weirdly misshapen, up on one side and flat on the other, as though his left hand side had been frightened.

'Any questions?' I finished, brightly. Dan was not going to know how sick I felt at seeing him, how my hands were bunching into fists at the sight of his face. There were a couple of well-thought-out questions from the writing group at the front, a long, and rather unfocussed diatribe on breaking into publishing from one of the mid-fifties men, and then Margaret was motioning for someone to turn on the tea urn and rattling a biscuit tin like a call to arms.

What are you going to do? You could run, make your excuses. Hide. But then, if you have to face him, if he's come here to find you, wouldn't it be better to do it here, in front of all these people, where he won't be able to deal those vicious little hurts with such precision? Even Margaret might come to your defence if you start getting personally attacked in front of her book group, although, looking at them, they may just take it as affirmation of the bonkers nature of writers.

'Tea, Winter? I've saved you some digestives here. The group can be rather lively when there's chocolate involved, so I thought it would be a good idea to put some back.' Margaret waved a packet and a loaded teacup. I tried to immerse myself in the conversation starting between two members, something, anything to stop my eyes from wandering over to that back corner of the room, where he lurked like a *Scooby Doo* villain, still seated, arms folded. *Waiting. For me. Chuckle, chuckle, laugh, throw in some advice, pretend just as hard as you can, Winter, that the man you can sense moving across the room doesn't exist.*

'Miss Gregory?' A hand on my shoulder. A touch so light that it almost shouldn't have registered, but it did, like the weight of an entire life. 'I wonder, could I have a word?'

So. This was it. This was how it happened. I turned slowly to face him. Didn't smile. Met his dark stare with one of my own. 'Anything you want to say, Mr Bekener, you can say here.'

Nobody else seemed to notice. No one could feel that cooling of the air as though a savage and very local climate change was taking place, or smell that sulphurous burning that pricked my nostrils, which was probably just whatever fancy brand of cologne Dan had chosen to wear but smelled to me like something satanic. They all just kept chatting among themselves, for all the world as though I wasn't slowly being dragged to hell.

Dan nodded. There was a tautness to him; I wondered if it had always been there. A wary set to his muscles, even in his face. His eyes seemed larger, as though he was shocked by something, his narrow face tired under the stubble. 'I just wanted to ...' his voice lowered even further, syllables dropping under his mild Lincolnshire accent. He must have been suffering some kind of trauma because he usually covered those giveaway vowel sounds with an assumed London jauntiness, he hated people thinking he was from some rural backwater, even though he was. 'I needed to see that you were all right.'

'Why wouldn't I be?' I answered, equally quietly. There were several directions this conversation could have gone in, and I didn't want most of them to be overheard. My heart had steadied now that we were actually talking, although there was a stripe of sweat down my spine that told me I wasn't nearly as calm as my autonomic nervous system would have me believe.

'With what happened. The way we split, the way you were, I was worried. And you went off without telling anyone at Shy Owl where you were going.' He raised a hand as though in an awkwardly unilateral shrug. 'We've got money invested in you and the new book, so I needed to know that you were working.'

'You didn't have to come in person,' I said around a smile. At least, my mouth was giving smiling its best shot. I had the feeling that my eyes were sucking any trace of humour from my expression.

'You've changed your phone number. I tried emailing but you didn't answer. You weren't giving much away on

Twitter or Facebook, so I rang your mum. She said you'd left France and gone to Yorkshire, I thought that was a bit of a desperate move, so I decided I ought to come up and make sure you ...' he tailed off. Margaret was standing poised by the urn with a slightly suspicious look on her face, watching us talking. 'That's my landlady. Does she have some kind of allergy?'

'It's her dress.'

'Bizarre.' Dan looked down at his feet. His boots were scuffed and muddied around the soles. 'I couldn't sleep,' he said, randomly.

His eyes looked almost bruised, their normal darkness shaded with insomnia as though he was wearing make-up and when he looked down like that I could see how hollow his cheeks were. *I will not feel sorry for him. I know how he operates.*

'You look tired,' and I was surprised, no, appalled, to hear how gentle my voice sounded. His eyes flicked up as though I'd scared him.

'I should go.'

'Yes.'

We both stood and looked at one another. 'And the book is going well? I can tell them that much, that you're on for the deadline?'

I averted my eyes. 'It's okay.'

His personality seemed to slip, as though the Dan I'd known before was under tight restraint, but still in there. 'Come on, kiddo, it's doing your head in, isn't it?'

No! No, Winter, don't you dare, don't give him so much as a sniff of your insecurity. He'll take it and use it to jemmy your life wide open again. 'It's got a bit ... stuck.' *You idiot.*

He took a cup of tea from the table. There were new

rings on his fingers, a plain silver band replaced the celtic knot I'd bought him and the thought that his life had changed, that things had happened, he'd bought things, without me knowing, made an accordion of my lungs.

'We need that book, Winter,' he said, his voice sliding underneath the warm-air rise of the conversations around us. 'Yeah, you're okay living on the back of *Book of the Dead*, but we're not doing so well at the moment. And I need ...' another tiny shrug, 'I need the work.'

Not the money. It wasn't money that Dan prized, it was the feeling of being needed, of putting his head down and grafting to put a book together. 'You could go freelance?'

Now those eyes were on me. In contrast to Alex's calm grey eyes, Dan's looked like the eyes of a mischievous child. He'd always had eyes that seemed to contain a gateway to another, far more chaotic, universe, as though a wild magic was barely kept in check within his body. 'Yeah, well.' That half-shrug again and a tilt of the head. 'Maybe I'm losing the edge there.' He sipped at the tea, but half-heartedly, and then put the cup down. Came in so close that I could smell a kind of frost-chill on him. 'I want *this work*. This book.'

I shuffled a hurried step back. 'Like I said, things are fine. Go back to London, Dan.'

On the far side of the room, Margaret, deep in conversation with the elderly couple, glanced over and frowned. I fixed a smile on my face and tried to look as though I was having a fun chat with a fan. 'I just need to sort a few things out and it will all go smoothly from there.'

'Yeah, right.' To my surprise he took my cup and put it down next to his. 'Let me help you.'

My adrenal glands nearly burned their way through my dress. 'I don't need your help.'

'You said that before.'

'And I meant it then too.'

'But ...' Then he sighed and folded the coat around himself again. The stiff fabric made an aching sound. 'I'm not just going away, you know that, don't you? I can't come all this way and then turn round, head back to London and say "oh yeah, she's cool, not writing anything mind, but I'm sure it'll come good in the end". Not to a bunch of guys who are pretty much existing on the money from the last book and pennies they find in the street. They need assurances, we *all* need assurances, that you're coming in on time with this one and that it's going to be worth the time and effort, right?'

I bridled. 'I know what I'm doing!' It came out far louder than I'd intended, and there was a lull in the conversation as a roomful of faces turned our way and I had to do the 'fun smile' again for a few moments until they lost interest. 'I said, I don't need your help, Daniel.'

Spread hands, like surrender, but I knew him better than that. 'Can't stop me hanging around though, can you? Just keeping an eye, cracking the old whip.'

I pursed my lips at him and tried to think of something cutting to say. 'I don't know what I'm going to tell Daisy,' I finally said and watched him freeze up, pulling his collar to his ears.

'You and she ... you're still talking to Daisy? After everything I said?'

'She's my *sister*. And you, you're *nothing*.' And I spun around and marched over to Margaret, turning my back on Daniel Bekener and the expression I'd seen radiating from his eyes, a confused kind of sadness and what looked like an underlying horror.

Chapter Thirteen

Daniel Bekener @EditorDanB
Why do some people not admit they need help?

MichaelJJames @TwistyMikeJ
@EditorDanB Work that syntax!

Daniel Bekener @EditorDanB
@TwistyMikeJ Srsly, what is it? If you need help, why go all
Snow Queen about it?

MichaelJJames @TwistyMikeJ
@EditorDanB Not everyone who needs help deserves it, think of
that?

Daniel Bekener @EditorDanB
@TwistyMikeJ I can't think like that. There's different kinds of
help after all.

MichaelJJames @TwistyMikeJ
@EditorDanB If this is what I think it is, give it up. You had a
shot, it backfired, let it go.

Daniel Bekener @EditorDanB
@TwistyMikeJ It wasn't what it looked like. There were things
you didn't know.

I sat up in bed and coiled the duvet into a knot around
me. There was a cold sense of dread sitting over my head

like a bad hat but an odd and conflicting sort of prickle of anticipation dancing between my shoulder blades at knowing that Dan was in Great Leys. I pressed myself against the chilly bars of the metal bed in which I sat like a Victorian orphan, trying to use the sensation to stop my thought processes, to distract me with physical pain from the circular torments that my brain was subjecting me to.

Dan is here. He's going to keep following, watching, digging and poking away at you like a terrier down a rat hole, on and on until you break. I groaned and bunched the covers again. *But he was perfectly civil this evening. No accusations, no nastiness and, let's face it, he could have been very, very nasty, given the way it all went wrong. But he wasn't. He was sad and tired and looked as though he genuinely meant it about coming to check that the book was progressing, rather than to hunt you down and persecute you. Maybe, maybe, that really is all he wants?*

Oh, come on, Winter! He clearly doesn't want you, *does he? He made that very clear back in London and nothing has happened to change his mind. He knows that you and Daisy are still in touch, and that was his ultimatum wasn't it – her or him? So, okay, he doesn't want to be back where you both were before, so it must be the book.*

I found that I was rocking slightly and forced myself to stop. To sit quietly and just breathe, feeling the cold night air singing in and out of my lungs, the soft, electric hum of my laptop and the ratchet-tick of the clock on the landing. Life. I have a life. Without Dan. I thought I would die of the pain and the horror and the loss when we split up, and the knife-edge terror of having to choose between my lover and my sister. I didn't dare admit to myself how close I'd come, how *close*, to choosing Daniel, to relegating

Daisy to my background life. I could hardly even get my head around the thought that I'd even considered it. But I got over losing Dan, I still have my sister and I'm still here, in my *The Wolves of Willoughby Chase* bed, with a half-written book on my computer. I can get through this.

I thought about speaking to Daisy, but didn't know what to say to her. Would she take my talking to Dan again as a kind of betrayal, or would she understand? She'd never really understood my relationship with him, she'd thought of him as some kind of rival. And, despite all my reassurances that I could have them both, that he was no threat to her and me – how could he be, she was my twin, my other half – she'd been right all along. So any conversation we had tonight would either be accusations or justifications, and I didn't think I could deal with any of that, not with the shock of him appearing out of the blue in the hall tonight.

I set the laptop to play some music, something suitably orchestral, while I lay down, trying to form the covers into something that didn't resemble a beached whale. I closed my eyes and tried to force my mind to worry about the far more pressing and down-to-earth problem of how to deal with Scarlet and the school bullies.

✉

From: DanBekener@ShyOwlPublishing.co.uk
To: GregTurner@ShyOwlPublishing.co.uk
Subject: Winter's second book

Greg, I've found Winter. And, you were right. I've seen for myself that she's still walking and talking and seeming to live a life; working, or at least saying that she's working for all her eyes tell a different story. She looks … I dunno, sounds stupid, but she looks somehow as if she's *tight*, strung out on late nights and bad dreams, like she lost a lot of weight very suddenly, not that she needed to but there's that kind of hollowness about her. Eaten out from the inside. And I don't know what's done it, if it's the writing, or even *me*, mate, yeah, not absolving myself from my part in the fiasco. So I laid it on a bit thick that I needed to work, that we need the book – okay, I know we do, but the way I told it you'd think we'd started taking out payday loans or something; Christ, sorry man, but I made us sound desperate just so I'd got an excuse to stick around and drag that book out of her.

So I'm here if you need me, playing a long game. Trying to respect the image she's putting across, hoping that she'll give me a free pass on what I said back in London, but I know she won't. She can't forget, our Winter, that's her problem. Can't forget, can't let go.

Anyhoo. Drop me a line if you need me, otherwise I'll be in touch.

Dan

✉

From: DanBekener@ShyOwlPublishing.co.uk
To: BethanyAnnBekener@wolmail.com
Subject: Life Up North

Hey, kiddo. How are you doing? Mum says you've made progress with the new chair and it's not trying to kill you any more – can't wait to see you whizzing around in it. Bet the dog is terrified! You're like a high-tech version of that remote control car we used to chase Django round with, remember? No wonder he finally chewed it to bits …

I've seen Winter. And now I think … I think I can do this. I can just be her editor – it's what she wants. The feelings aren't dead, they haven't gone away, but I can keep them down there. It hurts, but it doesn't rip me up like it did do. She looks rough, looks like she's come to a standstill with the book, so I'm going to stick around, make sure we get this thing done to deadline and then? I'm gone. I'm no kind of martyr, me …

Love ya

Danny Boy

Chapter Fourteen

'Sometimes it's not what's written on the stone that's interesting, sometimes the spaces that are left can tell us more about the person lying beneath, or, at least, they can hint heavily ... One Alexander Wright (1748–1813) had his stone erected 'by his loving and grieving wife, Mary', who clearly expected to be buried with her husband, judging by the space left beneath his epitaph for her own. However, the space is still there and Mary lies elsewhere in the churchyard, having overcome her grief to the extent of marrying a Thomas Fenwick six months after the death of her previous husband. Thomas must have swept her off her feet in a significant fashion – there are local reports of his having hired a coach and four to drive them to their wedding. They lie together beneath a stone much more ornate than that of the briefly-lamented Alexander ...'

—BOOK OF THE DEAD 2

It was a warm morning that smelled of the plums which seemed to hang on almost every tree in Great Leys, the air buzzed with wasps and a wind jangled the yellowing leaves. I squared my shoulders on the doorstep and went out, my notebook clutched to my chest and my pen rigid between my fingers as though I was off to attend some kind of inter-author jousting event. The road was busy, the pavements teemed with Stepford WAGS and children off to the school bus and there was no sign of Dan; my fingers loosed their grip on the biro a little and my shoulders relaxed a fraction. Of course there wasn't. He hadn't meant any of it – all that stuff about hanging around to get the book finished, he was just trying to freak me out, to rock the equilibrium of this little world I'd started to accrete around myself as though I was one of those naked creatures at the bottom of a pond, searching for things to barricade round me to keep me from harm.

In fact, knowing Dan and his dislike of wide-open spaces that didn't have a DJ in front of them, he'd probably headed straight back to London. *He looked tired. Stressed. Maybe he really was telling the truth about needing this book?* I shook my head against the little voice in my head, aware that people were starting to look at me strangely, poised here on my doorstep staring out into the morning busyness with my writing gear held in front of me like a shield, and I slammed the door behind me in a meaningful way and stalked out across the pavement.

The churchyard was a little heap of quiet, like an island in a sea of noise. The sun slanted down through the shading trees, making little patches of light and shade on the grass through which the headstones reared up to point long fingers of shadow towards the town like worn auspices of mortality. Not quite sure what to do with myself, other than try to occupy my mind, I leaned against the familiarity of Beatrice, letting the warmth of her sun-heated limestone seep into my jangling nerves.

'Hey.' The voice came from a dark bulk under the branches of overhanging cedar and made me drop my notebook into the long grass.

'Dan?' I put the mass of Beatrice between me and the shape, uncurling itself from where it had, apparently, been sitting cross-legged on top of a tabular monument to the father of a large local family whose high point had been opening a bakery.

'It's a graveyard. Who're you expecting?' There was a soft sweeping sound as his coat flicked loose of the memorial and he stepped forward into the sunlight, boots jingling. 'Mr "Massively Over-Compensating for Something"?' He slapped at the stone as he moved past it. 'Seriously, mate, that amount of curly writing? Never in a million years ... Might just as well have had "I made a fortune but had a tiny knob" carved on your stone.'

I was aware that my fingers hurt as they tried to dig into the solid stone under my hands. The stone felt a little like my heart at the moment, harsh and rough with scuffed edges. 'What are you doing here?'

'Oh, you know.' Dan's coat swung and coiled around his body like a solid mist, the buckled fastenings giving it weight and the light sparking off the silver catches. He flipped the collar up and hunched his shoulders, standing in the patch of sunlight that lay between us as though he knew the impact his slender dark outline would make. 'Like I said, just protecting my investment.'

Yeah, like I'm a 'thing'. Something to be watched, not a person. Thing. Anger tried to swell my throat. 'Everything is under control.' I bent to pick up my notepad without taking my eyes off him which meant contorting my body, and I saw the way his eyes hovered along the lines of my buttocks and his lips formed a growl shape. 'And anyway, I meant, *here*. How did ...' I stopped. I would not let him know how much his physical presence affected me. 'What made you think I'd be here?'

'Bloody hell, there are *other places* you could be?'

I felt my mouth betray me by trying to twitch into a smile and firmly stopped it. 'I could have been in the coffee shop. Or the library. Or bed.' The more I looked at him the easier it got, he wasn't the bogeyman my mind had built him into – cruel and warped and evil. He was just Dan, just the guy I'd just … Dan. My editor, the man who wanted this book written almost more than I did, the person most likely to understand the problems I was having with it. Whatever else he was, underneath, I didn't have to deal with right now. 'Or halfway to the nearest place round here that sells actual things instead of scented candles and pumpkins, which, I have to tell you, is probably York and that's a really long way away.'

A little of the darkness left his face, as though the mischief in his eyes had become the normal, 'knock on doors and run' kind rather than the 'knife them in the dark singing nursery rhymes' sort. 'What can I say? Intuition.' He gathered the coat around him, then hopped up to sit on another flat-topped tomb, biker boots up so that his knees were under his chin. He'd shaved since last night, I noticed, or at least hacked the stubble into reasonable order. 'Besides, the local coffee shop is still shut, I checked the library, and I knew you weren't in bed because I saw you.' He coughed and looked down at his knees, pretending shame. 'I'm staying with Mrs Hill up the street from you and from her guest bedroom you can see the curtains on your upstairs windows, so I knew you were up. Who's Alex?'

I dropped my pen now. 'Alex?' *Wow. He is quick. I'd forgotten that about Dan, that he could get squirrels to tell him where they'd buried their nuts, using only the power of his charisma and those wicked eyes.*

'Yeah. Mrs Hill mentioned that she thought you might be off to see Alex. I didn't like to say "who" because, well, you know me, never admit to not knowing something when you can always pretend and find out later, so who is he? She? Anything to do with the book or …?' he tailed off and tilted his head to regard me at an angle that made him look like a curious funerary statue.

'He's Mrs Hill's son. He and I ...' The memory of Alex's warm kiss and hot body must have heated my eyes because Dan twisted his mouth and stood suddenly on top of the grave.

'Okay. So. What's the plan for today?' He spread his arms wide and his coat flapped, he looked like a raven preparing for flight. 'Research, writing, what?'

'I don't know.' Something about the sheer energy of him made me feel as though he could somehow anchor me. 'But it's okay, I'll think of something. I just need ...' I made a sort of shrugging motion with the notebook still clutched to me. 'It's fine.'

Dan stepped a slow ring, arms still held out. His sleeves fell back and the tattoo of a circle and eight points gleamed for a second in a stray beam of sunlight on his wrist. Chaos. What Dan was really all about, and what he brought to everything. 'We can do this, kiddo. We can.' He turned his face to the sun. 'Yeah?'

'Don't, Dan.'

He finished his rotation and looked down. 'Don't?'

'Try to jolly me along. Not now. Not any more.' I tore my eyes away from his wildness, from that careful illusion of anarchy and pandemonium that he promulgated. 'I don't need your help and I don't need *you*.'

'Sure about that, are you?' And now he was so still, so dark, it almost felt as though the sunlight bounced off him. A black hole. 'Because I've tracked all your messages back to the mothership and it doesn't look as though there's a whole lot of work getting done right now. Last word we got, you were about halfway through and since then ...' Dan spun once more then jumped easily down, landing with a chink of metal and the sound of hollow earth. '... nada. Now I hate to get all "editor" on your ass but, hey, we have a deadline here, and it's beginning to make a ticking noise.' He made 'metronomes' of his two index fingers, wiggling them to and fro. 'You sure you don't want a little bit of input from One Who Knows, that might just get this book brought in, on time, and earning its keep?'

A deep breath. As though that would save me. 'I'd rather you were on the other side of the planet, actually, Dan. But yes, you're right, things haven't been going quite like I'd hoped.' I saw him give a slow smile and hurried to smack it down. 'Oh, it's nothing to do with us, with what happened, it's just that there's so much material here, so much more than I thought, it's like I can't pick out which people to write about.'

His hands went into his pockets and an expression came over his face that I might have expected to see on Scarlet's, a sort of 'deep thinking sulk', as though he was mentally weighing up options to see which was the most likely to get a positive reaction. 'Right,' he said, slowly. 'Right, yeah, okay. I see.'

He half-turned and swept the coat close around his body and there was a finality about the gesture that made something deep inside me ache like an old bruise. *Go away, Dan*, I thought, but somehow seeing him here, everything was different. 'Look. You can help me, if you must, but only if we can be professional about it. No being unnaturally "upbeat" about the book, no cosy little meetings like this or talking about ...' My voice fell into the unsayable.

'Daisy. Right?'

All I could do was nod and scrunch the paper under the tips of my fingers.

'I get that.' Dan closed the gap of grass that had stood between us, stitching its sunlight space with his darkness. 'And that's what's behind this?'

You can do this, Winter. This is the conversation you've rehearsed in your head over all those sleepless midnights. My palms tingled and dampened and my heart performed a nauseating double beat, but I held steady. *I can do this.* 'I hated you, Daniel.' My voice came out only slightly shaky. 'I mean, before, I … well, it was good, *we* were good. And then, the stuff you said' – and now the tremor was more of a catch – 'about Daisy, it made me hate you so much.'

He stopped moving. Just stood as though the words had frozen him. 'I never meant that to happen.' But his hands had come up in front of him now, that giveaway gesture he could never manage to control, pushing his cuffs back as though revealing that chaos symbol on his skin could somehow keep order.

'But it did. You became something in my head, some huge monster, but now I've seen you, now you're here, and now I've got, well, other things to think about besides the vile things you said about my sister, I've started to realise. You're just this bloke, Daniel. Not evil, not something to fear, just a really stupid bloke who doesn't know when to keep his nose out of someone's business, and who thought that isolating me from my sister would, what? Get you centre-stage? So, yes, for the duration of this book I can work with you, but on a professional basis only. Understood?'

'Whew.' Another step, and now I could smell the vanilla from his skin. 'Some nasty stuff coming out here, Win.' His voice was soft. 'For the record, I've only ever tried to help you. Nothing else, no agenda.'

'Right, so sleeping with me wasn't "having an agenda" then?' I dropped my voice to match his.

He looked down at the toes of his boots, collecting little beads of damp from the grass. His hair flopped towards his forehead, unspiked today and allowed to fall naturally; it gave him the look of an off-duty punk. 'No,' and his voice was soft. 'That wasn't agenda. That was something else.' A sideways look up out from under the hair, his eyes had an almost 'walled-in' expression. 'Never mind. Doesn't matter.' Another shove at his cuffs until his palm cupped the chaos symbol.

'It does to me,' I said, softly.

He lifted his head. The sun caught the edge of his hair and highlighted the side of his face, so he looked split, half in shadow, half in light. *Very Daniel. Never quite sure which side he comes down on.* 'Okay.' A slow nod. 'We'll be professional, get this thing done and then I'll let you get back to toying with the affections of Mrs Hill's lovely son, deal?'

'I am not toying with his affections!' But he'd done it, done the thing that Dan was best at – twisted the conversation away from the dark, away from pain and panic and into me being infuriated with him. To know Dan was to cultivate a really firm jaw from all the teeth gritting you had to do.

'If you say so.' Dark eyebrows lifted. 'Right, we're kicking this book into shape, yes? What's first on the list?'

'I've sort of promised to go down to the local primary school.'

'Seriously? Primary school? Wow. And there was you never so much as looking in prams when I knew you.' He kicked his toes against a tussock of grass and gave me 'wicked eyes', slightly hooded as though he wasn't quite sure how I'd take the lightness of his tone.

'It's a bit of a long story, but I think I can get a little girl some kudos if I go in and give a talk. Maybe stop some rather nasty kids from picking on her.'

Dan gave his head a quick shake as though flipping away a thought. 'Okay. Probably not such a bad idea, get yourself a bit of a rep around here, bit of a local base for when the book comes out. You won't need me to come with you – small children and I don't really mix well, unless it's nieces' and nephews' parties with cake and some suspicious old bloke dressed as a clown making things out of balloons.'

'Nieces and nephews?'

'Four.'

Why hadn't I known that? 'You never mentioned them before.'

He shrugged. 'No. Well. Maybe we kind of screwed up that stage, didn't we? The whole "taking home to meet the family" thing, what with your family being all spread out around the world, and my lot professional workaholics that think a day off is like admitting failure, well ...' He stopped staring down at his feet and gave me a sudden, and very steady, look from tawny eyes that held a hint of a challenge. 'Not taking any of it back, before you start to wonder,' he said, his voice very quiet. 'You and ... her. I stand by what I said then, Win, what you and Daisy have, it's not healthy, and that, I promise, is absolutely the last time I shall refer to your sister, okay?' With a squaring of his shoulders that told me he expected me to retaliate, he took a step back.

'Fine.'

His surprise manifested in a billowing of coat as his body moved inside it, and he looked as though he was about to say something; a frown flashed across his forehead and vanished behind his eyes.

'What you think of Daisy, or of me, or the relationship we have doesn't matter any more, does it?' I went on. 'As my editor you said you can work with me, anything else is just …' I threw my hands wide, the pages of my notebook scuttling and riffling like a nest of caffeine-addicted ants. 'As I said, just strictly professional.'

Another shot of the cuff, another rub of the tattoo. 'That's what I'm here for,' he said, then turned and was gone in a swirl of coat, like a traditional villain making good his escape, walking through the dew-laden grass without looking back. The cool air closed around him as though reclaiming its own and he was lost to sight before he even rounded the church building.

My shoulders slumped and I realised how tense I'd been all the time we'd talked. The sheer familiarity of him and the way he was had somehow fooled me into forgetting so much that I'd managed to function almost normally while he'd been in front of me, but now I could feel the low, hot burn of the anger and pain deep in my stomach again. An emotion that had been put on hold while Dan was actually there, as though his presence had functioned as a kind of damper, but now my mind was free to fan those flames into life again.

'Bastard.' My hands scrabbled a sheet of paper from the pad, nails raking it to strips, then my fingers curled it into a ball so tight that the molecules squeaked. 'Completely bloody *stupid* …' And whether I spoke about him or me, I couldn't have said.

Chapter Fifteen

From: AlexHillStone@wolmail.com
To: WinterGregoryAuthor@teddymail.com
<u>Subject: How are you?</u>

Hey, a first – I'm not going to apologise! Unless you feel that
I took advantage somehow but … no, it felt as though you
wanted me to kiss you as much as I did. Well, you didn't slap
me sideways, so I'm taking that as a positive thing, okay? But
it's all right, it was just a kiss, there's no implicit commitment
there, I'm not going to be making moves on you every time you
step outside your door – suppose you'd figured that out, what
with it being a couple of days since I've seen you. Anyway. No
stalker behaviour, no throwing myself on your mercy, just saying
that now I feel we've moved a step further on. And I wish, oh,
how I *wish* this could be a conventional thing, that I could take
you to the pictures, for a meal, we could walk in the countryside
together, have a lovely, leisurely time of getting to know one
another properly, but, you know, there's Scarlet. And my life
revolves, *has* to revolve around her, which means I'm pretty
much only free during the day, and not even much then, what
with having to get this building work finished before the bank
makes that kind of 'Ur-*ur*' noise on my business loan.

So, what I'm trying to say is, let's just see what happens, shall we?
Alex

I flipped the laptop shut and tried to ignore the chewing
sensation in my abdomen, as though my stomach was
working on a tricky toffee. *Alex. Yes. Let's see what
happens, take it slowly, be friends.* I could think the

words, even try to believe them, but they felt hollow and plastic. The last person I'd dated had been Dan, and that had been completely traditional. Well, no, not completely, he'd been my editor after all, given to throwing sudden ideas in the air to see if I'd catch them, but walks in the sunshine, holding hands, films and meals and ...

Stop it. I shook my head hard, trying to dislodge the image of Dan as my 'lost love'. He wasn't. Wasn't my anything, just an opportunist and then a betrayer, that was all. *So why do you keep thinking of him? You know now what he's capable of, why do you keep coming back to thoughts of him ripping around London, nipping down side alleys like a grown-up Artful Dodger, all in black and as wild as the wind? You see? You even keep thinking of him in romantic terms – what the hell is this all about?*

Schools nowadays weren't like they had been when Daisy and I had been children. There were intercoms and secretaries to get past, and appointment books, and a Head who couldn't see me because he was in a meeting but would bear my request in mind and I could telephone tomorrow to see what he said. It wasn't a big, brick building either, like our school had been, this one was built of pale sandstone, a single-floored square surrounded by playground where there was space for benches and little raised vegetable beds, and beyond were fields of cows and horses. When we'd been young it had been tarmac and car parks and huge high gates of wire, full of people coming and going, parents in classrooms listening to readers and drinking coffee, hadn't it? I was ushered from the building by a lady on her way to the photocopier (another thing I never thought of existing in schools), and we passed a classroom where I saw Scarlet sitting alone at a table, colouring as though her life depended on it, while everyone else clustered around the teacher, engaged in some energetic hands-up session.

My heart did that squeezing thing again and I must have hesitated because the lady showing me out gave me a stern look. 'If you don't have a CRB then we have to be careful about allowing you into school,' she said. 'The safety of the children must be paramount, of course.'

'Well, of course,' I muttered, wondering how deranged I looked that she'd seen fit to mention the Criminal Records Bureau check. I'd put my clean jeans on and tied my hair up and my sweatshirt, although a bit baggy, wasn't really serial-killer special issue, was it? But, as I was hustled over the threshold, my mind held on to that image of the little girl alone while everyone else was busy as a group, and I wasn't quite sure why.

'Maybe she reminds you of you.' Daisy gave her matter-of-fact opinion as soon as I told her about my feelings. 'Don't you always feel a bit like the odd one out?'

'Maybe.' I stirred soup while I was talking to her, to keep me busy, stop me from mentioning that Daniel had turned up. This conversation was about Scarlet, there was no need to upset my sister by mentioning his name. 'She looked so sort of lonely, as though she was concentrating on her crayons to keep from crying.'

'Hmmm.' A pointed kind of noise, as though something should be self-evident. It wasn't, but I decided to ignore that. 'So you suggested that you go in and talk to the class about writing? Must be nice to have a transferrable skill, I could never go in and talk about fashion to anyone at primary level. It would just have been a discussion about shoes or something, and don't all children wear trainers? Godawful things.'

'I don't think Louboutin make children's shoes, Daze. And yes, that's what I'm suggesting; it might give Scarlet a bit of clout around the place if they know that she really does know a real-life author. And …' I stopped. Stirred carefully, making sure with the tip of the wooden spoon that nothing was catching on the bottom of the pan. *I will not mention Dan.*

'You've seen Dan.'

'Yes.' *No point dissembling. No point saying 'how do you know?'. Identical twins, identical minds …* 'But I think it's okay. I really think I can work with him, just to get this book finished. It's giving me hell, Daze, I'm stuck and I just can't work out how to go forward with it and he …' Stopped again.

'Winter,' and she sounded sad. Not, as I would have expected her to, deceived or upset, just gave my name a weight as though it carried unshed tears. 'Remember. Just that. Remember what he did, how he was.'

The surface of the soup became agitated as the spoon swung back and forth in my eagerness to make her understand. 'But that's the point, Daze, I *do* remember! It's fine, now I know what he's like, underneath. I know he's a bastard, that he wants to keep us apart, so he can never pull that stunt on me again. We can work together and get this book done and he won't be able to draw me in like he did last time.'

'Hmmm.' And if the last 'hmmm' had been pointed, this one was positively serrated. Barbed, almost.

'Please try to understand. He's the one who knows what it's going to take to get the book done to deadline, he's got an interest in getting it finished – if I don't hit deadline then he looks as stupid as I do. He's the one who got the publishers to take me on even when they all thought *Book of the Dead* was a stupid idea. So he'll be professional, he won't want to risk me throwing it all away.'

'Would you? Seriously, Win, would you give the book up if Dan made a pass at you again? Chuck it all in and go back to writing advertising copy rather than go to bed with him?'

Soup slopped and my teeth gritted. It sounded as though my answer mattered more than it should have done. 'I don't need this book. I'll always have *Book of the Dead* to show I could do it, now I ... Yes. Yes, I'd give this up rather than get back with Daniel Bekener again.'

There was a silence at the other end, as though my sister was processing this. Then, 'I don't know. I don't think it's a good idea. He's ... he's a sexy piece, Win, you know that. All that wild charm he throws around, all that "look how I manage chaos" thing, as though he's got the secrets of the universe just revolving somewhere in his head. And the way he is, the way he can be so caring and gentle and then all hard like a great granite block ...'

'You remember, then.' My voice sounded rough, as though the memories cut away at the edges of the words, chopping into the meaning. 'Everything he did, and you still remember that about him.'

'Hard to forget, you have to admit. And that body ... well, he's got it going on, our Daniel, hasn't he, Winter? *Hasn't he?*'

'I don't want to hear this.' I broke the connection and ran up the stairs, leaving the soup still bubbling and the spoon slurred onto the work surface in a trail of monosodium glutamate.

Chapter Sixteen

From: AlexHillStone@wolmail.com
To: WinterGregoryAuthor@teddymail.com

<u>Subject: Not seen you in a bit.</u>

Hi, long time no see!

I hope our little moment hasn't put you off? I haven't seen you around lately. But then, I've been pretty much 'confined to barracks' myself; we're trying to get the final bit of the roof on before the weather turns (and the forecast is horrible, hope that doesn't put a crimp in your weekend or anything). Mr Moore told me about your suggestion that you go into school to talk to the kids about writing – he seemed a bit half-hearted about it, which I really don't understand, it's not as if we've got people queuing up to visit. And Scarl is missing you a bit. She asked if she could come by tomorrow, just to say hello, if that's okay with you? She knows you're busy … All right, I'll admit it, *I* sort of suggested that we pop in. I'm a bit worried about you. Mum told me that your 'editor' is B&Bing with her and, with what you told me about him, I just thought you might be hiding so you didn't have to see him. Which, yes, I totally understand, I sometimes wonder if I don't spend so much time working here just so that I don't have to circulate in society, you know. Like I said before, it's tough when everyone knows your business, and your family history, and having a stammer hasn't rendered me deaf, I can hear them all whispering behind my back about my sister being a bit 'warm under the pinny' as they say around here. They mean she was a slapper. Free with her affections. Which is pure cobblers, of course. Ellen was just young and she got away from Great Leys, something most of them have never done. Round here, everyone is married to someone they were at school with, and El having got pregnant by a guy from somewhere further than fifty miles away – it's as though she'd been sleeping with little green men from Alpha Centauri or something.

Sorry, sorry. And sorry that I'm sorry. I have no idea why I keep doing this, I start off writing an email just to check that you're all right and I end up carrying on about my family and my problems, as if you don't have your own with this 'Dan' bloke turning up. Anyway. Really meant to say, if it's all right with you Scarlet and I will call in tomorrow, to say hello. I might bring buns.
Alex

✉

From AlexHillStone@wolmail.com
To: LucyLoo@wolmail.com
Subject: Thanks
… for talking sense into me. I should go for it, of course I should. What's stopping me?
Al x

I tidied up before they arrived. While I didn't *think* Alex would report back to his mother if he found me living in paper-strewn squalor, with half-empty soup mugs and cups of coffee marking the path I'd been stalking around the little house like dots on a map, I didn't want him to find me doing a Howard Hughes behind drawn curtains.

I was working. I *was*. I'd uploaded most of the photographs of the churchyards onto my laptop and labelled them. I'd gone through the local history books that I'd got from the library and I'd made notes. Some notes, anyway. Proof was scattered around me, single pages torn from lined pads lay two or three deep like confetti from a giant's wedding, biros with the ends chewed to stubs had rolled under most of the furniture and books with Post-it notes protruding from marked pages stood in a tottering pile on the table. I left those, they at least made it look as though something proactive was going on, but I stacked the sheets of paper into a file and washed up the collection of mugs and cups. Then I pulled up the most recently worked on page onto my laptop, shocked to see that I had to bring it down from a folder that hadn't been opened for ten days. *Really? That long? But then, I've been doing research, I'll be writing it all up any day now. Ten days without looking at the book isn't so bad, it means I'll have perspective when I go back and re-read what I've done. Wouldn't do to get over-familiar with the material.*

There was a sharp tap on the front door and I had a quick glance around to make sure I hadn't left any half-eaten biscuits on any surfaces, and went to open it. As soon as I saw the dark head on the other side of the glass panel my hand fell away from the lock. *Dan. What's he doing here?*

'I can see you there, Winter, so don't try pretending that you've run away to join the circus,' he said, and I could see his outline hunch, hands going into pockets. The wavy glass that kept my privacy from people wanting to peer in as they passed made all the solid lines of his body look broken and abstract, as though there was a Picasso painting standing on my doorstep. 'Come on, kiddo, just wanting an update here, plus it's bloody freezing. There's a wind out here that's already given me a shave and a haircut and I swear that it's trying to file my nails as well.'

The wavering outline ghosted into a pose of huddling down into his coat and a pale blob of hand extended for another knock, so I opened the door with a sigh. 'What is it?'

'What it is, is about minus twenty.' Dan didn't exactly push past me, but he didn't wait to be invited in either; he did a kind of polite charge that made me step back inside the living room, and kept on coming. 'It's like the Arctic with better retail.'

I slid myself round the tiny table. 'I mean, what do you want?' I took it as a good sign that my hands weren't inadvertently trying to punch him, and that I wasn't sweating, although my heart was causing a tidal surge of blood to my cheeks.

'Thought I'd given you enough time to think about things.' He swept further into the room and tried to throw himself nonchalantly onto one of the chairs. 'Bloody hellfire, what's *this* made out of? Hacksaw blades and teeth?' Nonchalance reverted to a straight-backed wariness. 'Maybe I could be the first bloke to bring cushions to Yorkshire. I can see the headlines now: "Southerner brings soft-furnishing relief to a million Northern backsides." What?'

'Nothing.' I'd been staring at him, I knew it. Watching, because I couldn't help it. There was something about Dan's long body, the way his shoulders, broad in the embellished black of his coat, drew the eye. Something magnetic in his movements and the way his cheekbones broke dark stubble like plough blades in a night field.

'Well, come on then. Spill. What's been happening on the scribbling front? How are we looking on word count? And how the effing chuff do you manage to write anything sitting on these things?' He tried to hook a leg up over the chair arm but the over-polished wood and lack of any protective padding sent him spiralling around until he only just prevented himself from crashing onto the floor by grabbing hold of the table. 'This is *not* furniture, is it?'

'Everything is okay.' I flipped the laptop's lid down. Although he wouldn't have been able to tell how long it had been since I'd looked at the book, I didn't want him to have any ammunition to fire at me. 'Go away.'

To my surprise, Dan stood up. I thought, for one glorious moment, that he was going to do as I'd suggested, that he actually believed me when I said things were okay. But this was Daniel and I should have known better. He shucked off the big coat and folded it into a wedge, placed it back on the chair, then sat on it. 'That's better.' And then, '*Now* what?'

'It's just you without your coat on. You've *always* got that coat on.' Underneath, Dan was wearing a tight, black T-shirt, which made him look remarkably buff, and a pair of what looked like designer suit trousers. 'And no wonder you're cold. You should put a jumper on.'

'You've seen me without the coat loads of times, Win.' Almost as though he were pleased, he leaned back and raised his eyebrows at me. 'Hell, you've seen me in nothing but a Durex, why so surprised suddenly?'

I shook my head and forced my eyes to look somewhere else. 'Whenever I think of you, it's always the whole' – I waved my arms alongside my body to indicate a flowing garment –'thing.'

'So you do think of me?' His voice was very low and I was glad I was staring at the mantelpiece at that moment, not at his face. 'It's the image, Win. You know that. You, of all people, know you keep the image going because most people don't look any further than that. I'm the bloke in the coat and the boots, and that's all they need to see.'

'I didn't mean …'

'People only see what you show them. Basic psychology. No one wants to look any deeper just in case they see a reflection of themselves.' And then a sudden shifting noise as though he was moving us both away from a conversation that might hurt. 'So ... word count. Hit on any new material?'

I pointed at the books on the table, splayed out like a half-shuffled deck of cards. 'I've done some reading, made notes.'

'Aha. So no actual *work* eh?' He sounded amused and I had to look at him now. He'd got a hand raised, shoved into his hair as though supporting the weight of his head. 'Still got a deadline, girl, still need to hit it.' And then he was up, out of the chair and stalking around the room, that excess of energy that he always carried making the air crackle with his passing. 'This place. Dark. You need some light, some air, although probably not the stuff they've got going on out there, which is not breathable unless you're a penguin. You need space to get the ideas ...'

There was a slow, tentative tap on the front door, and he whipped around. 'Ah. A "visitor from Porlock". Hold the thoughts ...' and before I could stop him he'd opened the door to reveal Alex and Scarlet, hand in hand, on the step.

'I b-brought b-b-buns.' Alex held up a bag and then, realising it wasn't me standing in front of him, lowered it. 'Oh. H-hello.'

'Hey. Daniel Bekener.' Dan held out a hand, which meant Alex had to juggle the bun bag in order to shake. His gaze travelled over Dan's shoulder and into the room, where it settled on me in a kind of embarrassed wariness and his eyebrows lifted.

'Dan, this is Alex Hill,' I said. 'And Scarlet. And Light Bulb.'

Dan bent down. 'Hello, Scarlet,' he said to the hobby

horse. 'And hello, Light Bulb. I can tell that you must be a very bright young lady.'

Scarlet laughed. '*I'm* Scarlet,' she said and then flung herself past the men to arrive somewhere around my knees. 'Hello, Winter!'

'Daniel is my editor.' I made a face at Alex, who relaxed a little. 'He was just … actually, I'm not sure what he was just doing, but he was complaining a lot while he was doing it.'

Alex's presence had given me my confidence back. Dan wouldn't dare say anything personal in company, would he? *No. He's more of a knife-in-the-back man, not someone to drag stuff up when there's an audience.*

'H-have the b-buns,' Alex said. 'And w-we'll b-be going.'

'Oh, Alex, you promised, you *promised* if I was good we'd ask Winter to come to the RSPCA with us, you *promised*!' Scarlet was almost beside herself, jumping up and down in front of me and landing on my toes more often than not. 'And I was really good, Winter, honestly …' Even Light Bulb looked downcast, his ears seemed floppier than usual and it looked as though someone who'd watched more Kirstie Allsopp than was good for a person had attempted a repair job to some loose stitching round his mouth. He now had a ziggy-zaggy kind of smile that made him look a bit psychotic.

'I d-decided you w-were r-right about a p-pet,' Alex said. 'W-we thought maybe a g-g—'

'We're going to get a guinea pig!' Scarlet carried on bouncing. 'Tomorrow. Did you have a guinea pig when you were little, Winter?' And then, surprisingly she jumped a circle, 'Did you, Daniel?'

'I did,' Dan, equally surprisingly, answered. 'Two. And

then seven. And then, because my parents weren't up to playing "Guess how many in the hutch today", one.'

'Then you should come too, to help us choose.' Scarlet stopped bouncing, for which my shoes were glad. 'Because you know about guinea pigs.'

Alex and I exchanged a look of complicated horror. 'Scarlet, Dan is busy,' I said. 'Aren't you?'

Dan wiggled his eyebrows. 'Never too busy to help those in need choose a squeaky pet,' he said, and, to Scarlet's obvious delight, he jumped up onto one of the chairs and began to declaim in a hushed voice, 'This guinea piggy went to market, this guinea piggy stayed at home, this guinea piggy became Scarlet's ...'

'H-he's mad,' Alex whispered into my ear as we watched the performance.

'He's something,' I whispered back. 'I'm not sure what. Possibly unexploded.'

Scarlet laughed and clapped as Dan took a flying leap from the chair which sent him almost into the fireplace, where he stopped suddenly, and I wasn't quick enough to prevent him from picking up the two photographs. 'Nice,' he said.

'That one is Winter and her sister. They're twins,' said Scarlet, proudly. 'And that one is Winter's sister grown up. Her name is Daisy and she lives in Australia.'

Dan looked at the pictures, his head moving from one to the other. 'Yes,' he said, quietly. 'I know.'

Alex laid his hand on my arm. 'Scarl, I th-think we should g-go now.'

But Scarlet, immune to the atmosphere which was gathering around Daniel like a storm cloud, carried on chattering. 'They look exactly alike. There are twins in my school but they don't look the same because Hettie has long hair and she has plaits and Jacob's hair is really short.'

'Yes,' Dan said again. 'They do.' And now he was looking at the picture of Daisy in her bikini in that Australian sunshine, tapping one of his rings against the glass that held her in place. He laid the picture carefully back down on the shelf and carried on staring at it. 'Daisy,' he said, softly, almost as though the name hurt, and then he raised his eyes to find mine. Wouldn't look away, and the expression in his eyes was like someone laying a weight across me.

I did the only thing I could think of, changed the subject completely. 'So, RSPCA tomorrow?'

Alex's fingers still lay on my arm, stroking gently. 'Over at Yarton. About t-ten? If y-you're sure …'

'Of course.' Dan had flipped his mood again, and was pulling his coat from the chair to put it back on. 'We'll meet you there, I can drive Winter in my car and we can talk about …' and the merest pause, just a break in rhythm that only I would notice, 'work. We'll find you a guinea pig to rescue. Do you have the hutch and stuff? Only … guinea pigs? Tricky little critters, they might not dig and they might not chew but they can forge escape papers and be over the border before you can say "Supercalifragilisticexpealidocious".' He winked at Scarlet, who giggled again and then walked out of the door, dragging his coat around him as he went, and vanishing into the shoppers outside.

'T-that guy is w-weird.' Alex let go of my arm. 'No w-wonder you w-want to k-keep away from him.'

'He's funny,' Scarlet said. 'And he knows about guinea pigs.'

He knows about lots of things. Things that hurt. 'Let's open those buns,' I said.

Daniel Bekener @EditorDanB
Is there a word for when you do something and you don't know if it was stupid or not?

ElliottTravels @Tripsky02
@EditorDanB Yeah. Life.

Daniel Bekener @EditorDanB
@Tripsky02 Seriously, mate, I have no idea what I'm doing. Making it better or worse.

ElliottTravels @Tripsky02
@EditorDanB Sometimes things have to get worse before they get better.

Daniel Bekner @EditorDanB
@Tripsky02 And if they don't get better?

ElliottTravels @Tripsky02
@EditorDanB Then at least you know.

Daniel Bekener @EditorDanB
@Tripsky02 Wise, mate.

A.N. Editor Blog
You know that thing, when you go back to something and you think it's all different now and then suddenly it isn't? When everything comes roaring back at you to remind you of what was so great and what went so wrong, and it's all still there, going round and round like one of those fairground rides that you want so much to go on and then can't wait to stop so you can get off?

That.

Is it better to ride the tiger, or get off and look it in the face, tell it what it is? If I carry on riding this tiger – well, it could just run off into the darkness with me. And if I face it? Ah yes, looking her in the eye and telling her what is going on, tried that one. And yet, here we are again, giving it another go. Another attempt to explain to the tiger what is wrong. And why? Because I feel it's worth it, because, deep down, there is something here, something that means so much to me that I can't let it go. Can't turn that tiger loose into the jungle and watch it vanish, not when that tiger is wounded and in danger.

✉

From: AlexHillStone@wolmail.com
To: LucyLoo@wolmail.com
Subject: New arrival

We're doing it! We're getting a guinea pig! I thought about what you said about Winter's idea, and your hamster suggestion, but a hamster might be a bit too small, you know how excited she can get, and I worried that it might not stand up to the amount of cuddling I can foresee in its future, so we're off to the RSPCA in the morning. Maybe you could come by in a couple of days, say, after school? Pop in and say hi and meet our new arrival? Or maybe you'll be sick of hearing about it by then!

Mum says to tell you that she's ordered that book you wanted, and it should be in at the library by next week. I told her she could email you herself but you know what she's like.

Al x

I thought about faking every disease known to man and even a few that, I suspected, were actually diseases of sheep. *Daniel is worming his way back in, doing what he did before, being just there. Wild and unpredictable and around every corner, until you just have to give in and ride the crazy-train along with him. But at least now you know. Know what he's capable of, know that he'll whip around and betray you without a second thought.*

He double-parked the big silver car outside the cottage and leaned on the horn until I couldn't pretend any more and had to come out.

'Wow. Not sure if that counts as dressing up or dressing down.' He looked at me through wide eyes. 'Cute, but you'll freeze and I should know because I am wearing fourteen layers and my reproductive organs have *still* packed up and flown south.'

I was in pyjamas and an old silk kimono which I'd dragged on over the top. And he was right, I was freezing. 'I'm not coming. Well, I am, but not with you. I'll drive over on my own and meet Alex and Scarlet there, there's no need for you to come.'

Dan put his head on the steering wheel. 'And no doubt you're going to say that you've got work to do? Because you and I both know that's bollocks, don't we?' Now he raised his head and turned eyes that had lost the wide 'innocent appeal' look in favour of a cool heaviness on me. 'So. You sit here in this, well, it's got a roof and walls so I'm guessing it's a house but come on, the Borrowers want their place back, and you … what?'

A car, squeezing past on the bit of road Dan had left unencumbered by vehicle, beeped its horn and Dan responded with a raised middle finger, without looking. 'You trawl through your friends on Facebook, you head onto Twitter to tell everyone what a busy day you've got lined up, you drink some coffee …' He stretched across and opened the passenger door. 'And I'm offering you a ride out into the unknown. Well, unknown with guinea pigs.'

I hopped from bare foot to bare foot and tried to double the wrap around me. 'I don't want to go with you, Daniel. I said I'd work with you to get the book finished, not go cruising around the countryside in search of rodents.'

'We can work in the car. Now, go and put something on that doesn't make your nipples stick out like two stumps of Blu-Tack when the poster's fallen down.' I glanced down, saw that he was right and pulled the kimono even tighter around my chest. He gave me a bright smile and a wink and then nodded towards the front door. 'Two minutes. Go.'

I *wanted* to argue, I really did, but he was right, it was freezing standing barefoot on the frosted pavement with nothing but brushed cotton and a layer of silk between me and the increasingly intrusive elements, and I had the horrible idea that if I just slammed back inside and closed the door on him, he'd sit there all day, leaning on the horn and charming his way out of parking tickets. So, blue-fingered, I changed into jeans and jumper and the huge anorak and went back outside, where Daniel was chatting through the open driver's window to two women who were evidently asking him for directions.

'So where did you send them?' I hopped up into the warmth of the passenger seat as he buzzed up the window and waved the women off across the road.

'No idea,' he said, cheerfully. 'I told them I wasn't local but they just kept asking, so I made it up.'

'Poor women.' I looked back through the windscreen.

'Oh come on! I sent them down to the Tourist Info centre down beside the river – God, you really do think I'm a total twat, don't you?' He sounded a bit upset, wrenching the huge car out into the traffic rather harder than I thought it needed to be wrenched.

'I'm just going on evidence,' I said, tightly, and kept my eyes on the scenery outside the window. 'Whose car is this?'

'Greg's wife's. Astra got flattened.'

'What, left it parked somewhere you shouldn't, did you? Charisma won't rescue you from traffic wardens and the clamp brigade, you know.' He didn't answer, and eventually I had to look at him. Silence from Dan was like a bee with no buzz. He was just driving, but there was a jerky pull to the gears that gave away some emotion, a resolute straightness to his gaze out along the road. 'What?'

Now he turned. His jaw was thrust forward, bringing his lips into a tight overbite as though he was clamping them together. 'Winter.' His voice was the kind of level you could use to smooth concrete. 'I am your editor and I am trying to get this book out of you with as little pain as possible for both of us, therefore I hope you will take this comment as a one-off demonstration of my complete and utter fuckitude but *you are not the only person in this world*, all right? I get that you hurt, I get that you've got problems and that your life hasn't been a bed of kittens, but …' He crossed his wrists on the wheel, rubbing his tattoo on the back of the other hand. 'My sister Beth borrowed my car and got hit by a lorry. Head-on.'

I felt the horror pull over me like a too-tight jumper. When Dan and I had been … well, Dan and I, he'd talked a lot about Beth, so I knew that they'd been the closest of brother-sister combinations. It was down to her refusal to allow him to cruise along at school that had got him his spectacular results, excellent degree and, now, his dream job. Beth had been the only member of his family that he'd told about our relationship. I wished now that I'd had the chance to meet her. 'God, Dan, I'm sorry, I didn't know.'

'No. Well.' And then the flip, the 'alternate universe' Daniel coming out to play. 'She's doing okay, spinal injuries but, well we can hope, you know? And she gets to use this cool chair, it's like watching Davros coming down the road.' Banter in his tone but not in his eyes, they continued shaded and self-protecting. 'So. What's next after this book, any thoughts?'

I stared down at my feet. I wanted to keep my eyes from looking at him, noticing those long fingers on the gear stick, the way he steered by laying his jutting wrists around the wheel and turning with his forearms. Things about Dan that I used to know and had forgotten, and I wasn't sure if it was the fact that I had ever known or that I had managed to forget that disturbed me. 'Not really, no.'

'Your mum and dad, how are they doing?'

'Still divorced.'

'Yeah, I just meant … okay.' He blew out a little whistle between his lips. 'You are being chuffing hard work at the moment, love, you know that?'

'Work, Daniel. That is all I want to talk about. This book, in the here and now, nothing else. No "probing questions", no pretending that you even care about my life, all right?'

He winced at my tone. I'd sounded defensive. 'Right. Okay. So you're all about the here and now, are you? The past is, what? Gone? You sure?'

I sighed and turned to look out of the window. 'Shut up, Dan.'

We fell into silence for a few miles. I could see him reflected in the window I pretended to gaze out of, flicking me occasional quick looks and once looking almost as though he had raised a hand to touch my arm, but drawing it back in time to say, 'Hey, Yarton, this is us.' The car lurched as he pulled a tight right-hander and drew us into a car park to a cacophony of barking from a row of kennels. 'What's your man driving?'

'Alex isn't my man.' I scanned the parked cars. 'And I've no idea what he drives.'

'Looks he was giving me, he thinks differently. Maybe you want to watch yourself there, kiddo. Nothing worse than a relationship that one of you thinks is something when the other one thinks it's a fruit bowl, okay?'

'And this is about work, is it?'

An angle to the head that made his eyes look bigger, darker. 'Could be,' he said. 'Could be. Come on, let's go find them and start sorting that little girl out with a proper pet. I'm guessing that the hobby horse is a transitional object, yes? Mum and Dad separated, Mum left her to "go and find herself", little girl hanging on to Light Bulb as a reminder. Am I getting warm?'

'Except Alex is her uncle, her mum is dead, her dad isn't anywhere on the scene, and Light Bulb is part toy, part weapon … yes, you're spot on.'

'Freeoow. Take it back, kiddo, you are complicating your life like a fractal.' Dan jumped down onto the car park. 'Why? Not bizarre enough for you already that you've got to add a single dad and his offspring to the pile? How much does he know about you, this Alex? Enough to make a judgement call?'

But I'd seen Alex and Scarlet now, standing in the reception area to the rehoming unit, and I walked off to join them without speaking to Dan again.

'Please let me come home with you,' I muttered to Alex

under my breath as we watched Dan showing Scarlet how to hold a guinea pig properly. 'I don't think I can stand a return journey.'

Alex looked at Dan for a moment. Dan was on his hands and knees in sawdust in a pen of assorted rodents and rabbits, holding a brown and white guinea pig in an upright posture, so that it looked as though it was sitting on the palm of his hand, paws over his wrist. He passed it to Scarlet, positioning her hands so that she held it the same way.

'He s-seems okay. S-Scarl likes him.' Now Alex looked at me. 'I d-don't know, ob-obviously, b-but maybe … maybe h-he's not so b-bad?'

I felt my eyes widen. 'Oh, not you too! This is what he does, he suckers people in with the whole "I'm just adorable" routine and then, wham, next thing you know he's got you pinned to a wall and he's ripping your heart out with his teeth.'

Alex looked from me to Dan and then back. 'You d-don't think th-that you m-might be *overreacting* a b-bit?' he asked, carefully.

'Dan took it into his head that I was too dependent on my sister. Now, I don't know what made him think that, or why it was such a bad thing, but asking me to give her up in favour of him? That was just *wrong*. And me making the choice to stay with Daisy – what part of that is overreacting?'

Dan was making the guinea pig 'talk' to Scarlet, squeaking 'pick me, pick me!' and waving its paws in the air. As I watched his performance, he looked up and saw me looking, dropped me a wink that made my face heat up, then gave the guinea pig a kiss on the top of its head. 'Your choice,' he said to Scarlet, but I had the itchiest little thought that he'd heard what we'd been talking about, and the phrase had been directed equally at me. 'Just remember that you choose for life.'

Alex patted my shoulder. 'Y-you know him b-best,' he said. 'M-maybe he's j-just good with ch-children.'

'I want this one.' Scarlet took the guinea pig from Dan and held it under her chin. 'I'm going to call him Bobso.'

Alex took her to fill in the paperwork so they could come back and pick up Bobso the next day, leaving Daniel and I together in a room full of squeaky overexcited fur.

'I'm going home with Alex,' I said, watching Dan brushing wood shavings off his knees. 'You can leave now.'

Dan focussed on a small white rabbit which was attempting to dig its way out of the big plastic run. Scratch scratch scratch, then pause, then back to the frantic scrabbling at the corner where the Perspex walls met. 'Some things,' he said, still watching the rabbit, 'you can't escape from. You might be able to see the world out there, but however hard you dig you just can't get through to join in.'

'Was that meant to be allegorical or something? Because I think you are getting a bit too literary for your own good.'

Dan seemed to pull himself together. His gaze moved from the rabbit to me. 'Just your editor, Win,' he said. 'Just here to get the book done. Like I said before, no agenda.'

I waved an arm. 'Coming to help Scarlet choose a guinea pig is "no agenda"? Dan, do you even know what an agenda *is*?'

His shoulders came up in a shrug and he nestled his chin down into the collar of the coat, which was now liberally dusted with guinea pig pooh and little strands of white fur. '*Agenda sunt.* Latin. Those things which must be driven forward. Like you, Winter, and here I am just driving on with soft words and carrying the big stick of … well, I'm not really sure. Why *are* you writing this book? Wasn't *Book of the Dead* enough?'

'Just because people are dead doesn't mean their story is over,' I said, moving to one side to allow a family to come past and bend down to eye up the rabbits. 'Their graves tell a story too, and, if the last book is anything to go by, people are interested in previous generations; they want to know what their lives were like.'

Dan put a hand on my shoulder to manoeuvre me so that a young couple could come by on the other side. Arms around each other, they took up all the available space and Dan and I had to step closer together, almost forced to mirror their physical closeness. I was pushed into Dan's chest and the sudden feel of his body, the smell of vanilla and expensive body spray, the brush of his coat against my skin made me dumb for a moment. *So familiar. The scent of comfort that sat on the edge of challenge, a wildness that could bring sudden transformation from sitting over a pint in a pub to racing across a windswept heath. Daniel.*

He was looking down at me, smiling slightly at our forced proximity with one eyebrow cocked. 'Hey, just like old times,' he said, in a half-whisper. 'Remember?' And his fingers tangled in my hair, pushing it back away from my face, his other hand cupping the angle of my jaw, tilting my face up towards him.

My pulse was so fast it was a solid thing in my throat. I could feel the softness creeping now, starting beneath my belly button and crawling slowly up my body, bending everything I thought, everything I wanted, into cooked-spaghetti shapes. *Just fold. Fold into him, let his strength take the pain away.*

And then the image again, of Daniel on that bridge. Staring off into the distance as the wind danced in his hair and whipped tears from his eyes. *Making me choose.*

'What about Daisy?' I asked, softly, because my voice wouldn't come out any louder, as though that crawling malleability had reached my vocal chords. 'What about those things you said about her? Because *that* is what I remember.'

He took a couple of steps back, and his hands fell to their customary positions, pushed deep into pockets. 'Yeah. You're right. There's still Daisy standing there between us, isn't there?'

The brightly-lit room with the excited chatter of the children choosing a new pet, the smell of sawdust and incontinence all came flooding back in, washing the feeling of Dan away from my skin. 'Daisy will *always* be standing there.' I had my teeth gritted, and the space where his hand had been felt cold.

'Winter! We can come back tomorrow after school and get Bobso, they just want to make sure that we've got the right sort of hutch and a garden for him, and that he's got food and a water bottle.' Scarlet bounced back through from the far room and flung herself into the gap between Daniel and me.

'That's good.' I tried to give her my attention but it was hard with him standing there so full of things only half-said. 'Daniel has to go now.'

Dan bent down to the little girl's level. 'Remember, he needs to run on the grass, not just sit in a hutch all day,' he said. 'And things to nibble to keep his teeth from growing too long. And love. Lots of love – guinea pigs will purr if you sit them on your knee and stroke them, when they know that you love them.' Then he stood up again. 'Bye.'

Without another word, without any kind of leave-taking or indication that he'd see me again, he walked out of the room like a shadow walking away from the light. I must have been staring after him, because Scarlet had to attract my attention by pulling on my sleeve and half-dragging me across to Alex, waiting in the car park.

Chapter Seventeen

From: GregTurner@ShyOwlPublishing.co.uk
To: WinterGregoryAuthor@teddymail.com
Subject: Book of the Dead 2 – deadline approaching!
Hi Winter

Just touching base to let you know we've got your publication window all set for next June and we'll be putting out the first round of publicity after Christmas. I know Dan is up there but he's gone a bit quiet lately. To be honest I think he needed some 'personal time', things haven't been easy for him recently, so if you do see him then pass on my best regards.

Anyway. You've got another twelve weeks before we need to see that first draft. No pressure, but I'd like to know which way to angle the publicity, so if I could get a first look around Christmas, I can take it home with me and read through, make some calls.

I'm sure it's all going just great. Look forward to reading the finished article.

Best
Greg

I stared around the room. The books were in exactly the same position on the table as they had been when I'd tidied pre-Alex, and that had been three days ago, but, by using all my authorly powers, I managed to convince myself that this was a good sign. *At least I haven't thrown them out of the window.*

Why wasn't I writing? The question kept coming round to haunt me. I was having blindingly brilliant ideas, always in the middle of the night, but during the day it seemed almost more effort than I could muster just to turn on the computer and drink coffee. The book was two-thirds done, perhaps there was some miraculous way I could pad out the bits I'd written already, make them hit the word count and ...

You've lost it, Winter.

'Daze?'

'So you need me again now, do you? I was thinking you'd replaced me with Daniel.' A pause. 'Again.'

And horror dropped through me like a hot ball bearing through jelly. 'It was never like that. Please, Daze, don't. I need you. The writing's come to a standstill and Dan ... was here but I think he's gone again, and I don't know what I'm doing and everything is getting so fucked up and ...' The tears blotted out the words, 'And you're all I've got.'

'It's okay, Win.' Her voice was softer now, maybe it was because I was crying. I rarely cried. Daisy had always been the 'emotional' one, after all, and one of us crying fit to burst was usually enough in any situation, if I joined in it was like misery in stereo. 'Don't cry. No, it's good that you haven't needed me, totes. Sometimes I worry that you need me too much.'

I cried a bit harder. 'You're all I've got, Daze. You're like my still point, you know?'

Daisy sighed. 'Winnie, you've got Alex to talk to now. You're even getting yourself sorted with Dan, maybe it's time we had a bit of a break from one another.'

My heart set like a solid block in my chest. 'You mean not speak to you when I need to?' I imagined Dan's face. 'Dan would think he'd won.'

She sighed again. 'But it might give you another shot

with him.' She sounded mischievous now. 'Wouldn't it, Winnie?'

I suddenly had such a strong picture of her that it felt as though she was in the room with me, sitting drinking something with 'chai' in the title, draped in layers of fabric that would have made me look like a walking sample-book but made her look cutting-edge. Her hair was all unstructured, and the millions of thin bracelets she always wore were chittering and chiming whenever she moved an arm. I half-smiled. The twin thing still worked, even when she was annoyed with me. 'Now you are just winding me up, Daze. You don't want me to end up with Daniel, do you?'

Now she was trying not to laugh. 'Don't I? Maybe I can't wait to see you shacked up with Chaos Boy in a little flat in London.'

'No way.' But the panic was over, she was teasing me again. This had been just another one of our occasional spats, when one or other of us would try to assert some kind of 'single child' position over the other. I wondered if, sometimes, we didn't do it just so we could test the twin bond for strength, and then felt a cold shudder deep inside at the thought of what would happen if it shattered.

'Look, Win, do you want to get this book written? Or is it better to chuck it all in, admit that you only had the one book in you, hand back the advance and go back to telling people why they should buy the latest lawn mower?'

I could almost hear those bracelets now; Daisy fiddled with them when she talked and I'd always been able to find her in a crowd, just by following the sound – and then teased her it was like her version of cow bells.

'No, I can do it. I know I can. I'm just blocked.'

Daisy snorted. 'Come on, that's bollocks and you know it. You're holding up the book as a way of getting back at Daniel.'

'Am I?'

'That or at least getting his attention. And it's worked, hasn't it? He's there. Now you just have to decide whether you're not finishing it as a way of keeping him around. And what about your luscious Alex? You've pretty much done a one-eighty on him since Dan turned up. What's that about?'

'I've just been trying to avoid everyone, I think. I haven't even seen Scarlet much either.' I felt a sudden pang. Scarlet had made me promise to go over and see how Bobso was settling in, but I'd pretty much barricaded myself inside the House of Tiny. 'I'll go and see her today, when she gets back from school.'

'Good. That's a start anyway. And I suppose you'll see Alex while you're there?' Daisy sounded mischievous again, far better than that horrible wary tone she'd had at the start of our conversation. 'He's everything Dan isn't, and maybe there's your problem.'

'Wow, you are good at this aren't you?'

She laughed. 'It's what I'm here for, Win, obvs! Okay, now go and do,' and she was gone. But now I was smiling.

Daniel Bekener @EditorDanB
Jeez this is hard.

ElliottTravels @Tripsky02
@EditorDanB Well stop poking it then.

Daniel Bekener @EditorDanB
@Tripsky02 More right than you know, mate. Maybe I'll just leave it.

EastEndSmith @Barrowboy70
@EditorDanB Things are only hard if you care.

Daniel Bekener @EditorDanB
@Tripsky02 @Barrowboy70 You can really push an entendre, can't you? But could be right.

EastEndSmith @Barrowboy70
@EditorDanB @Tripsky02 Found something to care about at last?

Daniel Bekener @EditorDanB
@Barrowboy70 More like 'again'. Yep, going for again. Never knew it would be like this, never knew it *could* be. Will hang in.

A.N. Editor Blog
Christ. Christ, this is hard. A huge part of me just wants to cut and run now. Ha, the life of an editor – all of you following this blog for tips on getting published, you must be so sick of my internal monologues now. Yeah, the life of an editor, it's all glamour. All shiny books and grateful authors and the eternal fucking angst of how to spend the money.

No. It's not your fault and that's unfair. I made the fatal mistake of getting involved. Never happened before, I mean, I've run the whole 'girlfriend' thing (thanks for the comment, Jeremy, mate, but I'm pretty much straight as they come) but it's never been like this, never got under my skin, made me itch this way. Always thought that love would be clean, y'know? Uncomplicated. That you'd just 'know' and she'd 'know' and then it would be hearts and flowers all the way to the aisle and the reception in some country barn. I didn't think that you could get it wrong, I mean, what is there to get wrong?

Shit, do you want a list? You can fall in love with some girl who's got herself so truly fucked up that she can't even see you for what you are. And everything you say, everything you try, just makes it all that *little bit worse*.

Fuck it. Fuck it. Write to the market, if that makes you happy. Write to make money, write any kind of crap, I've got no advice to give you any more. I've got nothing.

f

Facebook

Alex Hill

This is Bobso, latest addition to the Hill family! S is madly in love, of course – we really need more excitement around here.

Picture of Bobso.

27 people like this.

Comment: Lucy Charlton We're having a barn dance up at school next week, you should come!

Comment: Matt Simons You could take black-lipstick woman. Show her how you can party in the Leas.

Comment: Alex Hill Seriously, Matt, that's pretty exciting around here!

Comment: Matt Simons Hey, Dundee isn't much better.

✉

From: LucyLoo@wolmail.com

To: AlexHillStone@wolmail.com

Subject: Barn dance

I was serious on Facebook you know. Come to the barn dance!

Bring Winter, if she wants. Remember us 'do-si-do-ing' at Matt's party that time? I want to see if you've still 'got it'!

Lu x

It was getting dark when I wandered my way over to the Old Mill. The shops were on the point of closing, the streets emptying of people. There were no bars or clubs opening, no lines of those waiting for the evening to get started and wind up into the frenzy of a night, just the pub filling a little more and the descent of a frost that made my heels crack on the pavement as I walked.

The lights of the Old Mill were muted but welcoming. The atrium was softly lit and a lamp glowed down from the flat; the office was in darkness except for the satanic red glow of the coffee machine's power light. I pushed my way in through the main door, and found Margaret and Alex standing just inside, surrounded by the smell of new wood and polish.

'W-winter!' Alex immediately came over to hold the door open for me. 'H-hello. J-just telling M-mum I wanted to f-f—'

Oh, Alex. No, stop it, Winter.

'Facebook you and ask you over,' Alex finished in a rush. 'S-scarl is upstairs, writing a s-story about B-b-Bobso.' He rubbed his face. 'She c-could have c-called him Andrew, for my s-sake.'

'How *are* you, Winter?' Margaret asked. Her tone was 'motherly concern' overlaid with wool from what was either a hand-knitted scarf or an anaconda with a really nasty skin condition. It was wrapped around her neck so many times that I wondered what she was going to do when December arrived. 'I suppose you're terribly busy, aren't you, although we haven't seen you outside much

182

recently. You should get out more, you know. Into the sunshine.'

'W-winter is a writer, M-mum, not a t-tomato plant,' Alex said.

'Hmmm.' Margaret looked me up and down. The scarf bobbed as though it had a life of its own. 'You're looking thin. I know thin is supposed to be the new voluptuous, but a young lady who appears to be a stranger to the sticky toffee pudding can never be attractive as far as I am concerned.'

'G-good job she's n-not trying to p-pull you then, M-mum.' Alex gave me a grin. 'You l-look fine,' he said, the grin broadening.

Since I hadn't even looked in the mirror before I left the house, I doubted this was the case, but it was nice of him to try to mitigate the effect of his mother.

'Winter!' There was a frantic rush of sock against wooden stair, and Scarlet precipitated towards us like a downpour. 'D'you want to come and see Bobso? He's got a *huge* hutch and a thing that goes out on the grass so he can be outside without getting eaten by foxes.' She jumped the last few steps and slithered alongside me.

Alex and Margaret exchanged a Look, and I deduced that they'd been talking about Scarlet when I arrived. And, knowing Scarlet, that she'd probably been listening.

'Yes, come and show me.'

'B-boots, Scarl. If you're g-going outside,' Alex said, and she sighed heavily, flouncing over to her wellies, which lay scattered just inside the doors as though lost during a particularly balletic moment. *Alex is going to have his work cut out when you're a teenager*, I thought, and, from the look on Alex's face, the same thought occurred to him on a regular basis.

'Daniel would like to know,' Margaret put a hand on my arm, 'whether it would be all right if he called on you tomorrow.'

I blinked. Had I somehow fallen though a wormhole into *Pride and Prejudice*? Focussing on her weird apparel meant I could ignore that little burst of heat that had gone off inside me at the realisation that Dan hadn't left me and headed back to London. 'Er, yes. Sure. Why didn't he just come round?'

Margaret gave a boa-busting shrug. 'He's giving you "space" apparently. To "think". I've told him what you need is a week of square meals and a turn around the Topping ...'

I mouthed 'euphemism?' at Alex, but he shook his head.

'... but he says that, where he's concerned, you need space.' She raised her eyebrows at me. 'Do you?'

I opened my mouth to say that what I really needed was Daniel and the uncomfortable feelings that he roused in me to go away, but I was saved by Scarlet dashing up to me, her wellies making 'pock pock' noises against her legs. 'Come on, we need to see Bobso before it gets too dark. Light Bulb is keeping guard on him in case of cats,' she said, and I was dragged through the doors and around the building to a small shelter, probably built for logs, but which now contained a hutch which looked as though it had been made for a nightmarishly large rabbit. Bobso sat in one corner, squeakily disgruntled at being disturbed halfway through a carrot. Light Bulb, even more lopsided than usual, leaned above the hutch like a corduroy angel at a rodent nativity.

I admired the guinea pig as much as I could, while Scarlet bobbed around telling me about how he needed his water changed every day and fresh food and bedding, and seemed to be taking the whole 'pet ownership' thing very seriously. She seemed happier and brighter than she had for a while, so I carefully brought up the subject of school. 'Has Mr Moore said anything to you about me visiting school?'

Scarlet paused in her recital of guinea pig no-nos, where she'd reached 'no citrus fruits', so may have been working alphabetically. 'He said to tell you that he'd email you.' Another bounce, which Bobso regarded with the equanimity that told me he was probably going to be a very good pet. 'And Daniel told me to tell you that he wants to see you but he doesn't want you to be frightened. He only wants to help you write the book, but he thinks you think that he's trying to make trouble.'

'Dan? When did he say that?'

'Yesterday.' Bobso received a soggy kiss on the nose at which he blinked his amber-button eyes, then began rotating his jaw around another carrot.

'Dan was here yesterday?'

'Mm. He came to help me put Bobso in his run. He's nice.' She turned her face up to me, a pale circle in the darkness. 'Is he your boyfriend now?'

'No.' I moved off, back towards the Old Mill. 'No, Scarlet, he's not, and he never will be.'

'Oh.' The sound her boots made slapping along her bare legs was like an amateur wobbleboard enthusiast having a practice session. 'He says he really likes you.'

'Oh … does he.'

'Mm. I told him that you had dinner with Alex and that you kissed him, and then Dan started laughing and said that Alex didn't know the half of it. What's the half of it, Winter? How can you know a half of something? 'Cos if you know something you don't know there's another half that you don't know, do you? You think you know all of it.'

Luckily we reached the doors just then, because otherwise I might have said something about Daniel that I regretted, especially to a little girl who seemed to regard him as only one step down from St Francis of Assisi. 'It's just a saying, Scarlet.' I held the door open for her. 'It's just Dan, stirring up trouble.'

'C-coffee?' Alex was waiting for us. Alone, so Margaret had probably gone home; that or been subsumed into Wool Hell. 'Upstairs, S-scarl. B-bath and b-bed, young l-lady.' Scarlet opened her mouth to protest, but Alex held up a hand. 'W-what did we d-decide?'

'That I'm only allowed to get up early to see Bobso if I get to bed before nine,' Scarlet recited. 'Night, Winter.'

The wellies hit various parts of the hallway and she slip-bounded her way up the stairs. The door to the flat closed softly and Alex let out a sigh. 'S-seems to be w-working,' he said, and looked at the floor. 'It's D-D-Dan's idea.'

'For God's sake!' Oddly, because I thought I was angry, tears needled behind my eyelids. 'That bloody man is everywhere! Margaret, Scarlet and now you. He's probably got all the Stepford Mothers in his pocket too.' A sudden and very unwelcome image of Daniel, smiling down at one of those immaculately made-up and turned out women, putting a hand out to brush her hair away from her face and moving in for a kiss ... my throat went hot and tight.

'He-he's j-just *nice*, Winter.' Alex opened the office door and the red light winked like a summons into Purgatory. 'He cares about a l-lot of stuff. About y-you.'

'Just coffee, Alex,' I said, sharply. 'That's all I came for. Not another one of Dan's remote-controlled chats, I've just had one from your niece.'

The coffee machine spurted into life, jetting a great torrent of steam upwards and groaning like an old man forced out of his chair. 'Y-you and D-Dan …' He was busying himself with preparing mugs of coffee, not looking at my face.

'I told you what he did, Alex. How could you ever think I would have any kind of thing again with a man who behaved like that? Apart from armed conflict.'

The coffee smelled good and my mouth began to water. *How long is it since I last ate? I'm losing track here and that's not good …*

'I s-saw how you w-were at the R-r- … at the pet place, and it l-looked to me as th-though you h-have stuff to s-sort.' He held a mug out to me. 'And y-yes, you told me about D-Dan and your s-sister. But it l-looked to m-me like more th-than that.' He raised his own mug in a silent toast.

My hand was shaking, I realised, when hot coffee began to slop over the mug rim, and I lowered it down to rest on my knee. 'Dan being an absolute bastard wasn't enough?'

Alex took a deep sip of his coffee, then looked at me through the steam. 'Un-unless there's more th-that you're not t-telling me, n-no, th-that's n-not enough.' Another sip. 'Is there?'

Despite the bitter coffee, despite the delicious smell sending saliva around my tongue, my mouth went dry. 'No,' my voice was cracked and hard. 'No.'

'Th-there's n-nothing else?' He was persistent, I'd give him that. But then, bringing up Scarlet would teach even the most indecisive person how to stick to their guns. 'S-sure? B-because no one c-can help you, W-winter, unless y-you admit a p-p-problem.'

And then I began to wonder what Dan had said. *How much* he'd said, and how he'd twisted things around.

'Look, thanks for the coffee, Alex, but I really ought to go. If I'm going to get the Editor from Hell dropping in tomorrow then I should get everything in order for a status report.' I tried to smile and be light, anything else would only fuel the fire. 'And also, incidentally, clear a backlog of cups that makes it look as though I've been hosting international coffee mornings all week.'

He gave me a complicated look, as though a smile was fighting with concern and almost winning, before being knocked to the ground by doubt. 'Okay.' He took the mug I held out and put it carefully on the desk, then moved in to give me a careful hug. 'B-but if you w-want to t-talk, Winter, I'm h-here.'

I gave him a quick return hug. 'Nothing to talk about,' I said as I stepped clear. 'Don't get caught up in Dan's games, Alex. I think he's looking for collateral damage.'

The complicated look took on shades of sympathy and disappeared as he raised his mug and started drinking. 'G-goodnight,' he said, softly, and I made good my escape.

✉

From: AlexHillStone@wolmail.com
To: LucyLoo@wolmail.com
Subject: Barn dance
I'd love to make the barn dance. Not sure about Winter though. It's a bit complicated.

✉

From: LucyLoo@wolmail.com
To: AlexHillStone@wolmail.com
Subject: Barn dance

Okay. Well, if you need to talk about things, you know where I am! Winter is lovely, Scarlet never stops talking about her and it's obvious she cares a lot for both of you but … sorry. Not going to say any more. She's lovely and it's a shame she can't make the barn dance. See you there.

Lu x

Chapter Eighteen

✉

From: DanBekener@ShyOwlPublishing.co.uk
To: GregTurner@ShyOwlPublishing.co.uk
Subject: Book of the Dead 2

Thanks for mailing Winter, mate. I don't want to scare her, but
hopefully it'll shake her up a bit and she'll realise that she has to
knuckle down, might make her a bit more responsive when I see
her tomorrow. At least, I'm hoping to, there's every possibility
that she'll have skipped out on all of us, so I'm pinning my hopes
on her staying to help out a little girl with bullying issues. Reckon
if it wasn't for that, she'd have run a while back …

Anyhoo. Yeah, to update you. I'm doing okay. Yeah, yeah,
you're concerned, very touching mate, very *Brideshead
Revisited*, but I'll be fine. I mean, the whole deal with Beth
getting hurt … but she's doing okay too, so don't need to worry
about me. It's Winter we need to worry about. Not just as an
author, if you see what I mean. We both know that there's plenty
more where she came from, after *Book of the Dead* everyone is
having a crack at writing Genealogy Fiction, we can fill that June
slot a hundred times over if we want, although, Jeez, don't you
ever dare tell her that, she's fragile enough already. No, she's
going non-functional on me.

I've got my … well, not spies, but people who are watching
out. And she's not eating, not leaving the house except when
she has to, and the awful, evil fucking thing is that I think I know
what's going on in her head. Win and I we were a tight team
back in the day … what am I saying, it's only been six months,
feels like a lifetime. Hey, we were good. And I know how she
thinks, how she works. She's pinning this all onto me, won't

leave the house because of me, etc etc, you know how it goes. And, yeah, I *could go*. Take away that excuse. But then I think without me to drive her on, even if it's pure hate that's keeping her running, without that …

Shit, mate, I dunno. I'll just do what I can, I guess.

Dan

I thought I was ready for Daniel. I was wearing my most combative jeans and a jumper that effectively hid most of my upper body; I looked as though Margaret had taught me everything she knew about fashion. I'd opened multiple files on the laptop, sorted the books so that disparate pages pointed to the fact that I was researching carving styles, and removed the latest half-dozen cups of cold coffee from around the room.

I actually started reading one of the books while I waited. I'd forgotten, yes, almost forgotten that I *enjoyed* this sort of thing, and I had sunk myself so deeply into the pages that the knock at the door made me jump.

'Dan?'

'Yeah, well, Richard Armitage was busy.' He stayed on the step this time, making no attempt to come inside. 'You look like shit.'

'You don't look so great yourself.' It was true. He looked … well, 'bleak' was the only word which sprang to mind. His normal restlessness seemed stilled as though life had tied weights to his limbs and his stubble had crept away from his chin and was now climbing up both cheeks like a cheap disguise. 'It's not your sister, is it? She …'

A smile that only engaged his mouth. 'No. Beth's cool.' And then the quiet again, so alien to Dan, who usually came on like someone had wrapped a stream of consciousness in a greatcoat and turned it loose.

'So,' I said, awkwardly. 'You want to talk about the book?'

'What, in comparison to standing on this doorstep with Swedish-export winds whistling into every orifice? Yeah, settle for that one.' He hunched his shoulders.

I stepped back to let him in. 'I'm getting stuff done.' I waved a hand at the open books.

'Really?' He was looking at the shelf above the fire, but I'd moved Daisy's picture upstairs to beside my bed to stop him using it as a conversational opener. His dark eyes raked around the room. 'Jeez. If you'd said you wanted to write in these conditions we'd have rented you a lock up in Camden. Do these windows actually, y'know, work? Or are they just stuck onto the brickwork for show?'

'It's cosy.' Why was I defending a room where I regularly sustained impressive bruises just trying to tune the radio? 'Snug.'

'Even Bobso's got better accommodation. At least he can turn round without having to go outside.' Dan whipped around and his coat swept a handful of biros onto the floor. 'Okay. So what have we got?' Now he perched on a corner of the table, one booted foot up on the seat of a chair. ''Cos that deadline ...' Arms flung into the air as though to avoid an oncoming train. 'I can see every hair on its chin.'

I indicated the books lying beside him on the table. 'Research. And I'm fifty thousand words in, so ...'

'Coffee.'

I stared at him. 'What?' *Confusion. That's what Dan's all about.*

'How much coffee are you drinking?' He'd dropped his head, seemingly to stare at his boots, and was rubbing the tattoo as though it itched, but now his head came up. 'Serious question, Winter.'

I had a momentary guilty thought about all the cups and mugs I'd recently rinsed and returned to the cupboard, but wild horses and a very large tractor wouldn't pull the truth out of me in front of him. 'Couple of cups a day. Why?'

Dan picked up one of my books, a floppy-covered academic work on gravestone lettering, and used it as a fan, waving it in front of his face like a literature-obsessed Regency damsel. 'And the rest. Oh, Winter …' and now his voice had a little hitch, almost sadness, which contrasted with the comical book-flapping, which was causing coloured Post-its to fall from the pages and rain around his feet. 'Do you really not know what's wrong here? Can you not *see*?'

'All I can see is a pillock losing all my marked places and sitting with his feet up on furniture which isn't even mine. I thought you were supposed to be helping me, not perching like a budgie that's been trained to make really abstract statements,' I said, pushing some irritation into my voice to stop him from seeing the swirling bewilderment that he was causing.

'Okay. Okay.' Dan slid off the table. 'In the spirit of the whole "Being Your Editor" thing, and not raking up the past …' He caught my eye and went on smoothly. '… or even mentioning it, before you throw something at me, I have to say that I don't think you're going to get any further with this one.'

I sat suddenly on the florally cushioned chair behind me. '*What?* You mean, call it a day?'

He shrugged and sucked his teeth. 'Gotta admit it sometime, kiddo, it's just not a goer.'

I narrowed my eyes at him. 'Is this some kind of reverse psychology thing, where you tell me you're pulling out and suddenly I get all incensed and write like a demon for three days without leaving the house and produce a masterpiece?'

Dan raised his eyebrows. 'That's Hollywood. This ...' He spun one of his coat-encompassing slow circles. '... isn't. Despite the fact it's built entirely of *some* kind of wood, that's probably just so they can burn it down when you leave. Plausible deniability.' He stopped spinning but his coat seemed to move independently for a few moments, as though it were a live thing in its own right, making a separate decision. 'See, what it is, Win ...' His hands dug into his pockets now as his head came up. His eyes, which seemed almost black in the thick light, found mine and held on. 'Sometimes you just have to cut your losses and I'm thinking now ...' A pause that made my heart beat almost sick-makingly hard in my throat for reasons I didn't want to think about, let alone acknowledge. '... maybe you're a loss too far,' he finished, so softly that the words seemed absorbed by the air.

I felt the lightheaded buzz that was all the blood draining from my face, the clammy sweat unnecessarily cooling my skin. 'But I thought ...' was all I could manage. My throat had gone dry. *What had I thought? That this could go on forever? Me not writing, Dan hovering in the background being all Dark Angel? Shit, had Daisy been right all along, was I using this book somehow to get back at Daniel? Using all this writer's block bollocks to control him, make him worried that he wasn't going to get his investment back – that his confidence in me was misplaced? Make him look stupid in front of all those who'd ridiculed the idea of* Book of the Dead *and then poured so much scorn on the thought of a follow-up that the project had almost sunk under its weight? Was that it?*

Dan was watching me. I'd always assumed that I knew

what was going on behind that straight, dark gaze. That, even with all the chaos stuff and the random moves and the spontaneous behaviour, I knew him. I suddenly realised that I had no idea what Dan thought about what was happening. *He's a stranger. But now he's a stranger who can take things away from you, things you know, deep down, that you really need. You aren't giving him that power, it's the power he's always had in the real world.*

'One day,' he said, softly, 'one day, Win, you're going to forget. It's going to fade and fade until one day you'll wake up and it will feel like it was all a dream.'

*No. No, I will remember. I will **always** remember.* And the mere thought of losing those memories, of any of it fading and dying made me breathe a little faster. And I realised why I was writing this book. 'Okay,' I said slowly, drawing in a deep breath.

He seemed surprised. Eyebrows raised and he pulled a face, then scrabbled a hand through his hair until it looked as though a poltergeist had had a go at it. 'You'll let it go?'

'I didn't mean that, it wasn't an "okay I agree with you". It was an "okay, I can do this". For *me* I can do it. For all those people who've got gravestones that people have forgotten about, all those humps out there in that churchyard that were once someone somebody loved.' I stood up. '*I* want this book. Never mind the guys back at HQ, never mind the readers and *certainly* never mind you. I'm doing this for me, and I will bloody well get that book in on deadline.'

'Well, that was unexpected. And I thought *I* was the king of the random.' He poked his tongue into his cheek, I could see the bulge. It was something Dan did when he was thinking very deeply about something, so deeply that, for a second, the image dropped and I was looking at the face of the real man underneath the manga-esque figure I was used to. The Dan that didn't need to make an impression or show a front to the world. The Dan I ... the man I used to know.

'Seriously. I *can* do it,' I said, and, even to me, my voice seemed to have a new certainty.

'I know you can. Just wondering if it's a good idea.' He spoke without looking at me. His eyes were flickering but seeing ideas rather than reality. 'Also wondering what the hell I just said there to kick you up the butt, because, fuck, I'm going to use that voice a lot more.' A quick flick of a sideways look. 'You know the coffee is you self-medicating, don't you? I mean, yeah, you're sharp, you understand what it's all about.' And suddenly he was standing very close, so close that I could feel that little static pull of his skin against mine. 'You know what you're doing.'

And I could feel that new certainty washing through my veins on a fizz of anticipation. 'Yes.'

A slow nod. 'Okay.'

I stepped away from him. *You're just a guy. Somebody I used to know, nothing else. Look, I can put clear air between us and not feel as though something is missing.* 'In fact, I'm going to start now. Go away, Dan.'

'Getting the message and the picture, Win, don't worry.' He tilted his head and looked down at me; it made his eyelashes slant across his cheekbones.

Yeah, I get it, you're attractive. But no more, Daniel. No more power over me.

'I'll check back in a day or so.' Now he moved across the room, boots jingling like a horse pulling into harness, to pause at the front door with his hand on the catch. 'Just remember what I said about the coffee. Ease up. It might feel as though it's helping, but it's really not, okay, kiddo?'

Like writing the books. Like coming here. 'I'll let you know how I'm getting on.' I reached for the door to do the 'hostess' thing of letting him out, but he'd already opened it and was halfway down the High Street before I got there.

✉

From: DanBekener@ShyOwlPublishing.co.uk
To: BethanyAnnBekener@wolmail.com
Subject: <u>Have you been reading those romance books again?</u>
Ciao, bella. How are you doing? Mum said you'd had a bit of a setback. Look, I'll come down and see you, sometime in the next week or so, okay? You just hang in there, kiddo, keep taking the tablets as they say. I want to see you buzzing around, seen enough of you lying flat on your back, tbh, you lazy moo!

Remember when I was home last time, what you said about Winter and the books? And I didn't want to listen? Hate to say it, kiddo, but it looks as if you might have been right all along. Guess I just didn't want to look at it like that. But I think we might be getting somewhere with the new one. She's pulled a bit of a turnaround on me and now she's promising that she's going to come in on time with it. Everything else between us has gone to hell, she gets all kinda jumpy when I'm around like she can hardly bear to look at me now. And every time she moves away from me, every time she refuses to see what's in front of her, it's like just another kick in the teeth for me.

I'm going to see this one through and then call it a day. Sorry, kid, I know you wanted this to work, I know you thought that Winter and I were going to be some kind of modern-day Tristan and Isolde, but it's never going to be like that with us again. Too much is broken and I can only stand so much. Reckon I've had enough now.
See you soon
Danny Boy

Chapter Nineteen

*'There's something that worries me slightly in the stone
erected over Thomas Parris, sheepherder of the district of
Fryupdale. It isn't the lettering, which is a pleasing italic
style, giving his last resting place a sort of 'handwritten' look.
It's the fact that his stone says merely 'near this place lieth
the remains of Thomas Parris who departed this life on the
twenty-eighth of February, 1818, in his seventieth year'. Near
this place? Couldn't they remember where they put him?'*
—BOOK OF THE DEAD 2

From: AlexHillStone@wolmail.com
To: LucyLoo@wolmail.com
Subject: Thanks
Thanks a lot for talking sense into me yet again. You're a star.
Al x

Alex Hill @AlexHillStone
@WinterGAuthor Got a message for you from school. Why not
pop round? Bobso has a surprise.

WinterGregory @WinterGAuthor
@AlexHillStone Sounds intriguing. #Amwriting but could come
tonight?

Alex Hill @AlexHillStone
@WinterGAuthor That's fine. Come after nine and have some food.

WinterGregory @WinterGAuthor
@AlexHillStone Lovely, see you then.

Matt Simons @MattyS
@AlexHillStone @WinterGAuthor Have a nice time, you two!

Alex Hill @AlexHillStone
@MattyS Shut up #sarcasmlowestformofwit

It wasn't just wanting to show Dan I could do it without him. Neither was it the realisation that I'd come to that I *really* wanted to write this book, to let people know about all those who were lying almost forgotten in churchyards across this area. It was more like a re-emergence of a passion that I'd used to have, a bit like falling in love all over again with a man and remembering what it was I'd used to love about him. The words, once I sat down at the laptop, just kept flowing out of me, as though something had dammed them up and they'd been swirling around in a backwash of lost plots but were now rushing over the barrier and carrying all the detritus with them.

I didn't even make a coffee. Dan's crack about 'self-medication', whatever he'd meant by that, had stung and I wanted to demonstrate, even to myself, that I could work without it. So, fuelled by nothing but a packet of slightly soggy biscuits and half a bar of chocolate that I found doing duty as a bookmark, I positioned myself in the light which managed to ooze its way in through the window and wrote for the whole day.

When I looked up from the screen, eyes itching and my fingers tired, I was surprised to find that it was almost dark. I'd been assuming that the gradual closing in of the light had been my eyes focussing so hard on the laptop that my pupils had somehow frozen.

'I'm off to see Alex,' I announced to Daisy. 'For a meal.'

'Uh-huh.' She sounded distracted, as though she wasn't really listening. 'So, you've given our Daniel his marching orders, have you? Does he know he's "outta here"?'

'I think he can infer it from context.' I felt different too. Lighter. As though the words had been weighing me down and getting them out of my head had been enough to allow my body to rise from whichever depths the arrival of Dan had forced them to.

'Maybe. But you know what he's like. Or do you, Win? Do you really know what he might be capable of?'

'Once this book is done, it doesn't matter. I never need to have any contact with him again, and he can say and do what he likes, it won't matter.'

'It might.' Daisy's voice was small now. 'If he drags me into things. If he starts ... well, he could spread all kinds of stories, couldn't he?'

'He won't, Daze.' I suddenly wanted to hug my sister. 'Honestly. It's hard to explain but he seems a bit different now. A bit ... well, I was going to say "softer" but that's not really a word you can use for Dan, is it?'

A bit of a laugh. 'Nah. Even Dan's soft bits are firm. So, what does he seem?'

I thought. 'More understanding, I'd say. Somehow. A bit less condemnatory. Oh, this sounds stupid, it makes it sound like he was a cross between some hell-fire preacher and Jack Dee, but it's hard to explain. Like he's realised something. So, no, I don't think he'll come after you, Daze, not any more.'

'But he won't let it go, will he? He might be all new

"squidgy Dan" but he's still never going to understand *us*, is he?'

'Like I said, it doesn't matter. I'll get this done and then we never need to have anything to do with him again, okay?'

'Okay,' she said, sounding small, fragile. Once again, and with full force, I wished my sister wasn't so far away. She seemed to wish it too. 'Maybe ... after the book ... you'll come and see me?'

You smell of jasmine and joss sticks. Your hair is frizzy at the back but you wear hats on bad-hair-days and nobody notices. You have a scar on your wrist from when you broke it falling off Jack. Hugging you is like hugging a collection of well-wrapped pipe cleaners and it's like coming home to myself. Like I'm not quite complete without you ...

'I thought about it earlier – I was so tempted to just shut up the laptop and leave it all, but ...'

'Yeah, I know.' A laugh. 'Don't worry about it. I'll see you soon enough, Win.'

'And we'll have massive cocktails with umbrellas in!' It was what Daisy and I always did when we got together, drank cocktails with stupid names and unlikely ingredients until we were giggly-drunk. 'Better go and get changed for Alex.'

'Something sexy? How about that little blue dress? Never failed you, that dress.'

'Hmm. Maybe. Not sure I really want to go the "sexy" route. Something a bit more old-school, perhaps.'

'The black one then. With heels.'

'All right, oh fashion queen, I'll wear that one.' And, laughing, I went off to rummage through my suitcase to find the demure-yet-sensual black dress.

The effort of finding it, sponging off some miscellaneous stains and then ironing it was well worth it. Alex's face positively flickered with all the different emotions that the dress seemed to produce.

'Y-you l-look very, uh, well. Wh-whatever it is, y-you look v-very.'

'I'll take that as a compliment.' I walked into the flat, my heels making hollow noises on the oak boards. 'It smells lovely.'

'S-supermarket's f-finest again, I'm a-afraid.' He gave a rueful grin. 'Tried a r-recipe th-that Lucy gave me, b-but …' A shrug. 'Had to t-tip it outside. C-couldn't p-put it in the b-bin, I w-went to s-school with two of th-the bin men.'

He was clearly straight from the shower. His hair was dark with water and his hug, when he greeted me, smelled of soap and shaving gel. The soft, woven shirt was in evidence again too, over black jeans that made him look taller and even more toned in the thigh department.

'Wine?'

There were two glasses on the worktop. One already had half an inch of wine in it. 'What, no Scarlet to keep you from alcohol poisoning?'

'She's at M-Mum's.' Alex gave me an unfathomable look as he handed me a glass. 'Th-thought it was only f-fair.' He tilted the bottle and poured me a generous measure. I hoped he wasn't trying to get me drunk, although, with the way he looked tonight, drunk wouldn't be necessary. He looked what he was, fit, tanned from the outdoors and cute. His hair was starting to dry in the warmth of the flat and little curls were forming around the back of his neck. I found my eyes fixing on them when he turned to pour his own wine. 'Ch-ch-, oh bugger, bottom's up!'

I drank some wine, feeling surprisingly shy. Here I was, dressed up nicely, here he was, dressed and behaving like a grown-up without responsibilities. A tingle of arousal got sucker-punched down by something I couldn't analyse.

'You said Bobso had a surprise?' I said to distract both Alex and me from the way my mind was running.

'Y-yes.' Alex held out a hand. 'C-come and see.'

It seemed natural to take the offered hand and be led down the stairs, wobbling slightly with wine and heels, and out into the yard. This time Light Bulb wasn't hovering over the hutch, but a carrot jammed into the wire mesh fronting showed that Scarlet was still taking her responsibilities as a pet owner very seriously. Alex let go of my hand and flipped open the 'bedding' area of the hutch to reveal a slightly surprised-looking Bobso, surrounded by six miniature Bobsos in assorted colours, which ran, squeaking, into the other end of the hutch.

'Is that a guinea pig or an amoeba?'

Alex laughed. 'B-bobso is now Bobsina.' He bent down and looked at the host of piglets. 'Th-they c-can run as soon as th-they're b-born.' The hutch was fastened up and double-checked. 'W-wish humans c-could do th-that.'

'I bet Scarlet is delighted. It's like "buy one, get six free". Still, Dan did warn you.' Mentioning Dan's name felt odd, as though he was some kind of spectre at the feast, lurking around in the shadows. As though his name could invoke him.

'Y-yes. H-he did.' Alex's voice had a strange tone, almost as though he was also feeling Dan's presence. Then he grasped my hand again. 'C-come on. I d-don't want to w-waste another d-dinner. Local w-wildlife can only t-take so m-much.'

Back in the flat, even with the lighting turned down low

and the wine bottle sitting between us, I still kept expecting Scarlet to burst through the door at any moment. It made me hesitant whenever Alex and I made contact, either both reaching for the wine or fingers touching when we pulled at the garlic bread in the middle of the table. He hadn't heated it for quite long enough and the garlic butter was still solid, but such was the mood that I didn't want to point this out.

'Mr M-Moore told m-me to ask y-you to g-go in next week,' Alex said, looking down at his plate. It was apparently boeuf bourguignon, as interpreted by the local supermarket, and not bad as long as you didn't mind shallots like eyeballs bobbing to the surface when you poked it. 'F-Friday? To talk about wr-writing.'

'Friday's fine.' I poked a suspiciously hard lump and had another mouthful of wine. It was going to my head a bit and I realised that I hadn't eaten much all day. All week, if it came to that. In fact, when *had* I last eaten an actual meal? 'And I'm sorry I was a bit rude to you yesterday, by the way. I'm just ... Dan has a bit of history interfering in my life, like I've said, and when you said he'd been helping Scarlet, well ...' I forked some more food. 'I could just see it happening all over again.'

'Okay.' Alex cleared his plate. 'N-no talking about D-Dan. Agreed.'

So we talked about life in a small town in rural North Yorkshire, about Scarlet, about places we'd travelled to and things we'd seen. Alex had, apparently, always been a hard worker, dedicated to his stone masonry and then, on the death of his father, he'd inherited enough to buy the Old Mill and attempt to rebuild it.

'It is beautiful.' I raised my glass to the softly-burnished wood, glowing in the dim lighting. 'It's like something out of *Country Living* magazine.'

'W-when I started rebuilding it I w-was engaged,' Alex said, and I almost dropped my wineglass. Then I tried to compose my face, even though I could feel the blood flushing my cheeks. He noticed. 'I d-didn't always sh-shut myself away, W-Winter,' he said, with a half-smile. 'Used to b-be quite a p-player in the old d-days.' He took another drink. 'B-but shit happened and now ...' A shrug. 'N-now I'm a s-surrogate dad with a st-stammer.'

'Well, I did wonder how someone as ... well, how you'd managed to remain single for so long.' The wine was definitely going to my head now. 'Who were you engaged to? Anyone local? Oh, stupid question really, there doesn't seem to be any escape from Great Leys, unless there's a tunnel committee I don't know about.'

'L-Lucy.' Alex dropped his head. 'I w-was engaged t-to L-Lucy. B-but I was a sh-shit to her w-when Ell d-died. C-couldn't cope, y'see?' And now he met my eye with a look like a challenge. 'S-Scarl doesn't know. P-please d-don't tell her. Sh-she knows we d-dated, she r-remembers that b-but we never t-told her it went f-further.'

'She said that Mr Moore didn't like you! I did wonder.'

Alex gave a slightly shamefaced grin. 'S-Scarl thinks she kn-knows everything. B-but f-for goodness s-sake, she's only eight! Lucy g-got a b-bit ... I'd d-disappointed her. Sh-she married the l-l-local "tough g-guy" and w-went off to l-live on T-Teeside b-but ...' A shrug. 'Wh-when she c-couldn't s-stand any m-more she r-ran. C-came back h-home. B-but I'd n-never w-want S-Scarl to know th-that Ell d-d- ...' He stopped and obviously mentally rephrased. 'That t-taking on Scarl put a s-stop to my life as it w-was. Sh-she doesn't n-need that guilt, she's g-got enough on her p-plate.'

'But Lucy still likes you,' I said, softly. 'Well, she still fancies you, anyway.'

Alex grinned more widely and shrugged. 'It's a sm-small p-place,' he said. 'Not m-much competition.'

I laughed and drained my wine. As I put the glass back on the table, Alex's fingers touched mine and this time I didn't pull back. Before I knew it we were both standing, and he was sliding his hands into my hair, pulling my mouth in for a kiss that went deep, as though sharing his secret past life had released him from some kind of obligation.

My hands gripped his shoulders. He was solid, all the muscle from building, from lifting stone and working it were tense under my fingers. His mouth moved against mine, words spoken that I couldn't hear, then his lips were sliding along my jaw, up to my ear. 'C- come with m-me.'

Into the passageway, the opposite direction from Scarlet's room, and in through a door that he shut with his foot, our mouths joined again, and then our fingers came to the party too, and we were groping like a couple of teenagers who'd seen the films and wanted to find out what it was all about. His hands slid around the front of the black dress then down to ruck the hem and stroke my thighs, while I unbuttoned his shirt and let the fabulous firmness of those muscles come out to play.

'Are you s-sure?' Alex whispered as he encountered the edge of my rather nice knickers. Not that I'd dressed for this, but under the black dress anything else seemed like taking chips to the palace. 'It's o-okay if y-you want to st-stop.'

I just gave a small moan and let myself fall backwards onto the big bed.

Alex grinned a devilish grin and came with me, propping himself above my body. 'G-good,' he said, carefully lifting the dress up over my head, so I lay in my nice underwear and nothing else, feeling the cool of the air against my overheated skin. A quick moment and he was naked there beside me, all tan lines and bunched muscle, hair tightly-packed from the centre of his chest down over his stomach.

Dan's skin was smooth. He didn't touch me for a long time, just lay looking down at me, with starlight visible through the dormer window behind his head and somehow in his eyes at the same time. No words, just the weight of his gaze brushing my skin and the long stretch of his body beside mine. Then a whisper, something in a language I didn't know and a cool tongue drawing designs around my navel. A soft sense of understanding, as though we didn't need any words now.

Alex was suddenly heavy. His skin smelled strange, still of the soap and shaving foam, now with added wine, but there was something about it that was off. Wrong. Something about the way his muscles flexed under the sun-tinted skin of his chest. My body screamed and shut down and I found I was curling my nakedness away from him, hunching myself into a ball to remove myself from his touch.

'W-Winter?' Alex moved across the bed, touched my shoulder. 'Are y-you—?'

'No.' I stood up, keeping my back to him. 'I'm sorry, Alex.' Tears were bunching in my throat, biding their time. 'I thought … I'm sorry, I can't do this.' I pulled my dress from where it hung on the carved oak headboard and dragged it on, not even caring whether it was the right way round. 'Sorry.'

Alex stood up. He was still naked, but the desire was obviously ebbing from him. 'Hey,' he sounded worried. 'I th-thought …'

I gave a half-laugh. 'Oh, no, it's not you. No, you didn't misunderstand, I *did* want to. At least, I thought I did, but when it comes down to it ... I can't.' The tears were making good their threat, overspilling my lids and tipping over my skin, hot and humiliating. 'I don't know what happened.' A bitter edge made my voice catch. I couldn't work out where the tears were coming from; my body felt desiccated, devoid of any moisture at all, as though the cold wind from the moors had freeze-dried me where I stood. 'Sorry,' I sobbed and, holding the dress closed across the front because I'd put it on backwards and the trendy slit back was revealing my treacherous body to the world, I ran out of the room.

Alex caught up with me as I kicked my shoes back on in the living room. 'It's o-okay.' He had the sense to stop in the doorway, not try to approach me. 'R-really, W-Winter. It's okay.' He had a bit of the 'talking to Scarlet' tone in his voice, carefully soothing, trying not to provoke. 'It's m-me who's s-sorry. I sh-should have r-realised.'

'Nothing to "realise".' I tried to calm my voice, to keep the tears from retching through the words but humiliation and fear and confusion were spinning my head too fast for me to have any control over anything much. 'I just made a mistake. You're lovely, really you are, but—'

'B-but I'm not Daniel,' Alex said, with complete certainty.

'NO!' I shouted the word and it seemed to be absorbed by the wood, as though nature wanted me to retract. 'No, it's not that. It's not him. It's me, Alex. I'm ... things are ...'

Alex sat down at the table, still naked. He rested his elbows on it and put his head in his hands. 'I sh-shouldn't h-have got involved,' he said, quietly. 'M-my fault. D-Dan said you w-were *fragile*. I g-got carried away.' Then, with a touch more humour warming his tone, he added, 'Y-you're fucking g-gorgeous.'

Despite myself, I almost smiled. 'Thank you. And thank you for,' I motioned with one hand, the other still clutching at my dress, 'for not pushing it. You're a gentleman.'

'L-Lucy might d-disagree,' he said, still keeping his face covered with his hands. 'Dan—'

'Look, he's not ... what else did he say about me?'

Alex looked up now. 'He said there were th-things about you that I d-didn't know. Th-that you weren't qu-quite what you s-seemed to be. That you are c-clinically d-depressed and not really c-capable of making d-decisions.'

'And I am going to kill him,' I muttered through tight lips. 'He's wrong. He's got himself messed up and he's trying to transfer a lot of stuff he thinks onto me. It's *Dan* that has the problems ... did he tell you about his sister? That she got injured crashing his car?'

Alex nodded. 'Y-yes.'

'Well, then.' I relaxed my hand a fraction and Alex's eyes swung back to my body as the dress revealed a little more than I wanted revealed. But, to his credit, he soon pulled his eyes back up to mine and he made no move to come out from behind the table. 'Dan's got problems and it kind of manifests in a personality disorder where he transfers his feelings onto someone else. It helps him to cope with life.'

'But y-you have to admit h-he was r-right about y-you. H-having problems? Otherwise ...' He made a movement with his hands to indicate both of us and our various states of undress. '... w-what just h-happened?'

'I changed my mind. That's all. I thought I wanted ... wanted sex. Then I realised I didn't. It's not you, Alex, you're lovely, but ...' I stopped and shook my head. 'It wasn't right.'

To my relief Alex smiled. 'O-okay.' Then he looked down and the rueful expression was back. 'Y-you'd b-better get back. I h-have to get in the sh-shower with some s-soap and a good imagination.'

'Thanks.' I thought about giving him a cheek-kiss goodbye, but he was still stark naked, aroused and not a saint, so I wiped my eyes on the back of my hand and smiled. 'Maybe I'll see you around?'

'Y-you'd b-better.' Alex stayed sitting, very firmly. 'S-Scarl will w-want to sh-show you the new f-family.'

With my coat covering the dress and my mouth still full of the taste of Alex, I walked home through the chilly, empty streets of Great Leys.

Chapter Twenty

From: NMoore@LeysschoolNYCC.org
To: WinterGregoryAuthor@teddymail.com
Subject: Talk to pupils about writing
Dear Miss Gregory

I'm thrilled that you have offered to come and talk to the children of Great Leys School about your writing career. As Mr Hill has, I hope, informed you, we would be delighted to see you on Friday afternoon, from 12.30 onwards. Please come to Reception and you will be escorted into school. As you write for adults, we trust that you will keep in mind the young age of your audience in school and understand that sales of your book within the classroom would not be appropriate.

Thank you for giving up your valuable time in the interests of education.

Yours

Neil Moore

Head Teacher, Great Leys Primary School

From: AlexHillStone@wolmail.com
To: WinterGregoryAuthor@teddymail.com
Subject: I don't know. Embarrassment?

I know, I know. Believe me, I feel like a total tit right now. All that bollocks I spouted before about 'taking things slowly' and 'just being friends' and one glass of wine and I threw that lot over the wall. See why I don't drink often? I pushed it too far, pushed *you* too far. I suppose … I suppose what it was I wanted you to know is just how hot you really are; I never meant it to go to the wire like that.

You're hot. You are a totally lovely woman, and I think hormones just got the better of both of us for a while, didn't they? And, yes, I totally get why you pulled back on me. I should never have even got that far and feel like a complete bastard for letting things get out of hand the way they did, especially if it compromises anything. What we've already got is enough, honestly; your friendship is worth so much to me and to Scarl, so if I've done anything to jeopardise that then I might as well gnaw off my own balls right now. It wasn't right, I knew it before I started, know you don't feel 'that way' as the problem pages coyly have it, about me. I can see it in your eyes and, hey, don't worry about it, not a big deal, like I said, friendship is more valuable than any amount of meaningless banging when you've got a small child in the mix.

Ultimately. Point of all this rambling. You did the right thing. I was a mindless, cock-driven bastard last night, and I am so glad, in this cold light of day, that you stopped me. I like to think I behaved with dignity and grace under pressure, but you know, if you never want anything to do with me again, I'll do my best to come to terms with it, but please, *please*, Winter, don't.
Alex

I got up late from a night of bad dreams. Dreams in which I'd been in bed with Alex but turned over to find he'd morphed into one of the faceless, nameless men that I'd slept with until I'd met Dan. And then he'd become Dan, teasing smile, dark eyes and open arms and the metal bedstead had clanged like a bell with all the sighing and turning over I'd done, but I fell into proper, dreamless sleep around dawn.

The laptop was still on. I crouched in front of it wrapped in the duvet from the bed and checked. Yep, all the work from yesterday was still there. And still *good*. I raised my eyebrows at it and tried not to notice the slight slick of stubble burn that adorned my chin from last night. Alex might have thought he'd shaved but he had the 'outdoors' approach to being clean-shaven rather than 'city man', which was so smooth I always suspected they slept in a silk bag.

Yep. Words, lots of them. Tentatively I sat down and doubled the duvet around me while I typed a few more sentences, and the next thing I knew the light was vanishing from the window and there was someone knocking at the door.

'Margaret, hello. Hi, Scarlet.' Margaret's frock *du jour* was a slightly startling bird-print but as I was wrapped in a duvet and still had bed hair, I really wasn't one to start pointing fingers today.

'Hello, Winter. Are you poorly?' Margaret looked me up and down. I couldn't return the favour without it looking as though her dress was taking flight, so I just smiled.

'Working. Got a bit caught up.'

'Bobso had babies,' Scarlet said, sounding sulky. Her school uniform was creased and there was a small rip in the hem of her chequerboard dress. 'But Granny says we have to give them away.'

'Well,' I said, gamely, 'I'll have one. And I bet you won't have any trouble finding takers if you ask around at school. They're so cute, just like miniature guinea pigs!'

'They *are* miniature guinea pigs,' Margaret said, stepping down into the living room and giving my biscuit-strewn workstation a sideways look. 'If you think about it.'

'I suppose they are. Would you like a biscuit, Scarlet?'

Scarlet accepted a HobNob, still slightly sulkily, and sat on a chair to eat it. 'Alex showed you the babies,' she said, her mouth looking as though only the biscuit was preventing it from pouting. 'It's not fair. *I* wanted to show you Bobso's babies!'

Margaret did the 'adult over the child's head' face. 'I told him not to tell her, but Alex has this "honesty" thing. Very admirable, of course, but I dread to think what would have happened if his father and I had been honest with him at times,' she said. 'But it's upset Scarlet dreadfully.'

Scarlet's lip was wobbling now, despite the HobNob. 'You're *my* friend, Winter. It's not fair Alex showing you Bobso and the babies – Bobso is mine too!'

Well, she did have a point. And Alex had sort of used Bobso as a lure to get me round there, so I was conceding that she was entitled to be a bit cross. Blimey, this was a tricky one. I gathered the duvet more closely around me. 'I'm sorry, Scarlet. I should have let you show them to me, of course. But what about Daniel? Has he seen them yet?'

Scarlet brightened a little bit. 'No! He was out yesterday so I didn't get to tell him, and he didn't come back to Granny's last night.'

I felt a tiny flicker inside me. *Where did you go, Dan? Back to London?*

'I told you, Scarlet, he went down to Lincoln, he'll be back later tonight.' Margaret looked relieved. 'Maybe you could show him the babies then.'

'Can I show them to you as well, Winter?' Scarlet finished the biscuit and the prospect of having someone new to appreciate Bobso's offspring had clearly cheered her up.

I don't think being in the same place as Dan and Alex is a great idea at the moment. There may be some kind of critical mass achieved. 'Maybe another day. It can't be good for Bobso to have lots of people poking around with

214

her when they've only just arrived,' I said, thinking fast inside my duvet-sausage. 'Show them to Dan and I'll come and see them … how about Friday? After I've talked to you all about writing.'

Scarlet bounced. 'Mr Moore said he was going to ask you to come on Friday. We had an assembly about it this morning and we're to think of sensible questions to ask you!'

'Just don't ask Winter if she earns as much as J. K. Rowling,' Margaret said, darkly. 'Mr Park asked a visiting author that at one of the book club meetings, and there was "an incident". Probably partly to blame for his wee problem, now I come to think of it.'

'Where's Light Bulb?' It suddenly occurred to me why Scarlet looked a bit less occupied than usual. 'Did you have to leave him at home again today?'

Margaret and Scarlet exchanged a look. Margaret's expression was nine-tenths exasperation, while Scarlet cast her eyes down after a few moments' contact with her grandmother. 'Lucy is fixing him again,' she said very quietly at last. 'His head came loose.'

A sudden memory of Light Bulb's increasingly-lopsided and psychotic grin. *Lucy mends him, does she? I thought it was Alex trying out some amateur embroidery skills. Lucy must be fond of Scarlet then, which bodes well if they ever try a rapprochement.*

'Scarlet was using him as a weapon,' Margaret semi-hissed at me. I had no idea why she bothered. Scarlet had no hearing problems that I knew about.

'Maybe things will get a bit better when everyone at school knows that you really *do* know a writer,' I suggested. 'Then if anyone is horrible to you, you can tell them that I'll make them a baddie in my next book.'

Scarlet's incoming smile went a bit ragged. 'But you write about dead people,' she said. 'Can you make dead people into baddies? Or ... or ...' Sudden enthusiasm crashed in. 'You could write about evil ghosts!'

'I blame children's television,' Margaret said. 'When Alex and Ellen were young it was all *Blue Peter* and *Doctor Who*, now it's drugs and evil monsters and whatnot. She's eight, she shouldn't know about evil ghosts!'

Scarlet and I shared a suppressed grin of complicity. When Daisy and I had been eight we'd been given an *Oxford Book of Ghost Stories* and had happily scared one another stupid for the next eighteen months with tales based around those we read. 'I don't know. They're good preparation for when life really does get scary,' I said without thinking.

Margaret sniffed and, on her bosom, a flock of flamingos took off. 'Let's get you home, Scarlet,' she said, holding out her hand. 'Alex will be wondering where we've got to.'

I waved them goodbye, Scarlet now looking a lot more cheerful than she had when they'd arrived.

![Facebook icon]

Facebook

Winter Gregory Author Page

Well, finally the new book is nearly finished. Here's a couple of pictures of some of the gravestones that are going to be featuring this time round – some fascinating stories have come out of being this far north.

336 people like this.

Comment: Cerys Grey LOVE those pictures! Spooky

17 people like this

Comment: J D Roxburgh When's the book out?

I saw his reflection in the glass before I saw him. A dark head, broken and distorted by the patterned glass in the door, seeming to be staring down at the ground. He hadn't knocked, but I opened the door anyway.

'Hello, Dan.'

'Hey.'

He looked a little bit better today, and I didn't know whether that made me glad or not. 'Saw your Facebook message and I reckoned the coast was probably clear for me to drop by.' A pause and then he looked up. 'You're done, then?'

'Yep.' Even I could hear the pride in my voice. 'It's going to need a bit of tidying up, obviously, but ... yes, I think it's pretty good.'

He stayed where he was, making no attempt to come inside. 'Okay.' Then, words coming out with a bit more of the 'Dan-style' about them, 'Look, I'm sorry. About everything. I never meant it to go this way, I never meant you to ... I never meant to hurt you, Winter.' Now he looked up and met my eye. 'Seriously. You are ... you *were* something special to me, and now the book is done and it's finally all over and everything ...' He tailed off and his gaze slid back down to the step at his booted feet. 'I just wanted it said. No unfinished business, you know?'

My body felt curiously heavy. As though the finality of his words had a weight that they'd laid on me, as though this ending was a thing of gravity that could be passed from one person to another. 'Do you want to come in?' was all I could think of to say.

'Probably not a good idea. I mean, I should ...' This

hesitancy wasn't like Dan either. It was almost as if another man stood in front of me, one who looked like Daniel, who spoke with his voice but whose thoughts didn't run like mercury through a head filled with impossible ideas but rather moved more at human speed. 'This is it, Winter. Email me the manuscript, I'll work on it back in London and get the edits to you, you never need to see me again. We're done.'

There was a dryness in my mouth and a fizzing sort of grey inside my head, almost as though I'd had a shock. *Dan's going. But Dan was always going to go. You've done what you said you'd do, the book is finished and now so are you and Dan as any kind of entity. Connection broken. It's what you wanted, isn't it?*

'Can I ask a favour? Before you go.' *Before it's really all over.* My fingers were tight on the door handle, sweating around the brass knob so that it slid like soap under my palm.

A faint smile from him now. A lightening of that terrible darkness that had drawn his brows down over his eyes and made his mouth look as though he'd recently eaten something mouldy. 'Anything I can do, Win, you know me, always ready to help ...' He tailed off as though he thought his words might be misinterpreted and cleared his throat. 'Yeah, I mean, if I can.'

'Come with me tomorrow to Scarlet's school. I'm giving my Authorly Talk to the kids there, and I'm not really sure that I'm enough to hold their attention. If you come and talk about books and what an editor does and everything, together we might raise Scarlet's stock enough to make sure that she never gets bullied again.' The words came in an unconsidered rush, almost bypassing my brain on their way to my mouth.

He put an arm up against the brickwork of the house, leaned against it. All the lines of his body relaxed and the smile on his face became softer. 'Wow. You want me there? Or did they ask you to bring me?'

It's an idea I've only just had, I didn't say. 'I just thought ... Scarlet likes you, she'd love you to be there too, and I'm not a hundred per cent sure that I've got enough material to talk to kids for an hour, I'm more used to speaking to adults and everything. I'm sure the school will let you in, they're all geared up for having one person, so I'm sure they could stretch to both of us on the premises, and you could maybe give them a bit of an idea of what an editor does, in case any of them are ever misguided enough to want to go into writing as a career.' Inside my head I tried to unpack what I'd said. Had I over-justified? Or had I made a reasonable case for it being a good idea to have my editor there as backup for my talk?

'Has she shown you the baby guinea pigs yet?'

As though he hadn't declined my previous invitation to come inside and had instead been waiting for some magic word, Dan stepped past me and down into the living room, where he slouched down onto one of the chair-shaped items of furniture. 'Oh, yes.' Feet kicked up onto the mantelpiece. 'Seen them, named them, we've even *brushed* them, even though I've told her that Bobsina will take care of all their personal hygiene needs.' A flash of animation. 'Maybe Alex should have got her something a bit more robust for a pet. Alsatian, Shetland pony, elk, something that way.'

'She's got a lot of love to give, that's all.' I went through into the kitchen and put the kettle on. 'But Alex is afraid for her. I think he's terrified of something happening to her, otherwise why not just get her riding lessons and have done with it?'

'Insight, you're making progress,' Dan said, enigmatically. 'Tea, one sugar, loads of milk. Why don't you take her riding? I'm sure Alex would trust you, after all, you and he are a bit tight, aren't you?'

I stuck my face above the kettle to let the steam give me a reason for the hot blush. 'We're friends, that's all.'

'Seriously?' Dan sounded as though he'd made a face. 'Thought he'd be your sort of thing these days, all shirt off and muscles and the stammer … buff and flawed, isn't that the kind of thing that all women dream of?'

A momentary image of Alex's naked body covering mine, a firmness of flesh so unfamiliar. 'We're just friends,' I said again.

Dan was quiet, and when I came back in carrying two mugs of tea I saw that he'd moved to sit in front of my laptop and was reading the manuscript from the screen. He'd got his 'editor's' head on. I could tell from the way his lips occasionally moved as he tried a phrase out, or twitched a cheek in a wince at a misspelling or casual use of grammar. I started to drink my tea, trying not to watch him through the spiralling vapour over the mug, but Dan snagged at my eyes like a rough piece of silk on a nail. His angular face with its cat-like cheekbones, those dark eyes like wormholes into another, more chaotic, universe. So capable of a sort of existential wildness and yet able to turn himself into a listening stillness when it was needed. A man built of mercury, of beating hearts and of lead.

'This is good.' He finally looked across at me. 'Really. Think you might have outdone *Book of the Dead* with this one.' Without even seeming to locate it consciously he reached out and picked up the mug of tea, draining it down in one long gulp. 'Knew you could do it, if I wound you up enough. Mail it over. I'll come to the school tomorrow and then head back to London in the evening, get this printed up and give it a proper once-over.' A tilt of the head. 'What're your plans now, then?'

I don't know. I couldn't see any further than finishing the book. I've been living here in a stasis field, every day the same in this unchanging place, surrounded by landscape that's been the same since the Ice Age gave up and went home, and I managed to convince myself that this was all there was.

'I ...' My hand shook a little and my mug dribbled some tea down the side. 'I'm not sure.'

'Okay. Well, keep me up to date, girl, because we're going to need you for publicity come Christmas – winding up to the final push when the book comes out. Don't leave the country, hey?' Dan pushed away from the table and stood up, looking for a moment, in his whirling coat, like the centre point of a tornado. 'I'm glad you got there in the end, Winter,' he said, softly. 'Knew you could do it.'

He reached out a hand and took mine, turning it over so that the tattoo flashed on his wrist and my fingers curled, unresisting, into his palm. With his other hand he removed the mug from my grasp and put it on the table. 'This is an effing stupid idea,' he said, quietly, 'but, hell's teeth, I have missed you so much.' Then he stepped a fraction nearer, caught my chin and held it while he lowered his lips down to mine.

A fraction of a second of the taste of him was all it took to plummet me backwards through time to the first time we'd kissed, sitting on the Embankment in London in the chilly spring sunshine. That had been a kiss of hope, of anticipation; a cautious getting-to-know kiss that had the brevity of melting ice creams built in. This kiss was its diametric opposite, a kiss of farewell, of longing. Of nostalgia for something that would never be again, a sad kind of sweetness. When Dan stood away again without speaking, I felt the tears choking their way up from the bottom of my throat.

He didn't even look back, just opened the door and walked out onto the crowded pavement and was gone in a flicker of black, as though the pale sun couldn't reach him, wherever he was.

Chapter Twenty-One

✉

From: DanBekener @ShyOwlPublishing.co.uk
To: BethanyAnnBekener@wolmail.com
<u>Subject: An ending</u>
I did it, Beth. It's over. Just a few loose ends to tidy, then I'm over
her. I am going to stay up north for a bit though, away from the
cities, to get my head clear. I know you said to try, to fight for
what I wanted but there's no point any more.

I can be all cool about it now, but it still feels like someone's
put their hand down my throat and is pulling my heart out.
Love
Danny Boy

B

A.N. Editor Blog
Finality. It's one of those words that looks different written down
– I always want to pronounce it finnallity in my head, like it's a
disease of fish or something. But in this case I'm convincing
myself it's a good thing. It's kinda like books, for anyone who's
still following me over here for writing advice. Endings are
always hard. Saying goodbye to those characters you've learned
to love, to identify with, sometimes there's this compulsion to
keep them around, keep the story going even when you know
it's reached a natural end. Even the ending of something you
didn't want is still a change, still having to pull back from the
spiral of chaos into movement in another direction, and the
ending of something you'd hoped would be more … well, yeah,
that one's a bitch.

But a proper ending, one with closure, that's different. If you can give a book, like a relationship, a decent send-off, observe all the proper rites and practices, somehow it makes it all less bitter. No one should ever walk away with unfinished business, and now I've managed to round my business off, ended my story. It's over, but it's decently over. I only ever wanted to help, to be there, to be *good* for her and in wanting that I let her in that little bit too far. Forgot to protect myself on the fall, so the landing when it came hit me harder than it should have, but now … now I reckon we're both on the rise. But separately.

So, yeah. Closure. Achieved. Not, maybe, what I wanted or planned, but for the best.

Daniel Bekener @EditorDanB
@WinterGAuthor New book out in June, mystery and graveyards @ShyOwlPublishing

Daniel Bekener @EditorDanB Sometimes this job is just too much

I sat in Mr Moore's office, with my bottom squeezed between rigid metal arms on a child-sized seat. I'd chosen to wear a wraparound dress with my hair loose today, so as not to look too much like another teacher, but from my reflection in the glass-fronted trophy cabinet I looked more like a witch who's had her broomstick stolen.

I stared through the window over a muddied field with battered goalposts and two lunchtime supervisors. These were ladies wearing unflattering tabards and a nursery-aged child attached to one leg, obviously trying to keep control over youthful border disputes with about as much success as people trying to round-up clouds. Beside me, on what was obviously an equally uncomfortable and undersized seat, sat Dan. He'd tried to make himself comfortable by tucking his legs as far under the chair as they would go and it made him look painfully perched, like a raven that's just eaten a golf ball.

'Do you think he'll be long?' he whispered out of the corner of his mouth. 'Only I'm getting cramp.'

'Shouldn't think so. He's only gone to take a telephone call, not marshall an OFSTED inspection.'

'Why, in chuff's name, do they not have adult-sized chairs?' Dan wriggled. 'I'm gonna be wearing this thing like an arse-cage.'

I looked at him, sitting there with his knees almost up against his chest, his hair tidy today although it still made him look a bit like a half-hearted punk, and the omnipresent coat curled around his slouched body as though he was being swallowed very slowly by a black python. My chest felt suddenly heavy. *So, this is it. The last time you'll ever be bothered by Daniel. Okay, he'll be around somewhere in the background, maybe a smile at a library talk or a cup of coffee fetched before a radio interview, but never like this again. Never so close that you can smell his skin, the dusty vanilla smell that makes you feel hungry for a food you've never tasted, or watch the way his tattoo appears and vanishes from under a cuff like a magic trick.*

I tore my gaze away and let it focus back out of the window again. 'We were early. Shouldn't think he wants to fetch the kids in any sooner than he has to. Look at them out there, it's like a warning against the dangers of e-numbers.'

There was a knot of children over at the field's boundary. One was Scarlet, I could tell from the fact that Light Bulb was bobbing about in their midst like a tourguide's umbrella. Within seconds they were ranged along the fence between school property and the field beyond, where two horses grazed, Light Bulb now propped against the rails.

'Just energy and enthusiasm.' Dan stretched and stood up. His chair fell back to the floor with a heavy clonk. 'It'll wear off soon enough, they've still got adolescence to get through, and a life of work and clock watching to look forward to.'

My mind flashed to the graveyard, remembering all those graves of those who had never got past childhood. All those who'd never had the chance to get bored with their jobs or disillusioned with life. Names which were now just stone-carved curios for the idle passer-by to wonder at, but had once been attached to people who'd run and skipped and yelled, hugged and cried and laughed.

'Win?' Dan bent in front of me. 'Hey.' The back of his hand rubbed gently along my cheek, wiping tears from my skin. 'Don't.'

The office door opened and Mr Moore arrived, sighing deeply. 'Sorry to have kept you waiting, but ...' Another sigh. 'The children will be coming in in just a minute, shall we go through?'

'Party face on, kiddo,' Dan whispered, holding out a hand to help me stand. As he pulled me upright I half-turned. Embarrassed by the tears which had caught me unawares, and overwhelmed by my sudden urge to lean into Dan's shoulder and let them fall, I didn't want to look into his face and see – what? Pity? Or the wavering fear that I wasn't going to be up to publicising the book? To give myself an excuse not to face him, and a few moments to let any redness of my eyes diminish, I gazed out of the window. A little girl, almost certainly Scarlet, was now standing on the top rail of the fence, the lower rails were occupied by half a dozen other children who looked as though they were encouraging her.

'It must be nice to have such a lot of space for the children to run about in,' I said. Meaningless small talk but it gave my throat a chance to loosen, and the tears time to head back to where they hid, permanently tangled among memories.

Mr Moore made a snorting noise. 'It's hard work. The farmer who owns the fields beyond used to have cows, but now he's put horses in there and it's a full-time job trying to stop the kids from feeding them.' He sighed yet again. 'I should have gone into dentistry, like my mother wanted. Right, let's get on, shall we?'

'Yes, I …' and at that moment a flash of movement on the fence made my stomach draw down into itself with a kind of foreboding. '*Shit*!' I turned and nearly fell over the small chair. 'We have to get out there.'

'Winter …' Dan's hand moved towards my arm but I'd seen it coming and dodged, made it out of the office door before either of the men had moved.

I heard Mr Moore say, 'Is she all right?' and Dan's murmured answer as I hesitated in the hallway beyond, getting my bearings, then ran down the school corridor towards the far end, where I could see a door out onto the playground, my stomach drawing tight against my ribs with the sick feeling of impending disaster. Then they were both coming after me, Dan calling my name on a rising tone that told me he thought I'd finally lost it, finally flipped into action, and the speed with which he was coming told me that he was terrified which way that action was going to end.

'It's Scarlet!' I called back over my shoulder, wrenching

open the door and flying out onto the tarmac playground, scattering footballers and skippers, who, clearly scenting some kind of drama, began chasing behind me, so that I headed an arrow formation of running people out onto the slippery mud of the field. My hair blew forward and into my eyes and my mouth, my carefully-selected-to-go-with-the-outfit boots spiked into the ground and slowed me, until I was lunging forwards in what felt like slow motion.

'Scarlet!' I shouted once, but only two of the girls at the fence turned round. One of the horses, bored enough to have come over to talk to the children, had its head over the rails now and, as I ran, I saw the terrifying sight of Scarlet swinging her way over the top of the sturdy railings and dropping onto the back of the horse, where she perched for a triumphant second. We were close enough now to hear her cry of 'See? See, I *told* you I could ride!'

I slithered to a halt, about five metres from the fence, everyone behind me coming to a stop at the same time in a sticky sound of cloying earth. 'Scarlet, you need to get off *now*.' I panted the order and began a slow, pacing approach, not wanting to startle the horse, a chestnut with the dished face of an Arab, its head held high now as it registered the sudden weight upon its back. 'Just slide down.'

One of the lunchtime supervisor ladies gave a stifled moan, but it was the only sound. Although there must have been close to sixty children and half a dozen adults crowded onto the slimy pitch at my back, the silence was unnatural. In front, Scarlet looked at me between the horse's ears. 'I said I could ride. And I'm riding, aren't I, Winter?'

Flick went those ears. *Please let it be a docile old beast,*

228

a schoolmaster, a companion horse for something more flighty. Please, please let her just slither down and end up with no more than muddy knees. 'You're not allowed over there. Mr Moore will be really cross.' I tried to appeal to the group's fear of teacherly reprisals.

'Scarlet wanted to.' A defiant girl with the rippled blonde hair and clean designer-label shoes that shouted that she had an aspiring mother. 'It was her idea.'

'Please, Scarlet. Yes, you've proved that you can ride, now please get down. If you get down I'll make Alex get you proper riding lessons.' I was nearly at the fence now. I could smell the hot, sour smell of horse-sweat and pounded grass from the paddock beyond overlaid with waxy canvas from the rugs the horses wore against the encroaching winter. So close that I could almost lay a hand on the Arab's neck, keeping my voice level and soothing, unalarming. 'And maybe, now he's come to terms with you having a pet, maybe when you're older he'll let you have a pony.'

'*Really?*' And Scarlet must have moved too sharply, or dug a heel against the horse's side because it peeled away from the fence, head up in fright. Ears flat to its head it spun into the centre of the field, Scarlet trying to crouch, both arms grasping out and trying to catch hold of the rug around its shoulders for something to hold onto. The horse put in two tremendous bucks, the first sent Scarlet slithering sideways, almost joining her hands around the horse's neck in an attempt to stay on top; the second flicked her into the air and she landed with a sound that made my heart give a heavy sick beat, spreadeagled face down on the tussocky grass.

I leaped over the fence, ignoring the bile that soured my breath and ran to where Scarlet lay. Bent down but didn't dare touch her. Behind me there was a sound of children shouting and crying, released from the immobility of apprehension by shock and fear and Dan's voice very calm and capable apparently calling an ambulance on his mobile.

'Scarlet?' I whispered, but she was clearly unconscious, smaller somehow in the middle of all this green, hunched with her arms bent awkwardly underneath her. 'Oh God.'

Dan came over the fence. 'They'll be here in five minutes,' he said, peeling off his coat and laying it carefully over the fragile little figure. 'Don't touch her.'

Mr Moore was suddenly there, a competent force to be reckoned with. He crouched down and laid a hand against the side of Scarlet's neck. 'She has a pulse. She's alive.' The note of relief in his voice wasn't just that of a teacher worried about Health and Safety policy and legal ramifications, but of a man who cared. 'She's alive,' he repeated.

My mouth was dry and I could feel the buzzing in the back of my head start to move to my ears but I fought it away. Kept my breathing even, matched it to the movement I could see in Scarlet's huddled back so I breathed with her, as though my effort of will could keep oxygen moving in both of us. In. Out. Shallow, but regular. A child was screaming somewhere, but there were scuffling sounds and low, careful voices as adults came to take control, moving the audience away towards the school. I didn't take my eyes off the little shape in the mud and the hoof-marked grass. Stayed low, so my body half-hunched over hers, as though my shadow could drive away any injuries.

'Winter?' Dan's voice seemed much further away than it should. He was crouching next to me, I could feel his hand on my shoulder. 'The ambulance is on its way.'

'I could see it happening,' and my voice sounded as though I was still back there. 'I couldn't stop it.'

'It's okay. It wasn't your fault.'

A drumming of hooves as the horse circled in, panicked by all the activity and still alarmed from Scarlet's sudden appearance and disappearance by the sideways set of his ears. I looked up and met its rolling eye. 'Can you make sure he doesn't trample her?' My voice sounded small, as though there wasn't enough breath for words and to keep Scarlet breathing. In. Out. The tiny movement that was the expansion of her lungs.

'Winter.' Dan's hand again, on my arm this time. 'Come over here.' Gentle pressure, but I pushed him away.

'No! I have to stay! I have to keep her breathing!'

But Dan was made of metal now. No longer flesh and bone and kindness, he dragged me towards the fence. 'The ambulance is here, they need space to get her out. Come on, Win, take it easy.' He cupped his hands either side of my face, forced my head up so that I was looking at him rather than the figures now on the grass either side of Scarlet's body. 'Come on, look at me. Look at me, Winter, hush now.' Soothing words delivered at a steady, even rate as though he were calming an animal. 'Ssshh. They're getting her to the hospital now, they'll do everything they can there. Better away out of this field, yeah?'

I didn't really register him coming in close, I was still shocked into perceiving images in a kind of blur which meant nothing. But he was right up against me, the fabric of his shirt silken against my face as he walked me into an embrace, the warmth of his body taking some of the chill from my bones and the way he locked his arms tight around me helped to steady some of the shivers that were rocking the length of my spine. 'I need … I need to be there at the hospital …'

'Yeah, 's okay, we'll sort this.' Dan's voice was an echo in my head. I heard him speak to someone over his shoulder. 'I'll drive over behind the ambulance. Nah, we're not family but there are reasons. She needs to be there, I think, for her sanity.'

'Alex,' I murmured, as the shakes spread to my legs and gravity increased its hold on the rest of me, trying to pull me down to the earth. Dan increased his hold.

'Mr Moore is on that. Lucy's going round to fetch him.'

'She fell, Dan. One minute she was there and everything was all right and the next minute she was on the ground.' My breath was catchy little snags in my throat, not enough to live on. 'And there was nothing I could do.' He was holding my entire weight now as the earth sucked at me, wanting me to join all those bodies under those stones beneath the dark shroud of soil in those graveyards.

'Winter.' His voice was sharp. 'Concentrate. This is Scarlet. She's young and the young tend to be bouncy, so stop seeing the worst in the situation. Come on, they're taking her to Newcastle, the Royal Victoria or somewhere, and we need to follow the ambulance because I have no effing idea how to get there otherwise.' Cautiously he removed his support until I was standing alone. 'Alex is going to be destroyed if anything happens to that little girl,' he said, half to himself. 'You need to keep the party face going just a bit longer, can you do that?'

I took a deep breath. 'I need to talk to Daisy.'

'Not now.' He snapped the words.

'Dan, I *need* to.' My sister would talk sense. She'd tell me that Scarlet was going to be fine, that the hospital would be able to fix her. Or maybe she wouldn't. Maybe she'd say that nature had to take its course, that perhaps Scarlet was unfixable.

'Later.' His voice had softened. 'Later, Win. You can speak to her when we get to the hospital, when we've got an idea of what's happening, okay? Now, come on, because that ambulance isn't going to wait and I went to Newcastle once and it confused the hell out of my GPS.' He smiled, and when I saw the smile I realised how hard this was for him. Not just what had happened to Scarlet, but my wanting Daisy. *Even now* – I could almost hear him say it – *even now you'd rather turn to your sister than to me.*

I let him lead me out to the road and we got into his car, starting up as the ambulance passed us with its lights flashing. The sight made me feel sick.

Chapter Twenty-Two

Daniel Bekener @EditorDanB
In the hospital hoping for the best.

From: DanBekener@ShyOwlPublishing.co.uk
To: GregTurner@ShyOwlPublishing.co.uk
Subject: Relocation

Sorry, mate, going to be a bit held up. There's been an accident, we're just waiting for news now. I'll be heading back to town soon as we know what's happening.

   Want to ask a quick favour – can you put the word out and see if anyone up this end of the world is hiring editors? I know there's somewhere in Newcastle – it's about 40 miles from here to there. I mean, not to spring this on you, but I'm thinking of, maybe, taking some more time up here. There's this kid, she's the one who's been in the accident, and I've got quite fond of her. Whatever happens with Winter and that's not looking good, mate, I mean she's good for turning the book in – I've had a quick read through and I think we could be sitting on a gold mine there – personally though she's a mess but I might stick around up here anyway. I can still work for Shy Owl, I mean, come on, you don't need my face around the office, just mail me the stuff! I just think it's about time I started to think about a future, and here is as good a place as any. I can be down with Beth in a couple of hours on the train if she needs me. Done it a couple of times from here, it's fine.

I'll be coming back to sort stuff out, maybe rent out the flat, check in, start the publicity machine up for Winter's book, and then ... think I just need a complete change, you know?
Dan

'We're just waiting,' I whispered. 'Alex and Margaret are in with the doctor now. She's got to be all right, Daze, she's *got* to.'

I glanced quickly over my shoulder to where Dan was sprawled across three plastic chairs in the waiting area. He'd draped his coat over himself and closed his eyes but I had the horrible feeling that he was awake and listening.

'You have to stay strong, Winnie, you know that. You can't fall apart now.'

'I know that. I'm ... I'm trying, but it's hard. It's ... she's so little. So frail. All those little bones, like she's just straws and skin, and it's not *fair*, Daze!'

My sister was quiet for a moment. 'Okay. Okay, yes, it's hard, she's a little girl and you are very fond of her and you're allowed to be upset.'

I blew out a breath that sounded too loud in this unnaturally hushed place. A low table held old copies of women's magazines, scattered as though bad news had washed over them like a tide. 'Poor Alex. He's devastated, and Margaret looks as if she's aged about forty years.'

'Yeah, you think it's hard for *you*. He's got it tougher, poor bloke. And what about Dan?' Daisy sounded wistful. Not sad, exactly, but definitely melancholy. 'It must bring it all back, his sister being injured and everything. Being in a hospital, waiting for news ...'

I looked over at Dan again. He'd given up the pretence of sleeping now and swivelled his body so that he slouched on a single chair. He was rubbing the chaos tattoo with the tip of a finger and staring at the wall as though his eyes couldn't take much more.

'Yes,' I said. 'It must.'

Talking to Daisy was calming me. She was sympathetic but everything she said was right, even about Daniel.

'You sound as though you care, Winnie.' Her tone was light, but I wasn't fooled. 'I mean, I don't want to bring that up when you're all distressed and stuff but remember. That's all. Just remember.'

I'd never seen Dan so upset as that night on the bridge. Crying into the wind, leaning over the parapet so I wouldn't see the tears, but I could hear them in his voice, see the pain in every line of his body as he made me choose. And now that man is sitting nearby, more pain, different pain, dragging at his limbs, pulling at his face as though grief has its own gravity. A shared pain now, not each of you in a separate cell of agony but together in a united agony of suspense and fear. 'I do. And I wonder if I didn't—'

A movement down the corridor, an opening door and Dan swung to his feet. 'Winter,' he said, softly, 'they're coming.'

'Bye, Daze.'

'Yes.'

And then Alex and Margaret were coming in. 'Ap-apparently the n-next few hours are c-c-critical.' Alex stumbled onto a chair and put his head in his hands. 'If sh-she comes round, then ...' He stopped talking, his words lost not to the stammer but to branching futures.

'We just have to wait and see.' Margaret sat next to him and stretched a cautious hand to stroke his shoulder. 'If she regains consciousness today, then things look hopeful. If not well, we cross that bridge tomorrow.'

'Why d-didn't I j-just let her h-have riding l-lessons?' Alex said to his knees. 'Wh-what was I s-so s-scared of?'

'You were just trying to keep her safe,' I said from across the room. Instinct told me to put my arms around him but he looked as though one person embracing him was enough and anyone else would just tip him over into claustrophobia.

Alex snorted. 'Y-yeah, and I d-did a cracking j-job of th-that, didn't I?' He shook his head. 'She j-just w-wanted to sh-show the bullies. To t-teach them a l-lesson.' He started pulling at a loose thread in his dusty shirt. 'Ch-Christ. I c-couldn't have s-screwed up more if I'd h-hit her on the h-head myself. El-Ellen w-would have k-killed me.'

'Well, Ellen isn't here,' Margaret said, sharply. 'And you've done a very good job of bringing Scarlet up, so don't start that nonsense. None of this is anyone's fault, except possibly those thoroughly nasty children that forced her into sitting on someone else's horse.'

Alex looked surprised under the general anxiety. 'D-do you th-think so? I th-thought you th-thought I sp-spoiled Scarl.'

'Well, you have, but a little bit of spoiling never did anyone any harm. You had piano lessons.' And suddenly there were tears flooding down Margaret's cheeks and she wound her arms tightly around her chest, as though trying to stop her heart from bursting out. 'I can't lose her too.' Her posture was rigid but her face had crumbled into ages of worry and loss. 'I can't lose her.'

'M-Mum ...'

'It's not fair! I've lost my husband and my daughter already.' Margaret put her hands up to cover her face. It looked as though she was trying to push the tears back inside her eyes. 'Why should I lose our little Scarlet too?'

The rigidity was gone now, fear and grief made her slump forward onto Alex's arm. 'You've done so much, tried so hard, why should you have her taken from you now?'

'It-it's all right, Mum.' Cautiously, as though he was a bit worried that she might bite, Alex scooped his arm around his mother. She seemed smaller, softer, less of a woman-sized package of loss-fuelled energy now, just a terrified grandmother in an out-of-control situation.

'All you ever did was your best!' Margaret raised a face that showed a mixture of anger and realisation. She seemed to be facing that moment when child becomes parent, letting Alex comfort her. 'You are doing your best, and Scarlet ...' A moment of choked-off words, as though saying Scarlet's name had the power to hurl her from us. 'She's growing up a fine young lady, which is all due to you.'

Alex sighed a laugh. 'W-wow. Th-thanks, Mum.'

'I miss your dad. And Ellen.'

'I kn-know.'

Margaret stood up, away from Alex's embrace. 'Do you know, I seem to be spending a lot of time in hospitals, one way or another, what with the dreadful Mr Park and his dribbly willy problem.' Although tears still streaked her face and her body shook with emotion, Margaret was back in control of herself. 'And I have found that they almost always have some kind of coffee machine, so ...'

Dan stood up. 'Yeah. I'll go.'

I might have known he couldn't sit still in a place like this for very long. Striding about, thinking was Dan's natural state. 'I'll come too.' The smell of the room was beginning to get to me, that institutionally-clean smell of bleach and fake flowers, and I didn't know what to say to Alex. There wasn't much I *could* say, not with his mother in the room. I wanted to tell him that his email was far more understanding than I had any right to, to tell him that friendship was all I could manage these days. But Dan was waiting in the doorway and I had to leave Alex, head back in his hands, to the somewhat more tender care of his mother.

We found a coffee machine on a corridor and Dan started feeding coins into it.

'Do you think Scarlet will be all right?' I asked.

'God, I hope so.' He handed me the first cup. 'Milk and sugar all round, I think. Now is really not the time for anyone to be fussy.'

'You're being very ...' I saw his face as he looked quickly up from the brown liquid streaming into another polystyrene container. He'd dropped some of the capable, in-charge attitude as soon as we'd left Alex and Margaret behind, and now he looked haunted. 'It must be awful for you, after ... after what happened to Beth. All this waiting around in hospitals and stuff.'

He left the full cup sitting in the machine and turned around to face me properly. 'Yeah?'

'Daisy said ...' I stopped speaking. He'd closed his eyes at the mention of my sister.

'Daisy said, did she?' He moved in until he stood so close that the fastenings of his coat knocked against my face as he breathed. 'And what do you think, hey, Winter? What do *you* think?'

I looked up into those black eyes, slightly hooded as though he was keeping his real thoughts hidden behind them and didn't want me to suspect what they might be. And suddenly he was not my editor, not the man who'd thrown my love away over the edge of a bridge in the night because he hadn't liked what I was telling him, he was just an unhappy man. As though all the images I'd kept of him in my head were gone, broken apart by the misery that he couldn't conceal; I looked into his eyes and through them to the person beyond. 'I think … what happened to your sister affected you more than you know.'

He smiled. 'Not quite. Nearly, but not quite. Y'see, Win, what it is, what happened to Beth it affected me more than *you* know.'

'Very enigmatic, Daniel.' The cup was hot between my fingers, the smell of synthetic coffee sour in my nose. 'Why don't you just tell me what the hell you are on about?'

He stepped back to push more coins into the machine. That look stayed in his eyes though. 'Can't. It might just make you … well, let's just say that *your* sister comes into things, okay? And I don't … look, let's leave it, hey? I'm not into pushing that rock up the hill again. I'll wait until we know more about Scarlet and then I'm heading back to London and that will be that, you need never look at me again, unless I'm on the publicity wagon when it wheels you around town, and even then my offensive presence will be well-diluted by all the PR bods and the hangers-on. Okay? We're done. You get what you wanted.'

I didn't notice my hands were shaking until spilled coffee burned its way through my sleeve. 'But what if that's not what I want any more?' I half-whispered, the words almost hidden under the background sounds of a hospital working away behind us, unheeded.

The sudden bang made me jump. Dan had kicked the coffee machine, his forehead resting against the coin slot and his shoulders hunched. 'This isn't fucking *fair*!' He turned around slowly and raised his head and now his eyes weren't hiding anything, they were letting tears slide out. 'Don't,' he said, softly. 'Don't do this.'

'Don't do what?' I was baffled. It felt … it felt as though he was leaving despite himself, despite what he wanted. He'd kissed me, he behaved as though he still cared. And yet, when I said that maybe I did want to go back, here he was telling me that he *didn't*?

'We're still where we were.' Dan straightened and used the sleeve of his coat to wipe his face. 'Nothing has changed. I want you, Winter, let's just put that right up there now, front and centre. I want you like I wanted you before. It's you, always has been. But I can't deal with the Daisy thing. Every time it looks like there might be hope, like you've let it change you, back it comes again and you're all "I've got to talk to Daisy about this". Y'see …' Now he was in close again, a cup of steaming liquid in each hand. '… until you admit you can live without her, I can't be part of anything with you.'

I stared at him. Underneath the relentless fluorescent lights he stood like a shadow. 'So, you're still not prepared to make allowances?' I said, slowly.

'I thought I could. But I can't. I want it to be *me*, Winter. I want you to turn to *me* when the going gets tough. I want to have all of you, not just the part that you can spare. I want to be the one you call on, I want you to be able to share how you feel with *me*, rather than … Shit. Let's get back. This isn't the time or place.' And balancing three cups between his hands, he stormed past me and back up the corridor to the waiting area.

Where we were met by Light Bulb, who was propped against the doorframe. Inside, Lucy, who'd evidently brought him from the school, was talking earnestly to Alex, but stopped when we came in, and looked embarrassed.

Dan handed round the coffees and the silence between us all wasn't only the silence of worry. Lucy and Alex kept looking at one another in a kind of deeply miserable way, while Dan and I avoided looking at each other at all.

There was a shard of pain under my ribs whenever I accidentally found myself looking at him out of the corner of my eye; he'd taken his coat off in the oppressive humidity of the hospital air and rolled the sleeves of his dark shirt to the elbows. His lean frame contrasted with Alex's hard-work muscles, which seemed to be drawing Lucy's eye like a magnet to iron.

'Can we see her?' I said, finally. 'I mean, aren't you supposed to talk to people who ... and Light Bulb should be in there, for when she wakes up, I mean.'

Margaret sighed. 'I should think so. We came out because the doctors and nurses were fixing up some machines, but they did say we could sit with her when they were finished.'

Nobody moved. It was as though, if we all stayed here in this room, Scarlet was still just 'asleep' and as soon as we had to look at her connected to drips and monitors, what had happened would become real. 'I'm going to just look in on her,' I said, finally. 'Take Light Bulb in. Let her know that Bobso and the babies will be all right while she's here.'

Everyone stared at me. 'Sh-she's unconscious,' Alex said at last. 'I d-don't th-think Bobso m-matters at the m-moment.'

'Bobso matters to *her*,' I said, firmly. 'And she'll be worrying.'

'Shit,' said Dan, quietly. 'Win, I don't think you ...'

But I didn't wait to hear the end of what he was saying. I seized Light Bulb around his stick and, carrying him like a floppy, corduroy-headed standard, went in to the room I'd seen Alex and Margaret come out of earlier.

Chapter Twenty-Three

The room was dark and, at first, all I could see was the bed. I took two steps across the squeaky lino floor towards it, saw the equipment surrounding the figure in the bed and all hell erupted.

A screaming noise, inside my head, drowned out the sound of the machines. My sister's voice, in agony, voices yelling and then I was yelling too, falling into a black spiral that sucked at me and still the voices. Still Daisy's high-pitched regular shrieking, as though the rhythm of making noise was keeping her anchored, both of us crying.

And then I was lying on the floor. Dan had my head cradled in his hands and was murmuring soft words and rocking. Alex was looming in the half-dark between the door and the bed, and Lucy and Margaret were peering around the frame with their eyes bulging, fear and curiosity forming a fence that stopped them coming any closer.

I stared up into Dan's eyes but couldn't speak. My mouth opened but when I tried to form words all there was was the shrieking and crying echoing in my mind and a huge weight shattering my heart from the inside.

'It's okay,' Dan was saying. 'It's okay, Winter.' He carried on rocking.

A thin, high-pitched sound cut through the air like a dentist's drill. Over and over, broken over breaths that pitched in and out. When Dan's hand tightened under my head I realised that it was me making the noise, although I couldn't feel it coming from my throat. Couldn't feel my body at all, only Dan's hands.

'What is it?' Lucy spoke around the doorframe. 'Some kind of seizure? Should I fetch a doctor?'

Dan shook his head. His eyes were fixed on my face. 'No. She'll be okay, she just needs ...'

'Daisy,' my mouth formed the name, spat it out. 'Daisy.'

'That's her s-sister,' Alex now, from the chair by the bed. 'Should w-we get in t-touch with her? I mean, if they're t-twins maybe s-something has happened to h-her that W-Winter is s-sensing?'

'We're too late.' Dan raised a hand and I saw him rub it over his face. 'I mean, you're right, Alex, but it's not happening now. Winter ... seeing Scarlet there ... Winter's had a flashback. Daisy's dead. She's been dead for five years.'

'No ...' I wanted to stand, to hit him, to deny everything he was saying. 'No, she's alive, she lives in Australia, she works in fashion, she ...' but my mouth and body wouldn't do it.

'But there are pictures.' Margaret sounded stunned.

'They're Winter. The one on the fireplace? I took that, on holiday, before I ... before I found out. She pretends.' Dan stopped talking.

'I said that.' A small voice, faint and faraway. 'I said that was Winter.'

'Scarlet?'

I couldn't speak. Couldn't move. It felt as though someone had blown my soul open with dynamite and left me paralysed and shocked, bleeding out on this floor. And everyone was clustering around the bed except me and Dan, exclaiming what a fright they'd had, and how did she feel, and she'd broken some bones and so not to move.

Dan picked me up, disentangled me from Light Bulb who had been jutting from underneath my legs all this time, and carried me out into the corridor. I closed my eyes against his shoulder.

By dint of walking down the hallway and kicking at doors until one opened, Dan found an empty room. He carried me inside and then laid me down on what felt like a dentist's couch. 'Okay,' he said, slowly. 'Okay.' He sounded as though he was panicking slightly and, through half-closed eyes, I watched him whirl around, rubbing at the back of his neck. 'Okay,' he said again. 'Can you speak?'

My lower jaw felt rigid. 'What happened?' My tongue felt artificial in my mouth, forming the words and pushing them out like some kind of manufacturing machine.

'Pure guesswork here, but I'm thinking ... what? You saw Scarlet and it threw you back to the last time you saw someone lying in a hospital bed all connected up? I mean, I never really found out the details, y'know, seemed bad taste and your mum just kind of outlined it for me but ... Christ!' He passed one hand around under his hair again, as though holding his head on. The other hand cupped his forehead. '*Christ.*'

I saw his face crumble, his hand come down to cover his expression as though he was hiding from me.

'Daisy—'

'Don't make me do this, Win.' Deep breaths; Dan was trying to control himself. 'Please. It's that night all over again. I love you, so fucking much, and I can't watch you doing this, pretending, amnesia, some fugue state, whatever ... I can't. It destroys me. Every time you say her name you're admitting that I'm not enough, that you have to keep that memory in your head to turn to, and I ...' A broken noise of a sob interrupted, not allowed to do its job. '... and I'm nowhere.'

'She's my *twin sister*.' The fragments that were what my soul had once been were piercing my heart at the sight of him. Gorgeous, chaotic Daniel. Now the chaos was gone. Had wheeled down through entropy into decay.

'Yeah, and what happened to Beth … that's why I came. That's what made me realise what you went through, what you were *still* going through; my sister was so ill, and if anything had happened, if she'd … if she'd died, I would have done anything to keep her alive. *Anything*. And I sat by her bedside and held her hand and I willed her to stay with us. And finally I realised where you'd been coming from. You kept your sister alive, Win, you kept her with you. I saw that, I saw how you kind of sheared off part of who you were, and you put it into Daisy. Twins, yeah? Two parts of the same whole. She was your other half, and you couldn't let that half go, you didn't think you could make it on your own so you kept her. And you're writing books about death and graveyards because you're trying to give a voice to the dead in every way you can think of because you can't face the fact that she's gone.'

He stopped suddenly, as though he'd been talking on a breath that had finally run out. His expression was exactly the same as it had been that night on the bridge, when he'd finally told me that he knew. My thirtieth birthday had been coming up fast, he wanted to organise a big party – friends, family. He'd found my mother's phone number in my contacts list and called her. Asked her how to get in touch with Daisy.

We'd been walking along the Embankment in the late spring warmth, arms around one another, and I'd looked up at him, my lovely, dark, anarchic Daniel. He'd stopped. Turned against the bridge and said he had something to discuss. I, stupid, romantic in my new feelings for him, had imagined a book conversation or – my heartbeats rising to match my pulse – some kind of commitment. A flat together, a house … And then those slow, measured words, spat into the water. *She's been dead all the time you've known me.*

Daisy and I were at home. She said she didn't feel well, she'd been off colour for days, we were heading upstairs so I could tuck her up in bed. And then she fell, dropping at my feet like an elegant bird and I was screaming and there were ambulances and hospitals and the long days and nights until there was no more hope.

But Daisy was part of me as I was part of her. I could no more exist without her than I could … I could …

'I love her, Dan.' It felt like hooks were attaching themselves to my insides, dragging them upwards. 'I love her.' And here came the grief, the sorrow that I never allowed because it would mean admitting she was truly gone. It poured up through me as though their source lay behind my heart rather than in my head. *She's never gone if I won't let her be. I can hold her, I know how she thinks, how she speaks, she is me.*

'And what about me, then, hey?' His voice was so gentle. 'You chose Daisy that night, Win, and I had to go because I couldn't bear to watch what you were doing to yourself. You wouldn't grieve—'

'You just wanted me to shut up and stop talking about her!' I yelled through the tears. 'You didn't understand.'

Dan came over. Very, very close, so I could see those black eyes, see the compassion that I didn't want. 'You have to let her go.' Now his voice was less gentle and more weighted. 'I do understand. Honest, I do. But she died. Meningitis is a bitch, Win, it was sudden and you had no time to get used to being without her. I stared down the barrel of losing my sister and I don't think I could have done it and walked out of that room the same man I went in. You have to let yourself be changed by it. Not forget, never that, Christ, no, you always had a twin sister, but you have to take on board what happened and let yourself move on.'

Let him go again. When Daniel is gone, none of this happened. We can be together, talk like we always did, and he …

But he's told them all now. They all know.

So, you don't belong here anyway. Go back to London. Or France, yes, go and stay with Mum in France again – loads of potential books in French graveyards; all those war stories.

Except it's nice here. Quiet and slow moving, it's easier to think. Not always having to rush from place to place, I can walk by the river when the writing isn't going so well and the hills are all moorland and stuff and it's like living in a calendar picture.

Whatever. But they're all going to feel sorry for you, and do that 'hushed voice' thing and treat you very, very carefully and start talking about therapy and counselling and that crap.

But it's Daniel. The man I fell in love with but had to leave. He's been in my heart, ever since; remember what happened with Alex, how I couldn't sleep with him because he wasn't Dan?

The door banged open. 'There you are.' It was Lucy, looking so down-to-earth in her school smock that Light Bulb bobbing in her hand was like a Photoshop blunder. 'Scarlet is asking for you, Winter.'

I could just run. Find a bus, find a train, leave this place and these people who know. If I can get away, then Daisy is still alive. Surround myself with crowds who never knew.

And then I thought of that little girl. Of her desperation to keep what remained of her mother close to the extent of putting life into that stick-and-fabric horse. Breathing life into the inanimate, because the alternative was too dreadful to contemplate. 'Yes.' I struggled to sit up.

Dan didn't look back. He walked past Lucy, shrugging himself into his coat as he went, without any kind of farewell and, as Lucy and I reached the doorway I saw him walk off down the corridor towards the entrance to the hospital. 'Dan,' I tried to shout after him, but my voice was a dry squeak. 'Dan.'

Lucy gave me a sideways look. She didn't say anything, but the hand not supporting Light Bulb gave my shoulder a quick rub and her mouth did a kind of straight-line smile. It was all the sympathy I could take right now, and I was curiously grateful for it.

'I found her, Scarlet.'

The room was brighter now. A nurse was fiddling around, doing something to a drip while Margaret got in the way, and Alex was sitting leaning towards the little girl, who I could now see had one arm in a plastic cast and a sling supporting the other. Her face was almost transparently pale. 'Hey,' I said, against the images that were trying to push forward in my head. *It's Scarlet not Daisy. This is nothing to do with that time, this is now.*

Everyone turned to look at me and the air thickened with their curiosity and doubt. Dan had just shown me up as not the person they'd thought I was. From being an ordinary, if such a word can ever be used about a writer, everyday person, I'd become something strange. Someone whose thought processes they couldn't even guess at. But they didn't matter now. None of it mattered now. 'Hey,' I said again. 'How are you feeling?'

Scarlet's eyes were on Light Bulb. 'I was riding, wasn't I? You saw me, Winter.'

I glanced across and met Alex's eye. He nodded slightly, but he too was looking inwards. Obviously re-writing his mental image of me, editing all our conversations, checking them over for any clear signs of my insanity.

'Yep. You were doing a good job too until that horse got over-excited and chucked you off.' I decided on matter-of-fact. No one could challenge me if I was more straightforward than a Roman road.

'Will you take me riding?' Her voice was faint now, her eyes closing. 'You're going to get Alex to give me riding lessons, you said.' Dropping towards sleep, probably induced by the drip towering over her head.

'I'm not sure I'll ...' I wanted to say it. To tell Scarlet, to tell them all that I was leaving. How could I stay, how could they *expect* me to stay, now that they all knew about Daisy?

Eyelids traced with pale-blue veins flickered and opened, with effort. 'You *said*, Winter. You mustn't lie, you know.'

Why not? My whole life for the last five years has been built on a lie ... The thought travelled down through my brain like a nail falling through water. There was a collective weight of eyes on me that almost buckled my knees. 'You're right. Of course I'll take you riding. When you're better though, you can't ride with ...' I looked her over, there seemed to be wires and tubes coming from all over. '... until you're all better.'

Scarlet smiled a smile of such happiness that everyone in the room smiled too, as though it was infectious. 'Mmmmm,' she sighed and her eyes finally closed. We were all silent for a moment, until the machine to the left of the bed began blipping a regular heartbeat and it was clear that she'd just gone to sleep.

'Th-thank you,' Alex said, quietly.

I tried to smile, failed. Inclined my head, and left the room.

✉

From: AlexHillStone@wolmail.com
To: LucyLoo@wolmail.com
Subject: I think you already know

I've been so scared, Lu, that I'd lose her. And now, now I nearly *did* lose her, but you were there, helping me through and I thought – what the hell is wrong with me? Like you'd let them take her just because you and I were an item, like you'd ever let her be second best. I am such a dick. I should never have doubted you and I should never have screwed up what we had, I should have trusted myself and I should have trusted you.

How was I so blind? How could I not see what was right in front of me? And how could you still care for a man who was so unkind to you back when Ellen died?

Al x

✉

From: LucyLoo@wolmail.com
To: AlexHillStone@wolmail.com
Subject: Because I've always loved you

That's all. xx

Chapter Twenty-Four

'In any graveyard there is always the one corner. Sometimes it's more than one, sometimes they are dotted around like small punctuations in the sentence of living, but they are there. Every line in their stone is carved so deep with their parents' unhappiness that it is hard to read, not because of illegibility but because of sympathy. In one grave, in one churchyard, there are nine children from one family, all gone within the space of six months, the result of a bout of typhoid that swept the region. In another lies 'George Smith, son of Henry Smith, aged 32 weeks'. How agonised those parents must have been, only able to count out the existence of their child in weeks ...
—BOOK OF THE DEAD 2

It took me two weeks to pluck up the courage to step outside the front door, and when I did I found the world had been brushed with snow. The far hilltops looked like iced puddings and the pavements of Great Leys had frozen lines on their edges where the snow had melted back. Nobody looked at me. It felt almost as though they averted their eyes, becoming interested in shop windows or the slippery conditions underfoot rather than look at the mad woman in their midst.

Sense tried to tell me that they'd always been like this, that I was just being paranoid, but it didn't stop me feeling as though I was moving in a giant circle of black loneliness that no one dared touch. I walked down the street and on to the churchyard to take a last look at the stones under their cardigan of frost before I packed my car and headed away. The stones were a constant, they'd still be here when I was gone as they'd been here for hundreds of years before I came; now they were also doubly immortalised by being in my book.

I stood in the corner of the graveyard where I'd first met Scarlet and Alex and rested my hand on Beatrice's stone, wondered how she'd feel if she knew that her inscription and history were, even at this moment, being read over by Dan in his London office. That the words I'd so carefully written to give her context and to show readers what her world had been like were being highlighted and underlined, crossed out and adjusted.

A pigeon clapped its way free of a tree above me as I walked out onto the frozen grass. It cracked beneath my feet into the quiet air and I saved up the sounds and the smell of cold air which tasted like metal on my tongue to tell Daisy. *Daisy*. I tried to force her image into my mind but it kept being overridden by Dan's face, that awful, sad, *destroyed* expression he'd worn in the hospital when I'd told him that I couldn't live without my sister.

I bent down and traced Beatrice's inscription with a fingertip. 'You're going to be famous,' I whispered to her. This little corner of a rural churchyard, with its sagging shoulders of wall and centuries old yew trees, now immortalised in the book, would be visited by readers from all over the world, if *Book of the Dead* was anything to go by. I'd had so many letters of thanks from parishes all over London who were now able to refurbish their churches from donations given by my readers that I was thinking they might make a book on their own.

'W-inter?'

I straightened up, almost guiltily. 'Alex?'

He shrugged. 'D-on't sound so s-urprised, I do live here.' A glance around. 'W-ell, not *h-ere*, but you know w-hat I mean.' He sounded different and it took me a moment to realise that his stammer was getting better. A slow delivery rather than a stoppered one. He looked different too, wearing a lumberjack shirt which didn't so much cover his muscles as focus the eyes on them one square at a time. 'C-ome and have a c-offee.'

I looked at him. 'I can't.'

I can't face you now you know. You'll stop treating me as just another person and start using that 'quiet' voice that people use when they think your sanity is in question. Treating me as if I've got a huge crack running through me that might blow open at any moment.

'S-o what? Y-ou were just g-oing to *leave*?' Alex came across the grass towards me. His footsteps tracked alongside mine in the frosty vegetation leaving a trail as though two ghosts had walked behind us. 'W-inter? Were you?'

I couldn't take the expression in his eyes and had to look away. I shrugged.

'S-carlet wants to see you. I m-ean properly see y-ou, not l-ike through binoculars.' He grinned and the tension that I'd been feeling began to seep away. 'But I w-arn you, it may be B-obso related.'

'She's home?' At least talking about Scarlet meant that we didn't have to address the Daisy-shaped elephant, although the presence of the tombstones meant that everything that had happened in the hospital was hovering just behind my eyes.

'Yep. Once th-ey established there w-as no brain d-amage, just b-roken bones and c-oncussion. H-ome and bored and c-onfined to bed. Well, s-ofa. Bed s-eemed un-necessarily p-unitive.' Alex held out an arm. 'Please.'

'What about what happened at the hospital?' I took two steps forward.

'Look. We're f-riends. Friends are allowed to screw up b-etween themselves, y-es? Your h-ead, my head, p-rivate spaces. We all d-o what we h-ave to to k-eep going.' He crossed the space between us and put his arm around my shoulders. 'I'm just s-orry that you and D-an ...' He stopped, and it wasn't a stammer stop.

An embarrassed silence fell. At least, it was embarrassment on my side, I really had no idea what Alex was feeling, although his arm across my shoulders was comfortable and reassuring. 'Yeah, well,' was all I could think of to say.

'So, c-offee? And S-carl? And p-robably Bobso?' Alex gave my shoulders a little shake. 'Come on, W-inter. At l-east say g-oodbye properly to a l-ittle girl who th-inks you're amazing.'

'Ah, guilt. Nice one, Alex.'

He grinned again and the feeling that I was tiptoeing along on drawing-pin tips finally left. He wasn't going to mention the whole Daisy thing, he was content to just let it be 'one of those things'. He didn't seem to regard me as being one step away from the psych ward, and he was prepared to let me see Scarlet. And he was right, I should say goodbye properly, it wasn't Scarlet's fault that I couldn't stay here any more.

No, it's Dan's fault. But Dan is gone. Over. If you'd had any doubt about that, then the way he walked off in the hospital, the way he blew your life apart in front of everyone who cared about you should have told you that.

He said he loved you and he walked away.

Scarlet was sprawled across the sofa, clearly wrestling

'taking things easy' into the ground. She'd got a set of model ponies spread out on the cover and was having a showjumping competition with them when we came in. Light Bulb, wearing a fabric rug that looked as if it had once been a dog-coat, was propped against one arm. His expression was now a re-stitched grin that looked as though he'd been at the vodka.

'A-nother visitor, Scarl.' Alex ushered me in. 'All the g-irls from school h-ave been round, it's been like P-iccadilly Circus. Or a T-opshop sponsored One D-irection fan f-est.'

'Winter! You came!' Scarlet leaped up but sat back down at a look from Alex. Her near-miss with death had clearly given her a temporary appreciation for discipline. 'Did you see Bobso? Is she all right? Are the babies all right?'

'Alex and I looked in on her on the way.' I perched on the sofa arm, a wary distance from Light Bulb. Falling on top of him in the hospital had given me some interestingly BDSM-style bruises on both legs which were only slowly fading. 'They're all fine.'

'I'm g-oing down to make c-offee,' Alex said. 'And to t-ell the guys to s-stand down from l-istening out for you, S-carl. Back in a m-inute.'

Scarlet waved a plastic-coated arm. 'I broke my wrist,' she said, when I looked at it. 'And my collarbone, and my ankle.' The cast was a mass of scribbles, pictures and get well messages written in glittery ink. 'No one else at school has ever broken so many bones.' There was a note of satisfied pride in her voice.

'Did anyone get into trouble?' I asked. 'Those girls who were bullying you?'

Scarlet bit her lip and her fingers fiddled with a plastic

Shetland. 'Shari said Mr Moore made them all go in his office and told them all I could of *died*. Emily Goodyear and Marissa Cheam cried, Shari said. I think Shari cried too, but she wouldn't say that, 'cos Shari is cool. Then they all came here and brought me chocolate and crayons and wrote on my casts.' A sudden broad smile. 'Emily said it was like *magic* that I didn't die. And Shari is my friend now, we're going to do riding lessons when I'm better, Alex says. Shari's got a pony called Dylan, but he was her sister's, so she has to learn to ride him properly, and I can ride him too, Shari says.'

I'd forgotten that, about primary school. I'd got so used to grown-up life, where you could just walk away from people you disagreed with; I could hardly remember what it was like to have to shrug off those slights and squabbles and then clean-slate your way into the future. 'Well, I'm glad it turned out for the best,' I said, moving a couple of equine outliers so that I could sit next to her, careful to avoid her equally-decorated ankle cast.

'I pretend that Mummy lives in my cupboard with Light Bulb.' Scarlet was looking back down at the plastic ponies on the coverlet, changing the subject with the ease of a child for whom all subjects are equal. 'Grandma and Alex and Lucy all told me not to talk to you about Daisy, but I think that's wrong. Like they don't let me talk about Mummy in case it upsets me, so I didn't tell them that I play games with her when I'm supposed to be in bed.' Now those grey, shrewd eyes met mine. 'It helps, doesn't it?'

My mouth twisted disobediently. 'Nothing really helps,' I whispered, fighting those hooks trying to pull emotion out of me. They stopped tugging for a moment, but when Scarlet looped her cast arm round the back of my neck, they gave one last, sudden jerk and everything came up at once, tears like sickness, welling in my throat and then pouring from my eyes, my mouth, driven by sobs that sounded like dry heaves.

Scarlet sat, half on my lap, resting her head against mine. She cried too, for a few minutes, but then stopped, seemingly impressed by the sheer longevity of my tears. I felt guilty, crying like this in front of a child, in front of *anyone*, usually my emotions were reserved for private occasions. Me, alone, supporting the weight of the loss of my sister. There was something curiously cathartic in having an audience.

Finally I reached the point of blankness, where there were no more tears and I'd stopped feeling. I'd cried my way beyond the pain for the first time, and there was a strange relief in its cessation. I'd got so used to that sensation that I was only half a person, that I was flapping about on the end of some balance whose counterweight had gone, its leaving was like losing five stone from my heart overnight.

Scarlet mopped at my face with a corner of her duvet and gave me a little birdlike kiss on the cheek. 'You've got snot all up your eyebrows,' she observed.

'Thanks,' I sniffed and furtively tried to do some damage limitation with the edge of the cover.

'Daniel said you never cried.' Another simple observation. 'About your sister.'

'He was right. I didn't cry at first because Mum and Dad … they were so devastated and I guess I was in shock. And then … then she was here.' I tapped at my chest. 'I never needed to cry because she was still here.'

Unselfconsciously Scarlet blew her nose on the duvet. 'I cry all the time about Mummy. I don't think she'd mind that really, she never told me off for crying before, but I don't want to feel sad because it used to make her sad when I was sad. I know Mummy's dead, I mean, we go to her grave and everything, but sometimes I can hear her voice talking to me. And she didn't *mean* to die, so I try to be happy.'

I put my arms around Scarlet's bony body and hugged her, hard enough to make her squeak and turn her injured side away. 'You could have died too.'

'But I didn't. And if I *had* died, I wouldn't have known how much everyone missed me, so I'm really glad I didn't.'

'You might have done.' I pushed her sadly chopped fringe out of her eyes. 'You might have been looking down on us all.'

Scarlet picked up a couple of the model horses. 'And then I would have been sad that you were all sad, and I couldn't do anything about it,' she said, reasonably.

'You've got a point there.'

Alex came back in balancing a pair of mugs. 'B-bloody machine, s-orry Scarl. Nearly t-ook my head off. Have y-ou two b-een crying?'

Scarlet bounced, within plaster cast limitations. 'Yes, but it was good crying, not bad crying, wasn't it, Winter?'

I took the mug that Alex held out to me. His raised eyebrows called for more than a simple 'thank you'. 'D'you know, I think it was. Scarlet was telling me about' – a quick glance from her and I realised that our conversation had been 'off the parental-figure record' –'things, about losing someone. About them not wanting us to be sad.'

Alex smiled. His face crinkled along those sun lines and made his smile look even wider. He was attractive, he was cute and gentlemanly and understanding, but Daniel was stuck in my heart like a fish bone in my throat.

'Lucy s-said, oh, y-yeah, Lucy and I, we're g-etting back t-ogether … she said th-at's why my s-tammer is getting b-better. Because I've l-ost the "survivor g-uilt" I had when Ellen d-ied.' He took a swig of the coffee. 'Nearly l-osing Scarl m-ade me realise, s-ometimes shit h-appens.' Another swig. 'S-orry, Scarl.'

'You shouldn't swear. It sets a bad example,' Scarlet said, solemnly.

He nodded agreement over his mug. 'You d-on't mind?' he asked, quietly. 'A-bout me and L-ucy?'

I eyeballed him, then Scarlet, and jerked my head toward the kitchen area. He took the hint and followed me. 'Seriously, I'm really pleased that you and Lucy are together again,' I said, at a hopefully Scarlet-avoiding volume. 'She's really mad about you and she cares about Scarlet, I mean, she's been fixing Light Bulb all this time …'

Alex looked over at the drunken, irresponsible expression sewn onto the corduroy face. 'Oh. I th-ought that was y-ou and Mum.'

'Seriously? You think I sew? For the record, Alex, I don't iron or cook either. Lucy will be good for you and Scarlet.' Memory threw up that image of him naked, all muscle and tan lines. 'Have you worked off your frustration yet? I'm so, so sorry about that night, I wouldn't have gone that far if I hadn't thought you were *right* but it wasn't you, it was me, being stupid.'

A really broad grin now. 'We … err, we g-et by,' he said and winked.

'They send me to Grandma's.' Scarlet chimed in, concentrating on arranging the ponies by size on the cover. 'They think I don't know, but they're,' she lowered her voice, '*making babies*.'

'*She's eight!*' mouthed Alex, with extreme emphasis and an astonished expression.

'Work cut out there.' I smirked back over the rim of my coffee mug.

'You l-ook better.' He tipped his head on one side and stone dust fell out of his hair. 'Somehow.'

I made a face. 'Thank you for not minding.' I kept the volume low, although it hardly seemed necessary when Scarlet had such acute hearing. 'That I lied about Daisy.' I dropped my gaze so I was staring at the blackness of the coffee in my mug, where bubbles rose and fell and swirled.

'Dan d-idn't tell, if y-ou were w-ondering. Not until the h-ospital. He j-ust said y-ou had p-problems, d-epression. He k-ept your s-ecret.' A smile. 'Even f-rom me and he kn-ew I was in-terested in you. He c-ould have really sc-rewed that up b-ut I think he w-anted you to t-ell me y-ourself.'

'I should have. I just can't … couldn't. If I tell people, then she's really gone, you know?'

Alex looked sadly over at Scarlet, who'd now brought Light Bulb into the game and was forcing him to take part in the competition taking place on the cover. It was like bringing a T. Rex to a dog show. 'Yes,' he said, softly. 'I kn-ow.'

Back at the House of Tiny, I sat on the bed. Well, part of me did, the other buttock had to wobble unsupported in the air, but I realised I'd got used to it. In fact there was something comforting in the confinement of the place – not just the house but the town, caught in its basin under the hills. London was great for invisibility. I could meet new people all the time, people who didn't know about Daisy, whereas here I suspected that it was only a matter of time before the gossip-grapevine meant that my entire life history was spread among the community, but there was a comfort in that.

I'd seen from Alex's experience how a small town enfolded itself around you. He could have moved away, gone anywhere, but he'd have had to explain every time, about the accident, Ellen's death, the cause of his stammer. Whereas here, all right, everyone knew your family back ten generations and remembered when your great-great grandfather had nothing but a pig and two bits of sheet metal, but everyone just shrugged and got on with it.

Living in a place like this means never having to say you're sorry. Whereas the anonymity of the big city means never having to say anything at all.

'Winter?'

'I can't do this any more, Daze. I know it's not you. I know it's just me, trying to put words in your mouth, remembering, not wanting to let you go.'

'Well, of course. But you've always known that, haven't you? It's not, like, a new realisation, is it?'

'No. But it's wrong. I need to … I need to stop. I need to face things. I need to stop imagining you as you would be now, with a great fashion job and a fabulous flat, all cutting-edge and stylish. I have to remember you as you were before … before you …'

'Say it, Winter. Say it.'

'Before you *died*.' There were no tears, not now. I'd cried them all out over Scarlet's pony-patterned duvet. 'When we were twenty-four and living at home. You were still making your own clothes out of boot sale leftovers and I was writing press releases for people who made plastic widgets, and I just wanted you to have the future you never had, Australia and famous people and a brilliant job in design!'

'You don't know what I would have done with my life. Maybe I'd have got pregnant by the boy down the road who smelled of cucumbers. Maybe I would have turned to drugs and vanished into a series of squats and unsuitable friends … you don't know. Stop trying to live a life for me and start living a life for yourself. Remember me as I was, okay, maybe I wasn't exactly living the high life, but I was happy. We were both happy. Remember me as happy, Winter. That's all.'

I smiled. 'Yes. I can do that.'

'And there's one more thing you have to do. You know what it is, don't you?'

I shrank inside myself with a feeling almost like nausea. 'I can't. Truly, I can't.'

'But you have to. Otherwise this isn't over, and it will never be over. You *have to*, Winter.'

You have to, Winter.

✉

From: WinterGregoryAuthor@teddymail.com
To: DanBekener@ShyOwlPublishing.co.uk
Subject:

I need to talk to you. There's so much I need to say, but I don't know how. I don't think I've ever known how, not since Daisy died.

I'm coming back to London for a few days to sort things out but then I've decided to buy a little place up here in Yorkshire. It's time I started living again … properly, but I don't think I can do that in London any more. I like it here. It's big and peaceful and there's just so much *sky* … There's a house for sale a couple of doors down from Margaret's place, nothing grand just a tall, thin terraced house near the river, but I think it's time I put down roots. Stopped floating around in that state of denial I was living in.

I know that too much has gone on between us for us ever to go back, but I've seen the way Scarlet has thrown off all the memories of the bad stuff she went through at school, a kind of 'forgive and forget' thing that seems so easy when you're eight, and I wondered if … if we could do that. If you could ever work with me again. I just want you to understand that I *couldn't* stop talking to Daisy, no matter how much I wanted to back then. She was all I had. And I owed it to her to keep her alive, here, inside me.

But now I know. I talked to Scarlet, about her mother and how she put part of her into Light Bulb to keep her alive, but now she's moving to real horses and Light Bulb is just a toy again. Just a reminder, a lovely, sweet reminder that her mother loved her. And I've got the memory of Daisy, I will have that always. Remembering us growing up, remembering what great times we had, how fabulous it was to have a sister that was a mirror image of me. *But she wasn't me*. She was herself, and I had no right to put a life on to her that she may not ever have lived. May not even have wanted.

You were right. I needed to let it change me. And I think I have.

Can we meet, one last time? There's something I want to show you. The fifteenth of next month, about ten a.m. www.FleetHill.co.uk.
Winter

✉

From: DanBekener@ShyOwlPublishing.co.uk
To: BethanyAnnBekener@wolmail.com
Subject:
I don't know what to do, Bethie.
DBx

Chapter Twenty-Five

'They say that no one is truly gone while someone who
lives remembers them, so is that why we carve such
elaborate memorials to the dead? So that those who come
after can see, can be curious? To show off the family
wealth and status by expenditure on someone who is
beyond caring about such things? Or so that, maybe, just
sometimes, someone will be passing by, look at a stone and
wonder about the person immortalised in script upon it?

Next time you walk through a graveyard, maybe
you will be able to see now, not an enclosure fencing
in the forgotten, but a field growing a crop of
memories. Every person buried there lived a life. It
may have been a small life, scratched out on meagre
farmland, or a life of excess and overindulgence,
but each of these people were remembered by those
who remained. From Augustus Rawlins, who only
lived for two days, to Samuel Nichols who lived to
be 107, someone remained to remember them.'
—BOOK OF THE DEAD 2

Mid-December was here with a vengeance. A biting wind travelled at ankle-height like a small bad-tempered dog and the air stung. I gathered my big coat closer around myself and walked on down the path. My footsteps echoed as though I was walking on tin.

I thought I heard someone walking behind me, but whenever I turned there was nothing but the air and trees, evergreen but slightly greyed by the weather which was now sweeping swathes of mist across the ground. I dug my hands into my pockets and walked faster.

And then, suddenly, there it was. All alone, near the wall. My knees buckled and I grabbed onto a convenient bench, sitting hurriedly so my weakness wouldn't show, although there was no one around to see, and I crouched forward with my head in my hands. *I should never have come …*

The bench creaked as someone appeared out of the mist and sat beside me. 'You made it, then.'

I passed my hands back over my head, smoothing my hair. Pretending I was adjusting my appearance, not hiding. My heart beat its way into my throat. 'You came.'

'Yup.' Dan stretched his legs out in front of him and stared at the watermarked leather of his boots. 'Did you think I wouldn't?'

'You didn't answer my email, so, yes, I didn't think you'd come.'

The damp air made his hair flop across his forehead and beaded the stubble on his cheeks in little balls of fog. He looked even more elemental than usual, almost as though he was part of this place rather than a visitor. He'd lost the big buckled piracy coat in favour of a woollen greatcoat with a collar that framed his face and a hem that brushed the tops of his boots. 'Sorry. Should've at least messaged you back but …' A sideways look at me that revealed his eyes were shadowed. 'I guess I couldn't think what to say. Had a lot of thinking to do all round, kiddo. But I decided, maybe, me being here would … there's some things that no one should have to face alone.'

'So you know that Daisy … that I …'

An inclination of the head and a half-smile. A hand came out of his pocket and touched my sleeve, curved over my arm until his fingers pressed against the flesh of my wrist. 'I handled it all wrong, Win. My fault, couldn't see the wood for the fire, should have hung around and tried to make it better but all I could see ... *all* I could see was you in that circle of hell that you'd built for yourself. I wanted to get in there with you, help you to tear it down but you thought you were happy in there, y'know?'

The fog was thickening now, isolating us in a sea of white. 'I thought I could keep her,' I said, quietly, and the mist damped my words still further, so it sounded as though I was talking into a vacuum.

'I know.' His hand retracted and lost itself somewhere back in a pocket.

Silence came down with the extra mist until the air looked like a pint of milk in water and sounded dead. 'And you know I'm staying in Great Leys? There's nothing back here for me, Dan.'

A nod. 'And you and Alex are ...'

A snort that I couldn't help. 'No, Alex and Lucy are an item. Such an item, in fact, that Scarlet keeps telling everyone they're getting married, but I think that's a way off yet. No. He's my friend, Dan, that's all.'

'Ah. Okay. Yeah, got it.' Some more silent staring at boots.

'Scarlet's had her first riding lesson, I've given a talk at the school and I'm opening the Great Leys Christmas Fayre next week. With a "y", Margaret was most insistent about that, something to do with standards, I think.'

'Uh huh.' A long fingered hand flicked beads of moisture off the coat. 'And you're ... uh ... I mean ... I'm guessing you're done with the writing about dead people now, yeah? Worked it out of your system, and all.'

I'd never seen Dan so uncomfortable before. His body

language gave nothing away, because Dan was always as edgy as a cat introduced to a puppy, but his refusal to meet my eye told me that he didn't want me to see how he was feeling. I didn't need to look in his face to know that he was working on taking the rejection as stoically as he could.

'Well, I'm not going back into writing press releases, I know that much.'

He glanced quickly at me, out of the corner of his eye. Jerked his head and water flicked onto the shoulders of his coat like diamond dandruff. 'Glad you're getting sorted then. No, really, I mean it. Glad you …' His voice tailed off into gruffness; he cleared his throat but didn't carry on talking, just shuffled his feet and hunched his shoulders up until it looked as though his coat was trying to swallow him. His elbows jutted, his hands were evidently digging so deep into the pockets that his fingers must have been gripping at his thighs.

I expected him to stand up then. To shrug, say goodbye and walk off like a shadow through the fog. But he didn't.

'You don't have to stay, Dan.' My voice sounded small.

Now he looked at me properly. Eyes like a night sky, carrying the weight of a universe of longing, met mine. 'Yeah, I do. You sent me that email. You asked me to come here today. And whatever you are to me, whatever I was to you, you shouldn't be here alone.'

Despite the location, despite the occasion, I felt something inside me pull open. As though the sun came through the fog and showed the possibility of summer, a crack in the relentless unhappiness that I'd felt for the last five years began to widen. *He came back for me. I blew him out on the bridge, and he came back, I rejected him in the hospital, and here he is again. Daniel. Knowing what happened, knowing why I did it, and yet still here. Maybe it's time to choose again, Winter.*

I looked away through the mist. 'You made me choose, Dan,' I said, quietly. 'You should never have made me choose.'

His look was deep now, intense, as though he was trying to read behind my words. 'I know. I was wrong. But you were going to tear yourself apart, and I couldn't stand by and watch that happen.' He stood up suddenly. 'I thought it would be me, y'see.' And now he turned, sweeping a great circle, hunching himself against the weather. 'I thought you would choose me.' His voice was so quiet now that the words were part of the mist.

It was time to decide again, and now I knew the right decision to make. 'I love you, Dan.' I spoke to his back. To the stiff-collared greatcoat of flecked black and grey wool, to the fall of his hair over the neckline, to the muddied heels of his boots. 'I wanted to tell you that night on the bridge. I wanted to say I love you, I wanted to say help me, but I couldn't, you made me choose and then you were gone.'

He moved slowly, turning to face me. He extended one arm and the wrist fell bare, his chaos tattoo dark against that pale skin, a complicated fractal of a mark that summed Daniel up in a series of lines and discs. 'And is it me now?' His hand touched my cheek and he bent so that the uncertainty in his words hung in the condensation that his breath left on my hair.

I looked into his solemn face, those big dark eyes temporarily without their mischief and steadily gazing into mine. 'Yes, Dan. It's you.'

And now he drew me up, through the frosted air, until our lips touched. This kiss wiped out the memory of the last kiss, the one I had thought was goodbye. In fact, it didn't just wipe it out, it tore it up and burned it then stamped on the ashes. He tasted of caramel and vanilla and the hands that held me were so much warmer than the day that it felt as though he'd stepped straight through from hell – but an interesting hell that was more pandemonium than any satanic realm. He blew out a sigh. 'Finally. Finally I can stop feeling like a steaming great pile of shit.' Black eyes flicked to my face and then away again, like nervous ravens. 'Because it's you, Win, like I said in the hospital. It's you, it's always been you since that day in the pub when you came flying in like some kind of possessed creature, all hair and legs and mad energy, and I looked up from my pint and it was kinda, "oh, there you are, love of my life, I've been waiting forever for you to turn up".'

'Overdramatic, even for you, Mr Bekener.'

A wicked smile that pulled the corners of his lips up and widened his eyes. He looked like an embodiment of the weather, ethereal, never still … but not cold. No. Not now. There was a heat in his grin that made my fingers tingle. 'True though, love. You and me, can it be you and me again? Can we do it?'

Now it was my turn to pull him in close. To let him see the new mischief that I could feel spark in my eyes. 'Oh, I should think so,' I said. 'If you don't mind moving to Great Leys and living next door to Margaret and the ocular funfair that is her wardrobe.'

'Already put the feelers out for work up that way.' Dan gave a small smile. 'And Daisy?' He ran a finger over my mouth, almost wonderingly.

'Wanted me to be happy, Dan. That's all.' And I raised myself up and kissed him this time.

When our mouths finally parted, he rested his forearms

on my shoulders, linked his hands behind my head and winked. 'Okay!' Then he spun so that we were facing the same way through the thickening air and he had one arm wrapped around me. 'Ready?'

'I think so.'

And together we crossed the grass to the lone marker. It wore its fringe of grass lightly, almost stylishly, compared to the stones around it and its gold lettering, undimmed by five years of exposure to weathering, shone like a beacon.

'Here lies Daisy Ophelia Ruskin Gregory, tragically taken from us in her twenty-fourth year. Much loved and much missed.'

I laid the red roses I'd brought against the headstone and stepped back. 'Is this the first time you've visited?' Dan coiled his arm around me again and pulled me into the warmth of his coat.

'Yes.' The roses looked too red to be on a grave, like a joke or a stage set. I made a note to bring apricot ones next time. 'I couldn't. I couldn't acknowledge she was dead, so how could I come to her grave?' I took a deep breath which shuddered. 'This makes it real.'

'You can cry if you want to.' Dan looked around the cemetery. 'I brought tissues.'

I shook my head. 'No. It's okay.' A few hot, fat tears gave the lie to my words, but I just brushed them aside. They were reminders from the past, that was all. *Remember me as happy.* I was going to have to work on that, but yes. I could do it. 'It's okay.'

[f]

Facebook

Dan Bekener is In a Relationship with Winter Gregory

1,427 people like this

Alex Hill is In a Relationship with Lucy Charlton
220 people like this

Alex Hill
Here's a pic of Scarl having her first jumping lesson!
Comment: Lucy Charlton She's a natural …
Comment: Winter Gregory That pony is a monster!
Comment: Lucy Charlton Will you come and help us choose a nicer one?
Comment: Dan Bekener As long as it's not Bobso all over again …

Remember me when I am gone away,
Gone far away into the silent land;
When you can no more hold me by the hand,
Nor I half turn to go yet turning stay.
Remember me when no more day by day
You tell me of our future that you plann'd:
Only remember me; you understand
It will be late to counsel then or pray.
Yet if you should forget me for a while
And afterwards remember, do not grieve:
For if the darkness and corruption leave
A vestige of the thoughts that once I had,
Better by far you should forget and smile
Than that you should remember and be sad.

CHRISTINA ROSSETTI

Thank you

Hello.

Thank you so much for reading my book! I mean, I'm assuming you read it, you haven't just flicked to the back to look for my author picture or something (seriously, don't. You'll go blind. Although there's probably a nice list of 'other books by this author' somewhere close by, if you're interested). I am the author. Or, as I prefer, The Author, because all us authors have delusions of grandeur – I, in fact, have a whole range of delusions and fixations which, if you pop over to my blog or follow me on Twitter or Facebook, you too will become familiar with. HobNobs. Tony Robinson (yes, the tiny, bald man who does Time Team). Doctor Who …

Where was I? Oh yes, the 'thanks for reading' thing. Anyway. Yes. I hope you enjoyed reading about Daniel, Alex, Scarlet and Winter in *I Don't Want to Talk About It*. Oh, and Bobso, of course. There aren't nearly enough guinea pigs in modern literature, are there? If you've got any opinions you'd like to share about the book, then please pop over to Amazon, Goodreads or any other bookselling platform and leave a review – it's reviews that other readers rely on to know whether or not they might enjoy a book, so you might just help someone else to discover their new Favourite Book.

Right. Kettle's boiled and I've just opened a new packet of HobNobs, so, if you'll excuse me …

Lots of love,

Jane

About the Author

Jane was born in Devon and now lives in Yorkshire. She has five children, five cats and three dogs. Jane is a member of the Romantic Novelists' Association and has a first-class honours degree in creative writing.

Jane writes comedies which are often described as 'quirky'. *I Don't Want to Talk About It* is Jane's seventh Choc Lit novel. Her UK debut, *Please Don't Stop the Music*, won the 2012 Romantic Novel of the Year and the Romantic Comedy Novel of the Year Awards from the Romantic Novelists' Association.

Jane's Choc Lit novels are: *Please Don't Stop the Music*, *Star Struck*, *Hubble Bubble*, *Vampire State of Mind*, *Falling Apart*, *How I Wonder What You Are* and *I Don't Want to Talk About It*.

For more information on Jane visit
www.janelovering.co.uk
www.twitter.com/janelovering

More Choc Lit

From Jane Lovering

Please Don't Stop the Music

Book 1 in the Yorkshire Romances

Winner of the 2012 Best Romantic Comedy Novel of the Year

Winner of the 2012 Romantic Novel of the Year

How much can you hide?

Jemima Hutton is determined to build a successful new life and keep her past a dark secret. Trouble is, her jewellery business looks set to fail – until enigmatic Ben Davies offers to stock her handmade belt buckles in his guitar shop and things start looking up, on all fronts.

But Ben has secrets too. When Jemima finds out he used to be the front man of hugely successful Indie rock band Willow Down, she wants to know more. Why did he desert the band on their US tour? Why is he now a semi-recluse?

And the curiosity is mutual – which means that her own secret is no longer safe …

Visit www.choc-lit.com for more details, or simply scan barcode using your mobile phone QR reader.

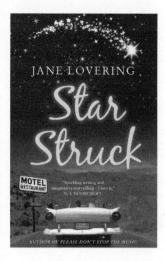

Star Struck

Book 2 in the Yorkshire Romances

Our memories define us – don't they?

And Skye Threppel lost most of hers in a car crash that stole the lives of her best friend and fiancé. It's left scars, inside and out, which have destroyed her career and her confidence.

Skye hopes a trip to the wide dusty landscapes of Nevada – and a TV convention offering the chance to meet the actor she idolises – will help her heal. But she bumps into mysterious sci-fi writer Jack Whitaker first. He's a handsome contradiction – cool and intense, with a wild past.

Jack has enough problems already. He isn't looking for a woman with self-esteem issues and a crush on one of his leading actors. Yet he's drawn to Skye.

An instant rapport soon becomes intense attraction, but Jack fears they can't have a future if Skye ever finds out about his past …

Will their memories tear them apart, or can they build new ones together?

Visit www.choc-lit.com for more details, or simply scan barcode using your mobile phone QR reader.

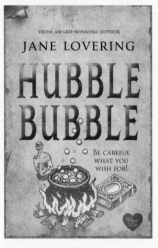

Hubble Bubble

Book 3 in the Yorkshire Romances

Be careful what you wish for …

Holly Grey only took up witchery to keep her friend out of trouble – and now she's knee-deep in hassle, in the form of apocalyptic weather, armed men, midwifery … and a sarcastic Welsh journalist.

Kai has been drawn to darkest Yorkshire by his desire to find out who he really is. What he hadn't bargained on was getting caught up in amateur magic and dealing with a bunch of women who are trying *really hard* to make their dreams come true.

Together they realise that getting what you wish for is sometimes just a matter of knowing what it is you want …

Visit www.choc-lit.com for more details, or simply scan barcode using your mobile phone QR reader.

How I Wonder What You Are

Book 4 in the Yorkshire Romances

"Maybe he wasn't here because of the lights – maybe they were here because of him …"

It's been over eighteen months since Molly Gilchrist has had a man (as her best friend, Caro, is so fond of reminding her) so when she as good as stumbles upon one on the moors one bitterly cold morning, it seems like the Universe is having a laugh at her expense.

But Phinn Baxter (that's *Doctor* Phinneas Baxter) is no common drunkard, as Molly is soon to discover; with a PhD in astrophysics and a tortured past that is a match for Molly's own disastrous love life.

Finding mysterious men on the moors isn't the weirdest thing Molly has to contend with, however. There's also those strange lights she keeps seeing in the sky. The ones she's only started seeing since meeting Phinn …

Visit www.choc-lit.com for more details, or simply scan barcode using your mobile phone QR reader.

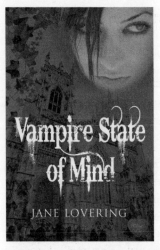

Vampire State of Mind

Book 1 in the Otherworlders

Jessica Grant knows vampires only too well. She runs the York Council tracker programme making sure that Otherworlders are all where they should be, keeps the filing in order and drinks far too much coffee.

To Jess, vampires are annoying and arrogant and far too sexy for their own good, particularly her ex-colleague, Sil, who's now in charge of Otherworld York. When a demon turns up and threatens not just Jess but the whole world order, she and Sil are forced to work together.

But then Jess turns out to be the key to saving the world, which puts a very different slant on their relationship.

The stakes are high. They are also very, very pointy and Jess isn't afraid to use them – even on the vampire she's rather afraid she's falling in love with …

Visit www.choc-lit.com for more details, or simply scan barcode using your mobile phone QR reader.

Falling Apart

Book 2 in the Otherworlders

In the mean streets of York, the stakes just got higher – and even pointier.

Jessica Grant liaises with Otherworlders for York Council so she knows that falling in love with a vampire takes a leap of faith. But her lover Sil, the City Vampire in charge of Otherworld York, he wouldn't run out on her, would he? He wouldn't let his demon get the better of him. Or would he?

Sil knows there's a reason for his bad haircut, worse clothes and the trail of bleeding humans in his wake. If only he could remember exactly what he did before someone finds him and shoots him on sight.

With her loyalties already questioned for defending zombies, the Otherworlders no one cares about, Jess must choose which side she's on, either help her lover or turn him in. Human or Other? Whatever she decides, there's a high price to pay – and someone to lose.

Visit www.choc-lit.com for more details, or simply scan barcode using your mobile phone QR reader.

Introducing Choc Lit

We're an independent publisher creating
a delicious selection of fiction.
Where heroes are like chocolate – irresistible!
Quality stories with a romance at the heart.

See our selection here:
www.choc-lit.com

We'd love to hear how you enjoyed *I Don't Want to Talk About It*. Please leave a review where you purchased the novel or visit: **www.choc-lit.com** and give your feedback.

Choc Lit novels are selected by genuine readers like yourself. We only publish stories our Choc Lit Tasting Panel want to see in print. Our reviews and awards speak for themselves.

Could you be a Star Selector and join our Tasting Panel?
Would you like to play a role in choosing which novels we decide to publish? Do you enjoy reading romance novels? Then you could be perfect for our Choc Lit Tasting Panel.

Visit here for more details...
www.choc-lit.com/join-the-choc-lit-tasting-panel

Keep in touch:
Sign up for our monthly newsletter Choc Lit Spread for all the latest news and offers: www.spread.choc-lit.com.
Follow us on Twitter: @ChocLituk and Facebook: Choc Lit.

Or simply scan barcode using your mobile phone QR reader:

Choc Lit
Spread

Twitter

Facebook